SUITORLAND

Freda Shafi

Fisher King Publishing

Suitorland

Copyright © Freda Shafi 2023

PRINT ISBN 978-1-914560-85-9
DIGITAL ISBN 978-1-914560-86-6

Published by Fisher King Publishing
www.fisherkingpublishing.co.uk

Cover image based on a photograph by
Roth Read Photography

In memory of Julie McSorley,

the strongest woman I ever met.

Chapter 1

Bash-A-Rat

11 November 1977

It was a routine Sunday in our Victorian terraced house on Shipley Road. The volume of Mum's cassette player was on full belt, playing songs from the 1940 Bollywood film, Mughal-e-Azam. "Jaldi!" (hurry!) I heard her anxious voice cry out, beckoning my two older sisters down to the kitchen from their bedroom. My eyes were stinging from chopping onions into small pieces for the chutney, which was to accompany the meal that day. My small fingers, freezing from the biting draft coming through the open door of the basement kitchen. The air was filled with the heavy scent of incense mixed with several curries cooking in tandem. My sisters could be heard giggling excitedly as they raced down the three flights of stairs from the attic to the basement. "It's your turn today." "No, it's your turn." I heard them tease each other.

By 'your turn' they were referring to whose turn it was to view the expected 'rishta' - suitor. A potential husband for one of them, was en route. He and his family were travelling all the way from Burnley to Bradford to see which one of my sisters might be an eligible match for their sons' hand in marriage. This was not an unusual scenario back in 1970's Britain. It was one of the only ways that Pakistani parents sought future partners for their sons and daughters. With four young women to wed in our family, we too were now part of this process.

As the youngest of five children, my job was to help cook the ample spread of food offered at the suitor meetings. It was often a small feast, made up of traditional curries and sundries, all created from scratch and served to the potential suitor and his family. My brother stood watching over me, grinning at the prospect of stealing a samosa, as they were carefully spooned out of the hot oil. He was wearing his Sunday best; brown gabardine trousers and a hand-knitted tank top to match, made lovingly by Grandma Kipling, our adopted English grandmother who lived next door.

I diligently awaited mum's next instruction, standing on the cold stone floor of our piecemeal kitchen, which was made up of mis-matched, salvaged cupboard doors that mum had put together herself, over the years. The tiny window above the stove let in more freezing air than the escape of pungent aromas from the ample pots of curry on the go. Today, there was also a batch of crispy pakora on offer, which I was eyeing up already, imagining biting into a pakora sandwich laden with my chutney and an ample dollop of ketchup. After the arduous task of helping mum create this spread, I always looked forward to tucking into the leftovers with impunity. Whilst visualising myself plunging into all the delectable dishes, I also remember hoping and praying silently, please 'God let him be the one!'

I had been helping mum cook for the suitors for a few years now; enough time for me to question this unusually bizarre ritual. My seven-year-old self often wondering how many families we would have to entertain for each of my sisters. It felt as if there had been too many comings and goings already. It was an accepted practice in our house that no one ever seemed to question. Was this normal? I was the youngest of mum's four daughters. There were three older sisters; all of them were impressive and more dazzling than me. Two of them, Laylah and Nailah were about to inspect the potential suitor.

There was an ample age gap between the older sisters and me; this, a result of mum being left in Pakistan for years before being reunited with dad in Yorkshire. Another accepted practice that enabled men who had been recruited to work in the textile mills to settle, before calling their wives to join them. For some it took a few months; for dad, it took a few years.

They were dynamite

I idolised my dazzling grown up sisters for everything that they represented and early on placed them on a pedestal. In my eyes they were mesmeric, dynamic, magnificent and exquisite young women. Both of them came bursting into the kitchen, looking perfectly groomed, in their fuchsia pink crimplene trouser suits, that mum had made for them a week earlier. The clothes fit exactly and were accessorised with beaded chokers and huge button earrings. Laylah's sharply tongued curls were flicked back off her face with precision, whilst Nailah's poker straight blue-black hair hung heavily down, sweeping her waist. Both of them with powdered creamy coloured skin, which was considered a desirable attribute amongst the Asian community. Thick kohl liner defined Laylah's feline eyes and only a smidgen of kajal swept across the inside edge of Nailah's almond-shaped eyes. Their glossed lips were all the rage, dispensed by a roller ball on the tip of a tube of gloss which fascinated me. I would often secretly steal it from their dresser and smudge more than the required amount over my own lips, in an attempt to feel their allure, as well as taste the cherry flavoured, sticky, gloopy glaze. Could they be any more marvellous? I asked myself, but more importantly, would I ever be like them?

'Slim and smart' as described in the handwritten adverts in the classifieds, in the matrimonial section of the Daily Jang newspaper, the only Asian newspaper at the time. These two words were always sure to guarantee interest from the mothers of prospective suitors. Mum anxiously scurried up to both sisters, straightening their hair and pulling at their clothes, pinching Nailah's tunic to make it tighter at the waist.

She nudged them once again saying, "Jaldi karrooo! - Hurry up! Go sit in the living room and wait 'til I call you." Whilst giggling and mimicking her, they both duly obeyed mum's fierce instructions. Meanwhile, standing on an over-turned Khyber ghee bucket next to the electric stove, I carefully dropped the last batch of samosas into the hot bubbling oil.

Those bright yellow ghee buckets were the most robust canister known to man. Once the ghee had been used up, they were washed out and re-purposed in so many inventive ways. Some became small seats, which mum would refashion by wrapping them in a thin layer of foam and then a layer of fabric from her stash; neatly stitching it to seal any evidence of it being an old ghee bucket. Some, when painted, became makeshift tables, and some, plinths, as I demonstrated in the kitchen today. There was never a fear of that base caving in as it could easily hold anyone's weight; it was that robust and durable. As I dropped the last samosa in from a height (bad idea), I felt an explosive splatter of tiny droplets of the hot oil on my tiny hands. "Oweeee!" I screamed, hoping someone would come running, but sadly, no one was paying any attention to me. That was when I thought, 'why do I get all the rubbish jobs?'

All the dishes were now ready to be plated on mum's finest China, which she had managed to squirrel into her 'sandooq' - large suitcase. We stood expectantly by the window of the front room. It was by far the best room in the house as it was carpeted, albeit in a hideous shade of bright green, over which we had no control. That too, another salvaged off-cut, which mum had retrieved from somewhere. We watched eagerly, whilst listening for cars, wondering if our visitors would be the next to drive past. Finally, the sound of an engine could be heard, and a car edged slowly into view, stopping at the gate. A bright yellow Datsun.

"That's them!" I screamed at the top of my voice, as mum shushed me, gesturing my sister Zainab and I to return to the kitchen and be on standby for her next instructions. On the way down, I peeked through the small slit of a butler sink window that divided this floor to the basement, to see a family, of at least six, including children, emerge one by one from the Datsun. 'How did they squeeze them all in?' I thought. As the doorbell rang, mum straightened her dupatta, veil, over her head. Her large ornate gold earrings, given to her by her father on her wedding day, were clearly visible. She was wearing her best midnight blue Benares shalwar kameez, a modest, elegant and traditional outfit. She took a deep breath to compose herself, as she opened the door.

"Asalam a laikum Mrs Rauf." I heard being said numerous times from the small crowd of people, male and female entering our house, one by one. The entire extended family had descended on us that day, even though we were told there would be only four visitors, at the most. 'Where are they all going to sit'? I wondered. They came in and all somehow finding places to sit or perch; edges of the one good sofa and various other ledges, functioning as makeshift seats. Mum came running down to the basement; her face panic stricken having only expected four people. She anxiously recruited us all to look for more chairs; anything we could find to seat people. "Hai-Hai" she whispered, an expression of shock, as I grabbed an old Khyber bucket onto which she threw a bright pink scarf to hide the stains. "That will do," she said and whisked it away. We all listened from the bottom of the staircase and heard the crowd continue to pass pleasantries. The usual small talk that we were accustomed to hearing at this stage of the suitor meetings.

The father of the suitor, Mr Baig, started with the more formal questions, which once again, we had heard before. There must have been a script somewhere for these awkward opening lines of conversation. "So, nice to meet you sister, thank you for welcoming us." Mum politely nodding in acknowledgement; her gaze lowered, not to make eye contact with him, only with his wife, Mrs Baig. He swiftly followed, with the predicted question, "But where is Mr Rauf today?" He was referring to dad; always a natural first question for the men to ask.

Mum paused for a moment as we all stood listening, from outside the room. For a few seconds I stopped breathing; always freezing with anxiety at this question, staring at my siblings wide-eyed. Dad no longer lived with us. He had left three years earlier, to start a new life somewhere else, leaving mum on her own to raise a family of five children. There was so much more complexity, pain, and trauma woven into this dark situation, but for now, that was the plain truth. Today, as always, mum would have to invent another excuse or more to the point an elaborate lie to explain his whereabouts.

After what felt like the most pregnant of all pauses, we heard mums voice, surprisingly confident; upbeat, if not slightly high pitched. She was well rehearsed at this, as she straightened her posture, sat bolt upright and proudly announced at the top of her voice, "Mr Rauf is on business today; he's delivering spices in Denmark." There it was - today's dad story. Trying to contain our sniggering, we collapsed, one by one onto the cold concrete tiles, with tears streaming from our eyes and rolling down our faces as we silently mouthed, "Delivering spices in Denmark!" At the same time, we were relieved that she actually made it sound plausible. We even visualised it, imagining it to be true - dad driving a heavy-duty truck, laden with spices from Pakistan, over the 5,000km route through Asia and Europe. What a road trip that would be. Mum was a convincing storyteller and a good liar. The visitors continued with their uncomfortable and prying line of questioning.

"Oh, that's very interesting, so Mr Rauf has a spice company?" Mrs Baig said, interjecting excitedly. Indian Spices in Britain had not yet become widely available, even in the Pakistani grocery stores, they were still pretty scarce. She was sure to ask what spices mum had in stock, in her own cupboards. Mum suddenly realised her lie today was probably not the best thought out; on the brink of backfiring. Anything to suggest you owned ample spices to another Pakistani woman was likely to get you ambushed into surrendering a few. Such was the scarcity of spices from the homeland. They were like gold dust. "Yes!" boasted mum and he is away a lot, even my spices are running out." Another impressive deflection from mum, followed by, "Anyway... you must all be really thirsty after that long drive, please let me get you some chai." Mum was, without doubt one of the most sophisticated, creative liars when it came to dad's whereabouts.

We all scarpered, as she made her way out of the room towards us trying to stay composed but looking anything but. "Cha, cha, chaaa – tea!!" This was the signal to get both sisters into the room for the expectant family. With the first course ready to be served, made up of sundries - a tray of tea and nibbles, known as 'nimak paray' which were basically small triangles of pastry, sprinkled with carom seeds and deep fried. One of the easiest and moreish snacks to create, simply with a few cupsful of all-purpose flour, a tablespoon of butter and a few pinches of carom seeds. It was brought together with a little water to create a dough; then kneaded and rolled out flat. It would then be cut into small triangular shapes and deep fried for a matter of minutes until deep golden brown. Served with hot chai, they made a perfect entrée and a good icebreaker to welcome our guests.

As we began to race around gathering plates and cups; everything the sisters needed to make their grand entrance, I watched them straightening themselves up. Mum tugged at them, to make sure they looked flawless, as they were ushered into the living room. "Siddha turro! - Walk upright!" she instructed Nailah who immediately straightened her posture, whilst Zainab and I continued to watch from the sidelines as they entered the room. There was a deafening silence as they walked in; you could a hear a pin drop. This was the moment the family were scrutinising my two beautiful sisters, superficially at this stage, for all their physical attributes. Then suddenly the conversation ensued, "Oh puttar - daughter, by God's grace 'bhot pyari' - how lovely you both are," announced Mrs Baig.

I heard a quiet giggle, with a hint of sarcasm from one of my sisters. The silence turned into full-on chatter; multiple conversations started happening simultaneously. Whilst we couldn't hear them clearly, it sounded as though things were going well. Zainab and I sighed in relief as we realised that stage one of today's 'mission suitor' was a success. The stage that Nailah and Laylah sarcastically referred to, between them as 'the sizing up of the goods.' I was too young to fully understand many of their coded sayings that they had coined between them. I sensed that not all was as clear-cut as we imagined and there were many reasons why.

The two sisters had come to England just over a decade ago from Pakistan. They were both thrust abruptly into this foreign country, greeted by a man that they both struggled to believe was their father. Overnight, Yorkshire became their new home. Having been left by dad at the age of one and two respectively, Laylah and Nailah had never been given an opportunity to forge a meaningful bond or relationship with him before he came to settle in England. They had been raised by mum and their grandfather, the closest male that represented a paternal figure. Life was good for them in those early years in Pakistan. Idyllic in fact, as they played in the beautiful open courtyards, running freely in the ample acres of land surrounding their home in Karachi, under the care and protection of mum's extended family. There, they were indulged; always surrounded by relatives - aunts, uncles, cousins and of course grandad's famous ice cream factory. Every child's fantasy.

England could not have been more poles apart from that idyllic world. They were forced to integrate overnight; fit in, navigate, without any preparation or warning. Cold, dark, dreary Yorkshire. It didn't help that they landed in the middle of winter. Freezing cold short days and long nights; nothing could have prepared them for this. The dark cobbled streets, dark stone buildings, blackened by soot from houses burning coal and smoke from the textile mills where dad worked. Rows of dark houses, a far cry from the clean masonry walls they had known back in Pakistan. If that wasn't traumatic enough, they were swiftly enrolled into the local Catholic school. The only two brown girls entering at the time, with limited knowledge of the English language, culture, and lifestyle. They were separated into two different classrooms, where they were unable to lean on each other for support, as they were unceremoniously inducted into 1960s racist

Yorkshire.

Children can be cruel at times, but children of racists, that could be another level of brutality altogether. Torturous savages in fact, who subjected the two terrified Pakistani girls to the worst ordeals. They were spat at, punched, their braids pulled out, called the vilest racist names that could only be concocted by the children of vile racists themselves. These atrocious acts were painfully compounded by teachers and staff who did nothing to intervene. Their complicity in the enabling, made the issue more painful than the physical and verbal attacks of their ignorant and obtuse classmates. Laylah quickly learned to defend herself. She was tough, unlike her younger, much softer sister who she fiercely protected. She learned how to physically fight back; push, punch, and tussle with anyone who chose to mess with them. After months of being prey to these depraved but not untypical acts of racism, the bullies turned their attention to the new brown kids. The Bangladeshi, Indian, East African and other non-white children that were slowly entering the school.

Being thrown in at the deep end, had its advantages. They learnt survival skills that were vital to getting them through the politically tumultuous years that followed; led by the politician Enoch Powell. Banners strewn across shop windows, graffiti on the wall opposite the house: PAKIS GO HOME! Get out, leave our jobs and F%^K OFF! Every brown person, irrespective of what region you came from in South Asia were called a 'Paki', to the dismay of the Bangladeshi's, Sri Lankans, East African Indians and Indian born Indians! If they were to be insulted daily, then at least let it be more relevant to their regional and cultural heritage. Had the British not heard of regional prejudice amongst the Asian community? This was a double put down. My sisters were survivors, quickly gaining a repertoire of new skills from self-defence, biting back and tolerance – in many cases they had no choice but to live with the verbal abuse and disparaging looks from the working-class community of Shipley. Welcome to Yorkshire.

They fought their way through those horrific years. They were tough, and eventually, it became easier. When three more children arrived in quick succession, with only a year between my brother and sister Zainab, the girls were given new roles as nurturers, carers, babysitters to their siblings who bought a much needed sense of joy to the household. The new arrivals even saw our neighbourhood open their arms to protect mum and become the extended family she had left behind. Sensing her silent cries for help from the confines of her home; humanity rose above racism.

1970's, Britain was now home. My sisters embraced everything, taking full advantage of the popular culture of the day. Music and fashion for them compounded their love of all things British. By the mid-seventies, they were more stylish if not iconic in Bradford. Many people knew of the beautiful Rauf girls. They were popular amongst the community, if not edgy; the 'It' girls of their day. Everyone who met them wanted to befriend them and, not surprisingly, every suitor that came to visit, wanted to marry them. But they would never accept any old proposition. Betrothal was based on far more than the credentials of those who visited our home. Parents would confidently rely only on their son's qualifications and their professions. But that was not enough. After everything my sisters had suffered, witnessed and braved; being discerning was their God given right.

In the kitchen, I continued to watch over the bubbling stove, knowing that two more courses of the meal would be expected to be delivered shortly. Today it was Murgh Masala - Hen Curry, a popular bird back in the 1970s. It was more flavoursome than chicken, especially in curry. By the age of seven, I was adept at making a masala for most dishes; it was pretty standard for me to create the base or masala for a murgh from scratch. Two medium onions peeled and chopped finely under the watchful eye of mum, a whole bulb of garlic, and a generous lump of ginger. The garlic and ginger bashed together within an inch of their life in a pestle and mortar. Sadly, for me, there were no fancy food processors back then. These three elements sautéed in ghee - clarified butter; a small cupful which covered them generously and with the heat of the stove, a golden-brown hue formed around the edges of the onion.

That's when I threw in a good grab-ful of cumin seeds (grab-ful: equating to a tablespoon) into the pan of hot onions and watched it splatter - making sure I safely moved out of the way. Followed with three to four roughly bashed up tomatoes, swiftly stirred in to form a paste. Then more spices thrown in - a teaspoon of each was ample; turmeric, ground coriander, garam masala and chilli powder to make the claggy paste. At this point, it was vital to keep that paste moving around, so it didn't catch the base of the pan. Once the spices released their aromas, which tended to stick to my hair and clothing; even the air around me hummed of it, that was the point at which the chopped bird on the bone was added. 'On the bone', for a richer and brothy flavour. Mum taught me to never leave the hen stationary in the pan for more than a few seconds. I used the wooden spoon to keep it moving swiftly, coating it in the paste and then watching the oil separate around all the elements in the pan. This usually took around ten minutes. Standing back again, to avoid a hot facial in the steam, I would throw in a cup of water. Then, lid on, the heat turned down, it would be simmered until amply cooked through. When cooked, a glassy film of oil settled across the surface; then some freshly chopped coriander from the garden would be sprinkled liberally over the top and left to penetrate the curry. It was always best when served with hot roti.

I gathered the necessary things to get this spread of food delivered upstairs on time; as always. As I did this, I heard my sisters running excitedly down the cold uncarpeted lower ground floor staircase, out of sight of any guests. They were giggling uncontrollably once again as they burst into the room in raucous fits of laughter. With her face glowing under the florescent light, Laylah belted out, "My name is BASH-A-RAT!" Nailah, hysterically exclaimed, "He's yours, I'm not marrying anyone with that name!" They were referring to one of the suitors, whose name was in fact 'Basharat'. Not an uncommon male name at that time.

It turned out that two brothers had come to our home that day as potential suitors. No one was expecting this. Suitor number one, Basharat, a.k.a. 'bash-a-rat' and suitor number two - Farooq, who apparently had been too heavy-handed with the Brylcreem hair lotion - another thing for them to pick on. Meanwhile, I remember thinking, what a bonus it would be if they both got snagged in one day. Course number two of the grand feast was ready. The meat biryani that mum and I had diligently prepared the night before. It all smelt and looked incredible, and it was plated to perfection. The sounds of laughter and chatter could be heard from the basement as more plates, top-ups of food and chai were sent back and forth. All the courses had now been successfully delivered and consumed. These visits lasted a few hours, more so, if the family decided we were the 'right fit' for them, as was the case with this particular family. Even though we had the final say.

As the meeting came to an end, I could hear the sound of footsteps walking from the living room to the hallway. I ran to catch a glimpse of them all as they left, to try and gauge the mood as they exited our home. As I peered around the wall next to the butler sink, I saw the family again, leaving as they had arrved, in single file through our narrow hallway. Each member held out a hand to mum, which she gently touched between her hands - a sign of respect; a positive one at that. It was obvious, that they were happy. The last person to leave, Mrs Baig, not only put out her hand, but she also outstretched her arms, holding mum close and whispering something into her ear that made her smile in acknowledgment.

I had to squint to get a better look when I saw something that struck me as odd. There was a samosa stuck to the back of Mrs Baig's dress, close to her bottom. Somehow a samosa had become wedged there, awkwardly; she must have been sitting on it. How else did it get there? It had, as expected imparted a halo of an oily stain which wouldn't wash away easily. "One less samosa for us," Zainab giggled from behind me. "What a waste," I growled as I started to tidy up the dishes with her. Zainab turned to me, disdainfully declaring something that I took light heartedly at the time, "Jesus Farah, I'm not marrying a Pakistani man if this is what we have to go through!" Her words didn't fully register until a few years later, when they would be reinforced in the most shocking way. But for now, I was more concerned with tidying away plates, until the next suitor day, whilst dancing to ABBA playing from the old wireless radio, positioned on a shelf in the kitchen.

Finally, it was over. The guests had left and Mum walked into the room looking proud but pensive. A slight quiver in her voice as she announced in a soft tone, which as a family we detected always spelt trouble. "They loved you both meri jaans - my darlings. But I'm just not sure," she continued. Meanwhile I was deflated at the prospect of more arduous suitor-searching. "Why mum?" inquired a bemused but not too perturbed Laylah. "Because there's a belief my darlings; you never marry two daughters into the same household." I thought it worked perfectly well in the film Seven brides for seven brothers, why not for these two? "Oh, is that right... why?" continued Laylah, once again, feigning concern. "Because, if one marriage fails, it will impact on the others' relationship, that's why my darling," mum concluded.

This was a superstition with a plausible rationale. Whilst mum had many irrational fears that she felt would jinx certain situations, there was some logic here. Given that both her daughters would be expected to live with their in-laws after marriage; if one marriage failed, it would impact the entire household. On the part of the suitor's family, the deal was both sisters' betrothal or nothing. As attractive as that deal sounded to me, it was for mum, a no-deal situation. Mum would reject this offer today. As she made her decision known, she seemed unusually calm. I detected from her calmness, that she was not ready to lose both daughters in such quick succession. Days later, mum as always, asked me to pen another letter to the suitor's family.

It read:

Asalaam-a-laikum dear brother and sister Baig,

Thank you for visiting. It was a pleasure to meet you. Your sons are wonderful young men by the grace of God. However, my daughters are not fully ready to commit to leaving this household together as you desire. It is not practical or favourable to them or ourselves, unless you reconsider. I do hope you understand, and we wish you all the best for the future.

Salaam

Mr and Mrs Rauf

The family did not respond; mum knew they were not prepared to reconsider the offer. But they did leave a lasting impression. Farooq, the Brylcreem boy, left a heavy oil stain on the wall where his head was propped throughout the entire meeting. Mrs Baig, another oil stain on the sofa from the wedged samosa. No matter how many times we attempted to scrub away both marks, the stains would always find a way of slowly resurfacing.

Chapter 2

Laylah

She embodied the essence of 1970s Britain. At eighteen years old, Laylah was the famous, 'It' girl of Yorkshire; an influencer of her generation and ahead of the curve in so many ways. Everyone who knew of her wanted to be in her company; enveloped in her infectious upbeat energy. She was exquisite in every way. Her long, naturally lustrous, raven locks hung loosely around her shoulders. The contrast between it and her dewy olive skin drew attention to her heart shaped face and features. Her carefully contoured thick kajel-lined eyes looked out from under an accentuated arched brow - a homage to twiggy and other famous models of that era.

I recall snatching any moment I could, to creep into her attic bedroom, when she wasn't there, to peek at her things. For a seven-year-old, it felt like gazing into another world - Wonderland or Narnia. There, I would carefully examine the many ornate bottles, placed with precision across her dressing table. A collection of soft musk scents; Fenjal - London, Paris New York said the label. This was sophisticated stuff; lotions and potions I had never heard of but loved to squeeze an ample dollop onto my grubby hand and sniff at it all day; imagining what it would be like to live in her glamorous, grown-up world. She embodied beauty, sophistication, femininity like no one else I knew. She was my hero and I idolised her.

With twelve years between us, I was more like a daughter to her than a younger sister. She was kind, loving, maternal and generous; often spending her weekly wages on toys from the markets for her three younger siblings. She cared and loved us all deeply. Unbeknown to us at the time, she carried immense trauma. No one would ever have imagined it from the mesmeric face she presented to the outside world. The carefully applied makeup, the well-coordinated outfits and the powerful energy she exuded, was a decoy. A camouflage which was her armour. Behind it was a frightened young girl. A girl in denial.

As the first-born child, she carried the can and broke the mould, paving the way for us all. She couldn't have been a better role model for her younger siblings. She smashed through a ton of glass ceilings and barriers facing not just brown and Pakistani girls of that era; she did it for all girls, all women. Self-assured and confident, she was not afraid to challenge the patriarchy when it came to standing up for what she believed was right. She was the first Pakistani girl to work at the then prestigious offices of the newly opened Imperium Stores in Bradford. She worked in the accountancy department, a male dominated profession at the time.

There she would be regularly undermined, whether it was being paid much less than her male counterparts for doing the same work (better) or excluded from management meetings. She was even assigned menial tasks that she would point blank refuse to do. "Why should I make the chai for these entitled twonks," she would recount to mum daily. After the one and only time her bottom was tapped as she walked past one of her co-worker's desk, she was the one reprimanded for giving him a black eye. She didn't mind the ticking off; it was every bit worthy of the joy she felt to have lamped Derek in the face. He certainly wouldn't be doing that again in a hurry. She fiercely defended herself and others from the injustices that she experienced and witnessed daily. Those routine racist battering's of the 1970's playground had been her fight club, her training academy, where she had learned to hit back; harder in every sense and it stood her in good stead.

"Don't try to be everyone's vakeel - lawyer," mum would timidly warn her daily. Wanting her daughter to quietly blend in and stay under the radar as many south Asian parents did back then. Mum saw any form of conflict with white people as an opportunity for them to 'send us back home'. "Don't fight with or in front of white people," we were told by an anxious mum, who it seemed was happier to see us acquiesce and be traumatised by some of the racist neighbourhood children who would often set their dogs on us. We would hear them cackle as we ran up the street to Master Qureshi's house; the local make-shift mosque where we learnt to recite our prayers.

Laylah was an aberration and a role model to many of the Asian girls. They admired her and often cited her to their own parents to justify that they too should be afforded the same 'freedoms' they saw her exhibit. Little did they know how much she had suffered; undergone to get to this point. She was loved and celebrated by her peers, but hated by their parents, who viewed her with disdain, seeing her as trouble. Mum would try her best to rein her in when a judgemental parent made a disparaging observation about her. "Try to stay low key and not to be the source of any shame or embarrassment for our family. Remember your roots, don't forget we are not from here, we have different standards and values," she would beg, in a desperate attempt to control her daughter. "Well, you brought us here mum, don't you think it's stupid trying to recreate the values from your home? THIS IS NOT PAKISTAN!" was Laylah's fierce reply.

She was right, our parents used their incongruent value system, muddling it with religion, in an attempt to control us. But worse still, justify their often-flimsy arguments as to why we were not entitled to the same rights here, in what was now our home - Britain. Entitlement worked both ways. Being 'other' culturally and religiously, we were targets of racists, who made us feel less entitled or able to access the same privileges given to the British. That part was elementary, it happened. Representation was not a thing yet; it was the 1970s. But then, imagine this being compounded by your own brown parents - reinforcing in you the belief that you were a subjugate and that you should be grateful for any crumb of entitlement thrown your way. They too were akin to the complicit teachers who turned a blind eye to the racist thugs.

Sadly, our parents did not help us to assimilate; if anything, they made us more alienated and 'other', in a society that they had decided to settle in and within which to raise us. I remember being told when asking mum innocently if I could go to my friend's house for tea. "You're not white you know." I did know but wasn't sure about the connection between skin colour and going to eat tea at my friend's house. Was it to do with religion? no; culture? yes. Was it a case of mixed-up values? most definitely. A whole array of arbitrary ad hoc, self-satisfying rules of the most confusing kind to our generation.

These were just some of the daily cultural and generational clashes that we had to naviagate; it was standard. However, there were other much deeper layers of strain between Laylah and mum. Theirs was a relationship that was splintered with complexity. Things we didn't know about; intense and ferocious arguments that manifested in terrifying screams that could be heard echoing from the cold stone tiles of the basement, up the four stories to the attic where we, the younger siblings would hide, amidst their rage fuelled exchanges. No one knew what triggered them; at our age, it didn't occur to us to ask. It was part of our normality; day to day family dynamics, in a house that was dominated by women with a fierce matriarch at the head of it. We just assumed that there would be many heated exchanges.

The clashes would always end with either Laylah or mum passing out, such was the intensity of emotions they each experienced; they would even forget to breathe in the midst of them.

We, the youngest three siblings saw these volatile arguments as opportunities to escape; to build imaginary fortresses around the immense Victorian terraced house. We would discover new nooks and corners that we never even knew existed, like the tiny box room under the stairs - was it a panic room of the Victorian era? Who knows. We would fashion imaginary tents and pretend that they were masts on a ship, using some of the best woven loom textiles from the mills that were destined for Saville row. We would rag them around the floors of the house to mum's sheer outrage. Mum was paid to unpick the imperfections from these rolls of material. Our games created more snags for her to unpick through the night. I wonder who ended up wearing the suits created from the expensive fabric, after they had been dragged through our dusty old house. We could be in another world, huddling together inside our makeshift fortresses, telling horror stories, whilst eating pocketfuls of spicy dried chickpeas; in our minds escaping, far away from the cold, dark terraced house we lived in.

Who could have imagined that a legume, in the form of dried chickpeas could be the tastiest snack you could give to a child? And they would actually enjoy it! I would watch mum soak a good few kg's of dried chickpeas that she would empty into a bucket from a hessian sack bought from Mrs Patel's shop. There were no pre-soaked tinned varieties back then, everything was from first principles. The chickpeas would stay in the water overnight along with a few tablespoons of salt. A pan of bubbling hot - scorching vegetable oil awaited these chickpeas which were carefully spooned in after they had been drained from the water. Enough splatters to pebble-dash the kitchen tiles if you were not careful. Each time, mum would forget to cover the oil, shrieking, "Satayanaaas! Destruction!" whilst grabbing old tea towels to wipe the tiles before the oil stuck hard as glue. The final destination of the deep-fried chickpeas, before our anticipating tummies, as we watched in amazement, was the secret spice blend. Not a secret to us, but to the other women of Shipley Road; no one got the balance quite right, which is why it became the most coveted recipe in Yorkshire. I knew it. In a large tray mum would spread a thin layer of 'kala lun' or black salt. It was the most noxious smelling sulphurous salt known to man, akin to a fart, but it was like gold dust to get hold of. Mum had smuggled a bag of it back from the homeland years ago. Only a tiny pinch required as it was potent. Then, came the other spices she had diligently ground by hand. Anar dana – pomegranate seeds; they become the most piquant pocket rockets when dried on the kitchen table - who knew? Another layer of hot chilli powder; there was only one strength back then and you had to be frugal with it otherwise you would know about it the next day, when queuing for the toilet. A few more layers of spices, ground coriander seeds, cumin, and mango powder known as amchur, that Mrs Patel reserved only for her favourite customers.

There it was, the most sought-after spice blend in Yorkshire that only I was privy to watch being assembled. I had the honour of mixing this classified magic blend with a flat wooden spoon until it was fused to perfection. A taste test involved sticking in my index finger and checking it as it sat on my tongue. First came the pinch of the chilli followed by the piquancy of the mango and pomegranate. Mum would do the same. It was right when we both decided it was right; our palettes were in perfect harmony.

The blend was ready to scatter over the crispy chickpeas, left to cool after removing from the hot oil they had danced and spluttered in, but surprisingly still remained intact. Mum holding one side of the tray, I the other, we'd swish these chickpeas around the spice blend until they were amply coated; then another taste test to ensure we had got it right. We would adjust the spices accordingly if required. These spicy little bombs were dished up in small cones rolled out of old copies of the Daily Jang newspaper. They were truly the best treat that the kids of Shipley Road lined up for hours outside our door to snag.

In the background, a secret love affair was taking place. Maybe this was one of the reasons the heated arguments happened. Love of this kind was against the rules, out of bounds for her daughters. The rules that mum had fashioned,

Freda Shafi

which were influenced more by fear of losing control than anything else. The rules were ineffective and incongruent but most of all frustrating to her grown up daughters, who were straddling two cultures, both so extreme in values. Inevitably there would be culture clashes of magnificent proportions. Whilst the secret love had no name; his presence was felt with the air that Laylah carried about her.

Unchaperoned clandestine meet-ups were disguised under the pretext of work. She volunteered at the Red Cross, which often saw her return late at night, to mum's suspicions and disapproval. "What kind of work goes on at this late hour?" mum would scold her as she crept back into the house, looking guilt-ridden. "I met the Queen mother today mum!" was Laylah's sharp excited response. "This late?" a puzzled mum inquired with a look of surprise and shock. Mum was a true royalist. She loved everything British and regal. The Royal family to her represented everything that she had dreamt about of England before she moved here. She even thought, whilst gawking endlessly at images of London and Buckingham palace from her home in Pakistan, that she would be living close by; neighbours with Queen Elizabeth, with whom she identified strongly. The queen wasn't that much older than her; she idolised her and jumped to celebrate any occasion that saw reason, such as the Silver Jubilee of 1976. Mum sat up all night sewing our red, white and blue dresses so we could attend the local celebrations wearing the royal colours and waving Union Jack flags. "Yes mum, they took a photo of me with the Queen mother. I'll show you when it comes out," Laylah continued.

Mum's intuition sensed what might be going on, but only let it go as far as it could; or as far as she had allowed for her daughter to explore a world that was strictly out of bounds. Enough to understand what the perimeter of love felt like, dipping your toe in, only so far to feel butterflies. And that was as far as it went. There were boundaries that she trusted us to observe; no physical contact, that she knew of in any case. Introductions to suitors were the only way we would ever meet anyone of the opposite sex. Two young people meeting outside of this protocol; would suggest something deviant had taken place and mum did not have the tools to comprehend or explain that to anyone, including herself. The introductory meetings were not just a respectable framework to find marriage material. You were likely to be matched with superior credentials. The second generation, that was us, had seen their parents hard toil, sacrifice and investment in them, pay off into their brilliant professional offspring. And brilliant profession was high on mums list of preferences for her daughters. She was not prepared to settle for any less.

Blood on the walls and the *No. 88 Bus*

His name was Junaid, Jo for short. The bus conductor on the Number 88, from Imperium stores to Shipley and he was madly in love with Laylah. They met on her daily trips to work; it was inevitable. She, the hottest ticket in town; no pun intended. Every inch of her dressed to the nines, exuding self-confidence, wit and charm. She was popular even amongst her work colleagues, many of whom caught the same bus with her daily. Dotty, short for Dorothy, was one of them, an older lady, in her late fifties. Dotty wore a fake plaited blonde bun that perched on her head known back then as a beehive. Her heavily powdered face, a few shades off her natural complexion was crepey where the powder collected in folds. A then fashionable thin black pencil line defined her hugely over exaggerated brows into an arch. Her look was akin to a drag queen. She and Laylah were thick as thieves as they giggled and gossiped throughout the fifteen-minute ride from Shipley to Bradford. Jo went out of his way daily, swapping rosters with his colleagues to make sure that he was always on Laylah's bus.

He, like many other men was dazzled by her. Everything about her was electrifying - her brilliance, her confidence, but what appealed to him most was her humility. She would talk to everyone on that bus, inviting them all to chat, to laugh and to be joyous with her. Jo never thought he stood a chance; surely, he was way out of her league? Invisible, if not insignificant. It was also the acknowledgement that he was flattered by; she noticed him, even when he was invisible to everyone else. On the day they spoke with each other; a small spark was ignited between them, and it grew quickly into romance. His clunky bus conductor uniform covered every part of his body bar his face and hands; enough for her to see the handsome young man hidden inside. She noticed his piercing oval eyes beaming at her every minute that she spent on that bus journey. As they spoke more with each passing day, the attraction spiralled out of control; they were soon besotted with one another.

Having newly arrived in the UK, with no real qualifications, or credentials to boast of, Jo was intelligent in other ways, and he was ambitious. He lived with his father in Bradford, in a heavily populated and tight knit community from a certain region in Pakistan. Mum once cautiously warned us, "These people don't marry outside of their own kind, either back home or here." We didn't fully understand what she meant, but it was a clear reference to a class divide. An archaic, ideology called baradri - brotherhood, which distinguished between certain classes, and regions. It caused huge divides in Pakistan post partition, often to maintain hierarchies, but more importantly, keeping wealth and traditions within a specific community. It could be likened to the way in which Royal families maintained wealth, class and position within a restricted parameter. Mum had friends within this community and knew from them, that they would not be open to marrying outside of their 'brotherhood'. Anyone doing so would always be considered an outsider and their life would not be easy.

So began a clandestine forbidden love affair, between two clans - the Montagues and the Capulets that never the twain should unite in marriage. Laylah and Jo were doing just that in hooking up. They were truly a modern-day Romeo and Juliet. The only other person who knew of their love was Dotty, who vicariously experienced this forbidden love, played-out like Heathcliff and Cathy, blossoming under her watchful fairy godmother eye. It was reassuring to have a maternal figure in Dotty, who unlike mum, helped them. Laylah fell deeply in love with Jo, despite the shackles and restrictions mum put on her, the eldest daughter. She knew she would be destroying the rigid paradigm that she had been burdened with. Her responsibility was to be the moral benchmark of conformity, a role model to her younger siblings. But this relationship was considered the opposite of those values.

It was Dotty in fact who came to our house to talk to mum about them, to gently persuade her into accepting a union of which she was not fully aware. Mum never showed any emotion around strangers. Instead, she sat and listened, nodding stoically as Dotty explained, wearing a florescent yellow tunic dress that lifted up to her thighs as she sat down. Mum sent my brother out of the room as he became overly intrigued with Dotty's long white legs on show that day; something he had never seen in real life. Dotty sipped her tea; leaving a dark red lipstick stain on the edge of the cup, as she began to explain the reason for her visit. "Well thank you for seein' me today, Mrs Rauf, I've come to talk abo..." "Yes, I know you are my daughter's friend Dotty."

mum interrupted. It was as if she was half expecting what was to follow. Dotty launched in without taking a pause for breath. "Mrs Rauf, Laylah's a lovely girl, I see her as my own daughter; I would never let her be with anyone unworthy and there is a young man called Jo, who is I promise you, so worthy."

'What the hell does she know?' I sensed mum thinking, whilst still nodding, with a painfully forced smile, as brown people did when they knew they were being patronised. Mum interrupted again, "Yes, yes, I know MY daughter well, she's a good girl, very clever, beautiful and our culture…" Before she could finish her sentence, Dotty, interjected, "Oh ah knoooow she is so polite." Her broad Yorkshire accent was beginning to grate on mum's nerves as she cut in again. "As I was saying, my daughter knows that there is a way we do things here and we will do it properly; bringing, his family to our home, so it's done with…" Mum struggled to find the next word, but she continued in Punjabi, looking over at me for help; "Izzat. She knows that we do things here with izzat - respect," that was the word mum was trying to find. "Yes, yes Mrs Rauf yoar right… iz-att!" Dotty tried to emulate the word phonetically, but got it wrong, putting the emphasis on the wrong syllable.

"So… I will ask Jo's father to come to see you with izatt?" she mouthed again, this time slowly, her eyebrows raised, sounding out the words like an instruction. Her face powder was beginning to show signs of strain through her many expressions; dried bits of powder began to crumble onto her dress. 'Is that what cakey makeup means?' I thought. I saw mum's irritation at this point. "Yes, yes, ok, don't worry; I will write to him, don't you worry, and I'll do it the proper way, my way," mum concluded; standing up, as if to usher Dotty and her tall beehive out of the door. "Oh, oh okay then. I'll pass the letter on then, shall I?" Dotty said. "No, we will take care of it." Mum's final words to her. She was aghast at Dotty's persistence in offering unwanted and unwelcome help for securing her daughter's suitor. Dotty tottered down the garden, looking back, giving us a brisk wave, "Bye then!"

She was endearingly naïve, to a point that she didn't have a clue how mum had viewed her that day; mostly as an interfering troublemaker, who she felt was leading her precious daughter astray. She felt Dotty was enabling Laylah's deviant behaviour; giving her the tools to go down a path that was forbidden. What did she know? mum thought and how dare this woman show up to patronise her on how to conduct her family affairs.

Another explosive argument between mum and Laylah erupted that evening, leaving mum between a rock and a hard place. She had no choice but to cave in, realising the consequences of standing her ground. If Laylah was to marry without her blessing, not only would she lose her precious daughter, but it would cause one of the biggest scandals that the Pakistani community of Bradford had ever seen.

The protocol had to be observed still - marrying by way of introduction; despite the fact that a suitor had already been 'chosen' by her daughter outside of this convention. So, for that reason, the introduction would have to be staged, and this way it would be wrapped in 'izzat' - all for show. Mum surrendered; realising she had no choice.

When the day arrived, Jo and his father came to the house to meet us, we had prepared a sumptuous feast and Laylah had prepared Jo to lie. Many lies. As if the clandestine clan-crossing wasn't enough, Jo's profession would also pose another sticking point for mum. Bus conductor was not on her list of approved suitor professions; certainly not what she had in mind for her eldest daughter. They simply had to cover it up. So, between them, they fabricated what was possibly the most far-fetched profession a young Pakistani man from inner city Bradford could aspire to. Jo had been promoted overnight from bus conductor to Pilot.

Knowing how adept she was at sniffing out a lie; this major role had been afforded some extremely careful research to get past the gatekeeper - mum. Laylah had enlisted the help of Dotty once again, to help them get their facts straight. Fortuitously, Dotty had a pilot cousin who was able to supply her with enough information to fabricate the basics required to pass a plausibility test at a very pedestrian level. It was quite the operation.

A feast fit for a pilot was prepared that day. 'Batera' or Quail, gamey bird, considered a delicacy and not easy to come by. These ones were especially reared by Mr Khuwaja the butcher. Intrigued, I went to collect the tiny quails with mum the day before; we needed two to warrant making a rich masala for this dish. I watched him dissect their innards and take off their head. Poor birds. We went all out on this feast. The strong flavour of this oily bird required bold flavours to disguise it. Mum taught me that the best way to get flavours soaked into meat was through overnight marination and we did just that. A pot of thick set plain yogurt made from scratch was used. The spices, a good teaspoon of each - turmeric powder, red chilli powder, cumin powder, ground coriander and two tablespoons of ginger-garlic paste, a small bunch of coriander from the garden, three smashed to smithereens green chillies and a teaspoon of Mrs Patels special garam masala. All in the pot with the yogurt. My favourite part was taste testing this marinade. I had to stop myself after three teaspoons; it was so insanely delicious. The quails were then ready to be thrown in and mixed together until no part was left untouched by the marinade. Then into the fridge to soak up all the flavours overnight. That was eighty percent of the work done, thank goodness. The next day, after the quails were amply flavoured, they were thrown into a simple masala. One onion, chopped finely with a teaspoon of the usual suspects; my spices: ground coriander, garam masala, turmeric, a pinch of red chilli powder and salt. Once sautéed, the quail was added; stir fried briskly for a few minutes before turning down the heat, covering it and letting it gently simmer until cooked through. Creamy and delicious batera. Served simply with basmati rice to fully appreciate this flavoursome bird.

When the guests arrived; there were only two - Jo and his elderly father. His mother had passed away several years earlier; he was the youngest child of a much older generation of siblings. This was also evident from the way his father staggered into the living room, unstable on his feet. His greying stubble, deep furrows around his face and jittery movements showed his advanced age; he was visibly old. Mum immediately felt comfortable with them both. They had a humble presence; unassuming people which was refreshing, compared to many of the families that visited us. After pouring the tea into her wedding China for his father, mum gently began her line of questioning. As I watched, I wondered, how she had managed to stuff this sixty-piece tea set into her suitcase from Pakistan, along with all the other loot that passed through customs.

She had already detected a certain vernacular; typical of the region she knew in Pakistan. It was the dialect of the people she had been told 'did not marry outside of their own clan'. There were certain definitive words of the forbidden clan here. Jo's father, ignorant that his son and Laylah were attempting a cover up today, slowly and shakily held his tea. He poured it into the saucer before loudly slurping it, unaware that three children behind his chair were creasing over with laughter, hearing him slurp and burp in succession.

"Puttar..." daughter, he began, looking directly at Laylah, "What do you do?" Laylah responded in English, "I work in the accounts department at Imperium stores uncle." He smiled, looking over at Jo, who was grinning with pride. His father noticed the palpable love between them, and he was accepting of it. He leant back into his seat; relaxed. It was mum's turn now. She turned to Jo and asked, "And you son, what is your job?" He too responded in English. "I am a pilot auntie." Mum feigned surprise but she had growing suspicions; something didn't sound right to her. The atmosphere became tense; the two lovers staring at each other across the room, not altogether admiringly now. This stare was full of dread, knowing that at any moment they could be tripped up by mum's calculated cross examinations.

"And Bhai jan," brother, addressing his father, she asked, "Where are you from back home?" There it was. The million-dollar question - no pussy footing around with mum. Jo and Laylah were now looking stunned at how this question had cropped up so early into the conversation. Laylah was hoping and praying that Jo had briefed his father, who replied instantly, "Kashmir." Mum paused and continued "Oh Kashmir... which part would that be?" There were many areas of Kashmir, the one she was angling at was situated on a certain side of the Mangla dam. She continued... "which side of the dam are you from," the only way to distinguish the socio-cultural differences between the two locations and classes.

Everyone knew exactly what 'what side of the dam?' meant. You were either in the rural part or the more built-up part, bordering a town known as Jhelum. Jo had forgotten to brief his dad. He was meant to tell him to say, 'the built up side of the dam', to disguise their heritage. He knew that an awful lot rested on his answer. He looked anxiously at his father. The answer he would give meant either acceptance from mum, which would signify an easy ride or judgement, which could mean losing everything he was here for today - that being the woman he loved - Laylah. It was the most nonsensical regional prejudice that ever existed he thought to himself; this flimsy line between approval or non-approval, which needed to be stopped with immediate effect. Maybe, it should be stopped today. But was he brave enough to do it?

Laylah glared piercingly, grimacing, praying for him to say the right thing. What was the right thing though? A denial of their heritage? A denial of who they were? Why should anyone be ashamed of that? A heritage which for them was not in the slightest sense a source of embarrassment or judgement. This was the death or glory moment. Even Jo began to rethink his answers. Why should he be in denial? That would mean living the rest of their lives this way; the wrong way to start any marriage. Why could they not be honest, rather than reinforce an already messy, convoluted set of lies? It was bad enough that he had lied blatantly about his profession. He decided in that moment, he was prepared to brave it and stand up for himself. It was the pivotal moment that would shatter or swing the pendulum towards a life of lies and deceit or honesty and integrity. Jo replied abruptly, with conviction and passion in his voice, "We are from Mirpur auntie."

He had stood his ground; refused to lie and he was prepared to brave the storm for the love of his life, announcing that he was in fact from 'that side of the dam', which mum had already guessed. The side she had made her assumptions and cast her aspersions over. Mum's expression turned from inquisitive to concerned. She interjected, "Well, we are Lahori's," from Lahore, to which Jo's father did not flinch; if anything, he looked calm and pleasantly surprised. Unconcerned with regional heritage, he was not judgemental, unlike mum. Trying to compose herself, mum realised she was on the edge of passing out, "PAAANII! - Water!" she hollered.

Hearing her, I ran to the butler sink to get her a tall glass of freezing cold water. Laylah was now looking visibly pale, clearly deflated by Jo's sudden proclamation and about-turn. He had stood up to mum, but more shockingly defied Laylah; refusing to play along with this degrading charade of denial. He had just driven a coach and horses through the lies concocted between them that had allowed him and his father into our home. No one expected mum's reaction as her face suddenly softened. She said gently, "It doesn't matter puttar - son." No one, at this moment was sure whether that was a patronising 'doesn't matter' or genuine 'doesn't matter', but it signified that mum had just announced that it was ok and there was even a possibility that he could marry her daughter. It was evident that he loved her.

Mum had sensed the desperation on the faces of these two young people. A desperation that was born out of being ambushed by her hard-line, inflexible rules and boundaries. Behind her stoic exterior and unwavering regulations, there was a woman who had once known tenderness, sensuality and love. Mum let down her guard. This was a glimpse of that tender woman. She saw the love between them; it was tangible. Despite his shortcomings, in her own judgemental eyes, she was convinced that Jo would cherish her daughter and more than anything, they would enjoy love in a way that she herself had never experienced. As they left the house that day; mum reached out to Jo and whispered in his ear, "Puttar, son, please look after my Laylah." He gripped her hand tightly, dropping his head down to hide the tears dripping down his face. "I will auntie, I promise; I promise." Shortly after they left, Laylah passed out with all the excitement.

The weeks that followed were dominated by preparations, lists, letters to relatives and writing invitations. Shopping for bridal fabric and all of the usual rituals and excitement that came with wedding season; this was a first for us. The first wedding in the house would surely be an incredibly special one in mum's eyes. On the day she realised that she hadn't bought enough Benares fabric for one of Laylah's dresses, everything changed. We should have expected what was coming when she caught the no 88 bus to Stone Abbey Road. Jo was working his shift. Not noticing her climb on the bus, he went over to her to collect the 10p fare. It was only after an irregularly long pause; he looked closer to notice mum staring at him wide mouthed. Everything had come undone within minutes of her climbing into his bus. No words were exchanged as she clambered off three stops early.

On returning home, she called up to Laylah, who was in her bedroom. Running down excitedly she asked, "Did you get the extra fabric?" Mum was furious, but she also anticipated the fallout of what was to come; knowing this was not going be easy. She calmly said, "I caught the number 88 today." Before she could reply, Laylah, once again, unable to catch her breath, fell to the floor and fainted. Whilst mum had backed down on her regional prejudice; she was not prepared to compromise or be made a fool by their blatant and deviant lies. She was also put out about the opulent feast and trouble we had gone to welcome them into our home. Unsure whether Laylah could hear her as she lay on the floor, mum continued, "I didn't mind that he was from 'that' side of the dam, I didn't mind that his culture is very different; what I did mind was that you lied about his profession and that you've been sneaking around for months Bas! - enough."

Laylah slowly came around, as I propped her head up. She sobbed, knowing there was no come back now. Mum added, "I bet you even lied about meeting the Queen Mother." Her final words on the whole affair as she left the room. The house shook as the door slammed dramatically shut behind her. The days, weeks, and months that ensued were filled with more dramatic, verbal attacks. We were in a war zone. Attacks between mother and daughter that saw Laylah broken, devastated; defeated. The house that was once filled with excitement, laughter and light suddenly became dark. Curtains around the house were drawn closed as mum retreated into her bedroom and did not surface for days. Mealtimes once joyous were now tainted with misery. Melancholy mealtimes, where everything tasted of sadness.

When Laylah sought one last meeting with Jo; her final goodbye, she recounted how he had taken a pen knife from his pocket, horrifically slashing through his hand then smearing her name in his blood over the walls of his room. LAYLAH LAYLAH LAAAYYYLAAHH!! Screaming her name with each letter drawn in blood, declaring this final proclamation of love for her. Endless, boundless, eternal love. Screaming until the sound had dried up from his throat, and no screams were left to be heard. Neither of them were equipped emotionally with what it would take to brave a life, a future together without mums blessing. They knew it was the end. No one would ever come close to that love, for either of them.

A few weeks later a photograph of Laylah appeared in the Telegraph & Argus. She wearing her Red Cross uniform and shaking hands with the Queen mother. Mum carefully cut out the photograph. Framed and mounted it on the wall.

Chapter 3

Was mum enough?

Pyar kiya to darr na kya -
I loved where is the fear in that?
Pyar kiya kohee chori nahee ki... pyar kiya -
I loved, I didn't steal anything; I simply loved
Lyrics from 1947 film Mugal-e-Azam.

M um listened to the song on repeat; the words forever etched in our minds. It was more than a song; it was her story. She had done nothing wrong; she had simply loved.

Had things been different for her, she would have been celebrated as a polymath. Gifted with a plethora of skills; she was a true renaissance woman. But instead, she chose to be low key, hiding under the radar and avoiding any unnecessary attention. This, the result of the resounding shame she felt after her married life was abruptly cut short. The sense of shame reverberated across many if not all areas of her life and resulted in feelings of frustration, denial and failure. It was the sense of shame mostly, that held her back, crippling her from realising her full potential as a brilliant woman. Mum was undoubtedly talented and adept, with a natural ability to turn her hand to anything. She was constantly perfecting and nurturing her skills; as a natural and intuitive cook, she would appropriate frugal ingredients to create the most delicious meals and banquets. As a homemaker, building and creating a comfortable and stylish home for her family. Much of her prowess and versatility was born out of scarcity and being suddenly thrust into poverty and necessity.

It had started very differently. She was the daughter of a wealthy businessman in Lahore and had a privileged life with an abundance of the comforts you would expect of a middle-class family in pre-partition Pakistan. Comforts, that included several servants to help around their beautiful house in a garden town, which was home to her family of eleven. It was understandable that on arriving in Britain, she refused to settle for anything less than the luxuries she had been afforded growing up. When the frugal years of Yorkshire kicked in, she did her best to re-create many of them, from a place of scarcity.

After landing in England in the October of 1966, her life took a dramatic turn. Everything from the moment she stepped off the airport bus, at the end of Southland Terrace, filled her with dread and a sense of foreboding. Starting with the freezing chill she felt on her skin beneath the ill-conceived chiffon kameez dress she was wearing to arrive, on a cold autumn evening, in Yorkshire. So much jarred her senses from the littered narrow cobbled streets to the oppressive looking dark stone of the back-to-back terraced houses, facing the Airedale train line. One of these small, terraced houses was to be her new home now. It couldn't have been more diametrically opposed to the beautiful military apartment she had just left behind in Karachi.

There was not much that gave her reason to be joyous at this moment, other than being reunited with her husband, after the long years spent apart. Was this really England… Yorkshire? Where were all the beautiful green fields, the hills, the beaches that she had seen in the photographs she had been sent by dad. How far was Buckingham Palace? She was not expecting this rude awakening, or the sudden cruel adjustment that came, without any warning. Unsurprisingly, mum was in denial for the first few weeks; the only things that motivated her, were her responsibility to her husband and two young daughters. They too were struggling to navigate this new world they had been suddenly jettisoned into. It was not an unusual scenario for wives of the first immigrants, arriving later to unite with their husbands after a period apart. Five years of separation was however, an unusually longer period than most. The 'separation' time was used by their husbands to find their feet in this new country, setting up home and a stable job before calling their wives to join them.

It wasn't easy for the men either, many of them arriving earlier and forced to live in cramped dwellings; sometimes up to twenty of them, sleeping on makeshift beds, wherever they could find a space, in the tiny houses. It was a means to an end; a temporary measure which enabled them to live frugally, save their weekly wages to put towards a deposit for a home of their own. Dad stretched this out for as long as he could. For him, the opportunity to explore and enjoy everything of swinging '60's Britain, was far more exciting than saving up for a new house. He was after all, free from his responsibilities, his wife and children, and he was ready to snag everything that this exciting country had to offer. There were no restrictions and no rules away from the daily grind of his work. But this freedom was not about frivolity, it was exercised to confront and deal with unresolved emotions, which stemmed from his childhood.

After his mother's death, he had only known hardship through circumstances that saw him homeless at the age of ten. He had become hardened if not embittered by those early years and learned how to survive on the streets of Sialkot. With no family to support him and disowned, even by his father, after his stepmother moved in, there was no exemplar, no moral benchmark to guide him in his formative years. He grew up questioning a culture that would allow this to happen. He questioned its values, its integrity and separated faith from religion - they meant two different things to him. Religion was indoctrinated but faith came naturally. It was faith that saw him through those early tumultuous years and taught him how to fend for himself and his younger sister. It was faith that enabled him to find his way as a teenager, when he enlisted in the army, putting himself through night school and working his way up to the middle ranks.

There was a resounding sense of life having cheated him.

Married life was not enough to make him feel complete; he was still unresolved. There was a bitterness and a sense of entitlement hanging over him. Coming to Britain, was the only time he had ever felt completely free, and he wanted to make the most of it. This, to an extent, the recompense for a cruel past that robbed him of his childhood. It was the justification that he needed to take advantage of his new-found liberation, in Yorkshire, but never enough justification for abandoning his family. His unresolved dark past had shaped his concept of life, love, relationships and values. His trauma, the root of his warped sense of reality and his vulnerabilities. He was searching for something and not surprisingly, was quick to snatch the opportunity to fill the labour gap sold to him by the representatives of Arthur Rambler Mills. They found cheap foreign labour in dad and many of other vulnerable men from the Indian subcontinent, mis-selling the promise of a 'better life'. It was a shock when they received their first pittance pay packets for the menial labour that the British workforce refused to do.

But despite this, life for him was good in other ways, during those early years in Britain. He was accountable to no one but himself, until Abbas, our maternal grandfather stepped in. He was enraged that his daughter had been left by his son in law to bring up their young family alone. Unbeknown to mum, her exasperated father purchased the airplane ticket for her and her two daughters to be reunited as a family once again. She had been told that the tickets had been sent by dad, but it was a lie. How could her father tell her that he had to beg her husband to take back his wife and their two young daughters?

Dad, Haider Rauf, was never in the running to be a suitor for the Deen girls of Lahore. It was a chance encounter at grandad's ice cream parlour, that saw him being introduced to the family. This handsome young army officer was welcomed quickly into the fold, viewed by her mother as eligible marriage material for one of her older daughters, not mum. Her sister, my aunt Zohra, was chosen, but fate had different ideas. Mum often said that it was written in her 'kismet' to be married to him. Her reference to fate and destiny was often used to validate life's many ebbs and flows. It was a form of surrender to instances where she had little or no control. Capitulation to kismet was easier than lamenting on life's tribulations.

Kismet was also the term used to define the rigid patriarchal framework in which she was raised. 1950's Pakistan, viewed women as subordinates, with no prospects other than marriage and propagation. On the day that dad visited her fathers' home, her kismet was cemented after an unexpected glance from him. He was brazen enough to inquire, "Who is that one?" pointing to mum who mischievously craned her neck to look back at him. She was the fourth, in the long line of sisters to be married. It wasn't her turn. The order would be disrupted if mum was seen to be jumping the queue; upsetting the pattern that had been diligently followed, up until now.

Somehow dad managed to persuade her father to give him her hand instead. He managed to break the rules on numerous counts that day. His army ranking enabled him to bypass protocol and he ended up choosing mum from the line-up of Abbas's daughters. Grandad allowed him to deviate the plan, giving his blessing. Within six months they were married in a small 'chat-kohta' - rooftop ceremony in Lahore. The early years of marriage for mum, were turbulent and traumatic from the stories she recounted of being a newly married military wife. She had never experienced love of this kind or the unexpected violence that came with it. The only romantic gesture she ever talked about was when dad threw her favourite flowers - freesias through the doorway at her, as she went about her daily chores. She also talked about the joys of becoming a mother, living with dad in their comfortable apartment in Karachi. The place her two eldest daughters were born.

But things changed suddenly after dad moved to Britain. Everything taking a more downward turn; starting with her being left alone, with no communication for months. It felt as if she had been left for dead. Where was he? Her daughters became her focus, her raison d'etre in those lonely years; she was determined not to be a victim of her circumstances and enjoyed the time she spent raising them in the comfort of her extended family. It took five long years before she finally joined him.

A year after arriving in Britain, my brother was born. Then a year later my sister Zainab. Then, to mum's dismay, within less than another two years, I came along. She vowed to have no more children, begging doctor Skelton to 'tie up her tubes'. With five children now, in early 1970s Britain, mum was settling in. The age gap between the older girls made it easier for her, as they were able to help with looking after their younger siblings; feeding and playing with us whilst mum worked from home for the local textile mill.

Grandma Kipling

Eventually, mum discovered a new support network in the neighbourhood, a surrogate family. Mrs Kipling, who we referred to as 'grandma', was mums guiding light and exemplar, helping her to fit in during those early years. She welcomed the beautiful bride of Haider. His card was marked after she heard the ominous cries from their basement and from there onwards, she kept a protective eye on mum, making no pretence of her disdain of dad. She threatened him many times, "I'll 'av you seen to if you lay another finger on that beautiful young woman," she warned him; telling him there was an army behind her and she was ready deploy her troops on him, if he stepped out of line. Her protection, kindness and generosity was the home that mum needed to anchor her in those early years. She was the only grandma, albeit surrogate, we had ever known, who filled the void of our biological grandparents. She made us gifts of hand knitted matching tank tops, gave us sweets and even English versions of our Pakistani names; telling mum, that we needed more pronounceable names for the English tongue, if we were to fit in. My brother was re-named Jason, Zainab became Stella; I was fine, my name was phonetically easier to pronounce. She also taught us how to make our first Sunday roast, something that mum had already surreptitiously tasted knowing the chicken was not halal. Grandma's method was genius, and it was a treat that we enjoyed once a week when we had an 'English dinner'.

Grandma Kipling's Roast Chicken bypassed the use of an oven, which was handy as mum never used hers. Her flavours were akin to an oven roast; it was clever.

All it took was a large pan with enough water to submerge the chicken - skin on. A whole peeled onion and two to three cloves of garlic; all boiled until the chicken turned from pale pink to magnolia - the popular colour of 1970s décor. Then in a flat frying pan, ideally larger than the chicken, a good few tablespoons of butter added. An incision made down the back of the chicken, carefully slicing downwards, then pushed down on the breast. It would flatten the chicken in a manner known as spatchcock. It was easier to cook in the second phase this way. That was when the chicken was placed face down onto the sizzling butter, to make sure every limb was seared to get the skin to turn golden and crisp all the way around. It took around 10-12 minutes. The stock from the pan would become gravy with the addition of a teaspoon of flour, butter and water. Grandma would serve this with boiled vegetables and mashed potatoes on the side. That was her easy Sunday roast.

As time went by, mum became more settled. The life she had left behind fading; becoming as remote as was her yearning for it. Her own growing family was now her priority and her tight social circle - the neighbourhood wives, a sisterhood by proxy. She built a family and a comfortable home for us. She built everything from scratch, including most of our furniture. During the still hours in the dead of night, she would often sneak out of the house with an old pram, that she kept hidden in the basement. She wheeled that pram around derelict houses close by, that were being demolished. There, she would salvage discarded frames of dining chairs, old settees, tables; anything that she saw with her imaginative eye that could be re-purposed. She would use the pram to transport whatever she could fit into it back home, in the dark; wrapping her head in a balaclava to make sure no one saw her, as she pushed it up the cobbled street.

I remember waking up to see carcasses of old settees and chairs, scattered around the basement. We never questioned it. Within days these shells would become the most beautiful pieces of dressed furniture that she carefully crafted using fabrics and off cuts that she collected over months. The old settee frame was transformed into a quilted leather sofa, resembling a Chesterfield. It was made by piecing together off-cuts of leather; the slight seconds which she stumbled on in the haberdashery shop run by a kind Polish man.

Jacek looked forward to mum's visits. "Hello Mrs, what you make today?" he asked mum coyly in his broken English. "I am covering my chairs," mum would respond, never conceding where she had salvaged them. He knew but acted ignorant, knowing of her hardship; he played along. He would often find a reason to give more than the yard of fabric she asked for. "I'll give you extra today, because it is a little frayed; there, you see?" he would feign to point out, whilst quickly scrolling. It was also obvious that he had a crush on mum. He admired her strength and marvelled at her creativity, skill and resourcefulness. Mum was as beautiful as she was talented.

She had fine features and olive skin, inherited from her middle eastern ancestry. A slender nose, light hazel brown almond-shaped eyes defined by a sweeping contour of surma - natural kohl, from the steel pot that she kept on a shelf in the kitchen. She had the same hairstyle her entire life, which saw her fine blue-black hair pulled back into a low bun and pinned carefully, with a few strands hanging around her ears. She was confident in her skin, never wearing makeup, only a thin layer of Astral face cream, which sat glimmering on her sharp cheekbones. Her clothes were appropriated to fit in just as much as the English versions of our names. She re-fashioned all of her Pakistani clothes, cutting the long kurta dresses into short tunics, which she would wear over trousers. The English men would often glance her way admiringly, as she walked past them into town with a child or two in tow. She held herself with confidence, poise and grace.

Mum embraced Britain and loved much of its cultural offerings which included TV shows of the 1970's and of course music. When her marital woes and regular clashes with dad became too much, she would find solace in music - the Indian film music she had grown up with, was replaced by power ballads of Mary Hopkins, Helen Reddy and Elkie Brookes. I would hear her softly humming and singing the lyrics of songs she loved, whilst working on the fabric sent to her by the local mill. She spent hours with her tiny tools used for 'burling and mending', plucking out the imperfections in the fabrics, correcting areas where the loom had slipped and left a hole.

'Those were the days my friend… I am woman… Pearls a singer'. These lyrics would get her through some of her toughest times. They also helped her to learn to speak English; there were many new words and expressions as a result. Much of her vocabulary and many phrases in fact, referencing the songs she loved.

'I can't live, if living is without you…'

When dad left…..

You don't realise how much space is occupied by someone, with few belongings. When dad left, there was distinctly more light flooding our home . There was space to play, to run, jump, and to live freely, in rooms we never explored in our four story Victorian terraced house on Shipley Road. "If you don't make him leave, I will take the young ones and go, and I won't come back until he's gone," I heard Laylah beg mum one day whilst holding me close, tightly pressing my small frame into her hip. Mum was standing opposite us, facing downwards with a pained and anguished expression. She was deep in thought, torn, knowing that this would be the biggest decision of her life.

I remember feeling confused and thinking why? The atmosphere was tense, and austere; it felt as if we were on the brink of a revolution. This was an ultimatum. It was 1977 and I was only six years old when dad left our home and our lives. Not only he, but all reference to him including the word 'dad' itself, was banished from our vocabulary. A juxtaposition of emotions followed which left our home divided; both sombre and jubilant as we were forced overnight to adjust to his absence. We were unsure of how to deal with the conflicting and complex emotions that saw my older sisters silently relieved and the younger ones, including myself confused and torn. My memories of dad were vague, too few in fact to formulate any semblance of a father figure or to define a sense of loss. But there was a clear and palpable void - that I do remember.

His departure could be sensed on mums face too. The furrows between her brows softened, her sense of relief dissolved the strain from it and replaced it with a calmness and serenity. The solace also swept across her body language making her movements lighter and sprightly. With his things now gone, there was room to play and move around, in a way that was not possible before. Everything felt so much lighter. But there were also dark days when I would catch mum breaking down, dramatically, in the arms of Laylah or Nailah. They, her crutches, became replacements for dad - carers and providers, if not surrogate husbands. There was no counselling for families like ours. Mum was alone, left to deal with her new reality and a new sense of freedom.

Free however, only to a point that she allowed. She never fully embraced what this liberation meant or could have meant for her. Having only known trauma, shackles and limitation; freedom did not feel like a safe place to her. She would regularly second-guess her decision, breaking down, wanting him back. Was it Stockholm syndrome? It took many years for her to step out of the prison that she had built in her own head. Victims of trauma never really fully recover, which explained why, some days it felt as if we were living in a bipolar household, seeing two extremes of mum. Either euphoric or debilitated by sadness. With dark days aplenty, she would close the curtains and lock herself away, leaving us all to fend for ourselves, knowing that somehow, we would all be ok.

That was when I took full advantage of having the kitchen to myself. Knowing that she wasn't hovering over me, I would raid the pantry looking for ingredients to experiment with and invent new things to eat. Food that made us feel better, usually involved sugar; to lift the mood and bring some joy, more so if we could scoff it in front of the TV or in the tents we made from her rolls of fabric. For me, this was my escape from the sobriety of the early days of dad's departure. I experimented with ingredients and flavours, putting twists on some of mum's traditional recipes. I wondered what would happen if one of our favourite savoury snacks became sweet?

That was when the sweet samosa was born. This was truly one of my best accidental discoveries. Whilst rummaging through the pantry looking for brown sugar, ready to make caramel popcorn, a bag of semolina that had been stacked on one of the higher shelves fell down and landed on my foot, as if by serendipity. Semolina was such a versatile and inexpensive grain; there was always an ample stash that was used in many sweet and savoury dishes. With it, we made sweet dishes like halva - one of my favourite desserts that could even be eaten for breakfast with puri's - small flash fired chapatti. Making it involved taking a few cups of semolina in a saucepan and stirring in lots of butter over a moderate heat. When it started to clump you could smell a distinctive aroma of butter on the edge of burning. That was when water was added, just enough to break down the clumps before turning down the heat. Then sugar; a cupful would give this dessert enough sweetness. Mum used to add dried fruits on occassion, and a cup of chopped nuts and shaved coconut for texture. This was just one example of a frugal dish that could be stretched to feed a family on a meagre budget. This halva would last us several days. It may not have been the same as eating a chocolate pudding, but we never once complained.

The puri - small roti's that we would usually eat this with were smaller versions of roti, but more decadent. Made with plain wheat flour and flash fried by dipping them into hot oil for few seconds. It would be eaten together by taking small pieces of puri and wrapping it around the halwa, one bite at a time. I often wondered how it would taste if the puri was replaced with samosa pastry, encasing the halwa and deep frying as you would a regular savoury samosa. So that was exactly what I did. The halwa had to be cooled down first before placing it into a small half roti; the edges sealed as a regular samosa. Then deep fried until golden and crispy before removing from the oil. Some extra fine sugar sprinkled over the top. These pocket rockets were the best thing to come from mums' 'self-pity-parties'. The fact that they were so cheap to create; we would make hundreds of them and store them in old biscuit tins in the dark cellar, where no one else but we knew about them.

Just one of the many experimental dishes born out of down days. As time went by, they began to diminish as mum grew stronger and began to kick back. It was the space that she had needed to lament, to grieve and to slowly take back control. There was no time to be wasted as now there were more pressing issues to be dealt with. With four daughters, she realised that she had a mammoth task ahead of her - finding suitable husbands for each of them.

Chapter 4

YORKSHIRE - Stani's

What are we mum?
Indian song from the film Shree 420
Mera juta hai jaapaani, - *My shoes are Japanese*
Ye patalun ingalistaani, - *These pants are British*
Sar pe laal topi rusi, - *I have a Russian hat on my head*
Phir bhi dil hai hindustaani! - *But my heart is Indian*

WE changed the last line, screaming out in tandem:
Phir bhi dil hai - YORKSHIRE - STANI -
But still my heart is *from Yorkshire!*

And if ever we made it into the Oxford dictionary…

OUR DEFINITION: Yorkshire-stani: A hybrid that combines East and West, pertains to those born in Yorkshire in the late 1960's and 1970's. A most unique blend that combines Yorkshire Grit and Pakistani hot-headedness.

Earth and fire; we fashioned a new breed from these two divergent cultures, which boasted dual everything - language, fashion and culture. It wasn't an overnight success. It took years in fact, to evolve and navigate our way through the murky waters of being British (Yorkshire) and Pakistani. Straddling these two cultures was not easy; we wobbled between them from one day to the next. And if trying to find your identity amongst these polar extremes wasn't hard enough, throw in some befuddled cultural values; then add a few knotty boundaries. The limitations placed on us served only to confuse us more. Unpacking it all was not for the faint hearted. We tried our best to fit in, but we were square pegs in round holes. Discombobulated.

Like the song lyrics suggest, we were bits of everything - hybridised. You would imagine that this much bounty and richness was something to celebrate; but sadly, the 1970's were just not equipped for that. We blew like feathers in the wind between the two cultures. We didn't identify as Pakistani, nor were we fully British either - whatever that meant. Britain itself was changing, as a result of the mass immigration, with more influences beginning to infiltrate and stretch the definition of what it meant to be British. So instead, we created a new paradigm which was unique to us, taking the best from both worlds and fashioning our own way forward to become cutting-edge and ground-breaking.

A distinct manifestation of diverse influences permeating the mainstream, came through food. Bradford was fast becoming a curry capital, with its long roads of newly established Indian restaurants and green grocers. There were many new emerging communities in Yorkshire, which we knew of, simply by observing the demographics of our own street. Italian, Irish, Polish, West Indian and Bangladeshi, with many bringing their own version of 'curry' into the city.

This melting pot of cultures also gave birth to the concept of fusion flavours.

A phenomenon that saw dishes being appropriated; often unrecognisably from the original. One such phenomenon happened when curry was appropriated to suit the British palette and the chicken tikka masala was born. It came about one day when a sauce for the 'dry' chicken tikka pieces was requested. It was invented specifically for that dish; made with a rich tomato and yogurt sauce to bring moisture and a saucy element. It tasted particularly good and took off. It was even hailed as a 'national dish'. Proof that appropriated dishes were as good, if not better, especially when they become popular in the culture from which they originated, as well as to the British public.

Even the Chinese were serving up their own style of curry sauce, with chips. After Chung-yu's mum, who owned the local Chinese chip shop introduced us to her Indo-Chinese curry sauce, we were on a mission to crack that recipe. This was not Indian curry sauce, nor was it Chinese. It was a hybrid; like us. It tasted sweet, with strong undertones of Chinese five spice and of a generic blend known as curry powder. Invented by the British, we stayed well away from that blend in our curries. But for curry sauce - the chip shop variety, it was perfect and could be used to rustle it up in minutes.

All it took to create, was a small onion, roughly chopped with a teaspoon of crushed ginger and garlic; fried in butter to start with, until it looked translucent; not too brown as with all other scenarios involving a fried onion. A jug of stock was made using a stock cube and into that, a heaped tablespoon of cornflour, a teaspoon of curry powder (the stuff we only reserved for this dish) and a half teaspoon of Chinese five spice added. Mixed with a hand whisk to take out any lumps, then poured over the fried onions. It could be sieved for a super smooth sauce, or the onions, left in for texture, as we liked it. This, the fastest curry sauce, from start to finish, was poured over hot chips or eaten with a bowl of jasmine rice, as mum liked it. Who knew curry could be so diverse?

Blend in don't stand out

'Blend in don't stand out' we were constantly being encouraged by mum. It was her mantra. Because standing out posed shame as well as a threat. The threat of being targeted by the growing racism as spouted by Enoch Powell; the politician who spread his bigoted diatribe, recruiting the far right to kick back at growing numbers of immigrants. The National front was a terrifying prospect to us. If we saw a skinhead wearing Doc Martins, we would run for it. Did they even know how and why we came to being in England? Probably not, but we were not equipped to stand up to them at the time. We didn't have anyone in a position of prominence representing us, certainly no one who might have enough influence to make a difference or to defend our rights.

The only south Asian person who had any influence on the British public was Madhur Jaffrey; an Indian TV chef who brought curry to everyone's dining table. She was popular, amenable and one of the only brown faces on TV at the time. She gave us a reason to celebrate our food and be represented authentically to the masses. She showed diversity and complexity through the richness and history behind each dish she created. Even we learnt something new from watching her. Curry and south Asian food became a culinary experience to many, a journey that was more than just a 'blow your head off' spicy dish after too many beers. She gave it a cultural relevance and gravitas; celebrating it as it truly deserved. She became my hero the day she made a 'Cocktail Kofta'. Genius! An Indian spiced meatball served on a cocktail stick. Something she said, would be served as an entrée at her dinner parties. I imagined her dinner parties being as exuberant as her. She made a kofta sound sexy, classy if not upper class and she elevated the status of Indian food to the British population. After Madhur, I never had to explain or justify curry - the smell, the look and taste to my friends ever again. She was the one who made me proud of my culinary heritage.

But some things still took a while to evolve and be accepted. One of them being our religious festivals. They were low key if not dumbed down. We kept our festivities moderate and quiet, sharing them only amongst family and our close-knit community - mostly our neighbours. The

English people we knew referred to Eid as 'Your Christmas' even though it had nothing to do with the birth of Christ. The only way it could be understood, appropriated; explained.

Language was another interesting subject for our generation. English was our first language obviously, but with mum, we spoke Punjabi and Urdu with guests, as it sounded more eloquent. There was no compromising on that. Early on we had to figure out the differences in syntax, expression and vocabulary. It came intuitively when raised in two cultures, but still, not a skill to be undermined. Without knowing it, we were experts in semantics and never fully appreciated the advantages of having another language as well as another culture. We were too busy juggling the contradictions and dichotomies. But having another language enabled us to view the world through a much more colourful lens. We could actually feel words; experience them differently across our other languages. They resonated and evoked emotions which equated to feeling them at a different level. We had another set of tools to draw on, which enabled us to process, feel and experience the world through our unique cultural heritage. It was empowering, although we didn't see it that way at the time. That would come later.

We even invented our own vernacular; well at least mum did. She tried her best to speak English, but it would be delivered to us in a unique combination of broken Punjabi, Urdu and English. Wherever she couldn't find the right word, there it was, a Punjabi word in its place or vice versa. And we would reply, using English words pronounced in an Indian way, as if that would make it easier for her to understand. I imagined it was the same labyrinthine experience for many of the other migrants in our neighbourhood. We felt at ease with our fellow diaspora; we knew that we were all facing the same barriers, confusion and racism. Strangely enough, we never discussed our hardships; we didn't feel the need to. It was an unspoken bond, an empathy between us that cut across race and religion. We were all united in our otherness.

But a new culture was born through us.; one we created. Navigating through ignorance, shame, and the overt racism of that era, to evolve and grow into ourselves. We would eventually embrace our identity and celebrate this unique blend of being Yorkshire and Pakistani. It would become our superpower.

But for now, we were proud *Yorkshire-stanis*

She acquiesced

She may as well have married Jo.

Letter from Raskshan Line, Karachi, Pakistan, dated 8th August 1978.

Salaam dear sister,

We are writing to you, with the permission of your father Abbas Deen.

We wanted to introduce our eldest son, Murad; age 25. He is working with Kolheed air base as an engineer and has very good prospects.

We understand that you have four daughters; of which your eldest is still unmarried. With respect, we enclose photos of our son, who you may consider as a potential rishta suitor for her.

We patiently await your response.

Ibrahim Murad

I remember the day they arrived. A batch of photographs bound together with string. It looked like a chronologically arranged, whistle stop tour through this family's history. It was organised in a way that showed them evolving through the years. They began with old sepia photographs of the parents carrying small children. Then more photographs of them a few years later with the same children, but now older and in various settings. The last few photographs showed Murad on his own; as a grown man standing in front of buildings in Lahore and various other, what appeared to be, staged scenarios. He was without doubt, an extremely handsome young man.

Mum casually left the pile of photo's sitting on the dining table. We all hovered over them as she knew we would. It had been six months since Jo and Laylah ended their relationship and she was slowly coming out of her dark place. She knew she had to start to move forward. At first, she didn't make it obvious, but she too had more than once casually flicked through the pile of photos. It was mum that started the conversation one day.

"Would you ever consider anyone from back home?

Mum asked. "This is my home mum; do you mean *your* home," Laylah's reply. For so many reasons, Pakistan was still considered home for mum. She had spent more of her life there, than in England so her rationale made sense.

Several days went by before the conversation recommenced. This time it was Laylah who started it. "Who are these people and how do they know of us; of me?" "Through your grandfather, they approached him," was mum's reply. She continued, "Baba-jaan - Grandad would never allow anyone unsuitable to approach us, he's a good judge of character; they must be a good family." Laylah grabbed the pile of photos and pulled one out that showed Murad standing in front of an airplane; behind him a sign saying 'Kolheed air base'. She examined it closely, her eyes darting from left to right, scrutinising it. I was wondering whether she was comparing him to Jo, for whom she had fabricated a similar profession, as a pilot. How ironic. Was this karma playing out? Their lie had come back to laugh at her; here was different man, a strange suitor standing beside an airplane. It was not her darling Jo. She slapped the photograph on the table in front of mum. I sat poised, quietly watching, wondering what was coming next. She leant forward, looked at the photograph, then at mum. Her expression turned from defeat to resolute.

"OK. So then, how do we do this?"

She surrendered

She had made her decision, and it was now definitive. Was it the prospect of, as mum put it, returning "back home" that was the pull for her? Escaping everything in England, which now felt empty and pointless. Was it the fantasy of starting from scratch, far away from cold dreary Yorkshire? That and the probability of more underwhelming suitors, that were never going to be Jo. It was more likely the latter, which drove her decision.

She was worn out; frayed from chasing her hopes and dreams. They had not delivered the fulfilment that she had imagined and she had reached her threshold. Realising that all the fighting, pushing, and breaking away, trying to refashion the parameters of being British and Pakistani, had come to nothing. It was not worth the fight anymore. She had reshaped the mould over the years, but sadly not broken it. She was now tired, depleted and ready to throw in the towel. Love was not everything it was cracked up to be. So, she acquiesced.

Laylah recalled the day that she travelled from my aunt Zohra's house in Lahore to Karachi to meet Murad for the first time. She was waiting in a taxi, with three of his four sisters; a customary get-together for the girls to introduce the bride to be to her prospective groom. There was a lot of excitement in the car as she eagerly waited to meet the handsome young man she had seen in the photos. This was finally 'it' for her. It was more or less a done deal, there was no going back, all the arrangements were well under way for this wedding.

As the girls were beginning to sing verses from a traditional bridal shower song, Laylah looked out of the car window, "Jiski biwi lambi uska bhi bada naam hai," *The one whose wife is tall is a fortunate one.* She noticed a small, spindly figure of a man heading their way. He was wearing dark brown checked flares, a pin stripe tight nylon shirt, which was open to the third button down, revealing his chest, and aviator sunglasses, covering almost all of his face from his nose upwards. His dark hair was wispy, unruly and sparse. It was parted, too far over to the right, sweeping across his forehead and the top of his head - *a comb-over.* Who was he? As he edged closer, Murad's sisters began to clap and sing even louder. It was beginning to feel extremely hot and claustrophobic in the car; Laylah took a few deep breaths as they chanted:

"Kothe se laga do, seedhi ka kya kaam hai."
If you stand her against the wall, there is no need
for a ladder
Mere angne mein tumhara kya kaam hai
In my courtyard, what is your purpose?

The last line, beckoning a response from the man who was now standing at the car door, opening it. "Mera kaam, hai aap ka khawand" - he chanted, as he swayed his head from side to side - 'My purpose is to be your husband'. This man was Murad. Everything from inside the car felt as if it was now spinning around her, including Murad, which made her nauseous. Laylah passed out.

It was a combination of the heat in the car with no air conditioning, together with the shock of seeing her future husband for the first time. He looked nothing like his photographs. Firstly, he appeared much smaller in height and frame; his hair thinner than expected for a man of his age. He was a lot skinnier, if not emaciated from the appearance of his concave chest as he stood upright. It turned out that Murad was older than we had been told; ten years to be exact. The photographs had either been taken a long time before or doctored. In some, it was now evident, he had been wearing a toupee.

She slowly came around after being carried back from the car to the house and was laid under a ceiling fan for more air. His mother dabbing her forehead with a cold wet flannel. "Beta tikh hai?" - Darling, are you ok? she asked. Laylah took several deep breaths; sitting upright to compose herself. "Yes, auntie I'm ok," she said. But what she wanted to say in fact was - *is that really him? Your son Murad?* The words of the song still playing in her head: *The one whose wife is tall is a fortunate one.* He was indeed the fortunate one, on many counts.

Everything had been arranged and paid for in Pakistan for this wedding. The venue, the clothes, the food, all of it. Such was Laylah's confidence in this suitor before she had even seen him in the flesh. It hadn't occurred to her to have a back-up plan. She had let herself get swept away into the fantasy and escapism of it all. The delusion born out of defeat. Leaving England, to go back to her roots and start a new life from scratch, was not meant to kick-off this way. This was not how she had imagined it.

A primal tug: a place to call home

Laylah and Murad did spend time together in Karachi before the wedding, connecting through familiar territory. Days spent walking through the old parts of the town that she remembered as a child. Meena Bazaar, the place she had spent much of her happy, carefree childhood with grandad, in his ice cream parlour. That was no longer there; he was too old to keep it going and had retired. It was now replaced by street vendors selling kulfi, kheer, seviyan and sherbat. All the traditional Pakistani cold desserts and drinks were now being made in mobile street stalls. She had loved grandads' sherbet; a cool drink made with a sweet syrup known as roo hafza, mixed with water and ice. That and the gola ganda - snow cones that were a hit with the street kids. She and Nailah had roamed these streets, sucking the life out of this frozen treat made of crushed ice, magically mounted onto sticks and sprinkled with rainbow-coloured sweet syrups, probably containing a long list of chemical food colourings, but they tasted good.

She could still taste it now, walking down the narrow passages of uneven pavements, which had closed in it seemed; shrunken over time. It was dirty, grimy, hazy and smoggy; no longer clean and uncluttered as she remembered it. It had definitely worn down and decayed over the years. The street markets were crammed together; kapra clothing bazaars with rows and rows of multi-coloured loose fabrics. Benares, Shanghai, silk and chiffon, all hanging from the stalls, baking in the intense heat of the midday sun. The aromas of food being cooked outdoors mixed with the petroleum used to generate the heat. That inimitable soft scent of sandalwood that permeated the air, from the moment you landed in Pakistan. It lingered on your clothes and even penetrated the sandooq - suitcase that carried everything back home from this country.

The street foods were the same - gol gappay, samosa chaat, doodh patti. The sounds and scents of her childhood washed over her as she revisited the place where she had only ever felt safe; loved and happy. The horns bellowing from the chaotic, undisciplined traffic, random tannoy announcements emanating from offices and the Adhan - call to prayer echoing in tandem from different mosques across the city. With every step she took, she was being transported back to a place that did not feel foreign to her anymore. She felt a primordial tug. An inexplicable sensory reflex, pulling her, anchoring her to this familiar territory. It was already imprinted in her DNA. This was beginning to feel like a place that she could once again call home.

Despite his physical appearance not meeting her expectations, Murad was a kind and caring man. He seemed genuine, sincere and confident in himself. He wasn't the engineer on the aircraft's we had been 'con-vinced' to believe by his parents. He was an air conditioning engineer; contracted to the airline. She may as well have married Jo after all. If it wasn't so tragic, she would have roared with laughter all the way back to England, back into the arms of Jo. But she didn't. The world of the suitors had played a real number on her. The one saving grace in this situation, was that Murad was in awe of her. And for now, that was enough. What else was out there for her? She didn't care to know. This would be the biggest leap of faith she would ever take.

Only mum and Nailah attended their wedding. It was too expensive to fly the three younger siblings out. It was a traditional Pakistani wedding, stretching out for days and nights, with all the ceremonies and customs diligently observed and celebrated. I cried my eyes out when mum left us at home; begging her to smuggle me into her suitcase, but it wasn't to be. We were looked after by my uncle Raad, who travelled up from London for the week to stay with us. Mum trusted him to observe only two things whilst she was away: 1) to make sure we were safe and 2) to make sure we were fed. That was it. Uncle Raad did not have a clue how to cook, so I pretended I couldn't cook either. Such was my dismay at being left behind, not to see the wedding of my beautiful big sister, my role model, my muse. My idol. Each day we ate Birdseye beef burgers, sandwiched between white bread whilst mum was gone, and we loved them. Uncle Raad tried to convince us they were halal, but they weren't, and he insisted we never utter a word about it to mum on her return. And we never did.

Chapter 5

The sisterhood

Miner's strikes, coal shortages and picket lines of the 1980's saw a fuel crisis of a different generation. Our reliable coal fire became redundant and was decommissioned. The dark copper cabinet-style fire had once been a dependable powerhouse, for heating old water pipes running throughout the entire house; generating heat, hot water and even served as a stove that baked poppadums in thirty seconds. It was also, as mum discovered a makeshift tandoor - a large Indian style urn oven; a raging furnace, where mum would bake her naan bread. But now, it was replaced with three bar electric heaters, dotted around the house, with fake plastic coal accessories that would light up every time they were switched on. Certainly not as pleasing aesthetically or as productive as the original cast iron fire.

Too young to fully understand the impact of these strikes and the changing economy, life continued as normal. Frugality was not unusual for us; mum knew how to cope in extreme circumstances. Resourcefulness was second nature to her. She would make a feast from a handful of frugal ingredients in the same way she could turn an old broken settee into a Chesterfield. The Thatcher years also saw an end to British manufacturing. The worsted industry came to a complete standstill leaving Arthur Rambler's Mill at the end of our street to slowly decay; windows smashed and even a fire in parts where the local thugs congregated to smoke and drink. This thriving worsted community that was once made up of almost all nationalities - Pakistani, Italian, Irish, Ukraine and Polish, was in decay.

Despite all of this, there were many happy memories of our neighbourhood. The women of Shipley Road were all fiercely strong matriarchal figures. I vaguely remember the fathers; they were shadows behind the women who all vehemently ruled their roosts. The Bhaska's, a Hindu family, our immediate neighbours; Mayuri the mother, a simple humble lady who kept her doctor husband in check with one shrill scream that we could hear through the thin walls between our houses. The Sandhu's, a mixed marriage couple, an unlikely pairing back then that produced the best-looking offspring we had ever seen. Olive skinned, tischen hair and aquamarine eyes. Sofia Sandhu was a strong loud Italian diva and Raaj her husband, a Sikh alpha male, which made for a very volatile relationship.

They too could be heard arguing daily, at both ends of the long row of Victorian terraced houses. She would screech in Italian, "Va al diavolo!" He would retort, "Kuthi bhaunk," both equally offensive phrases, whose meaning wasn't known until we were older. The O'Sullivans - an Irish family, the mother an opera soprano, who would belt out falsettos effortlessly as she hung out her washing. She bred children every single year; with her husband Fergul, a waif thin figure of a man, who looks-wise, was not in her league. I wondered what the dynamics were between them. There were ten of them living in a three-bedroom house and showing no signs of stopping either.

The Lombardi's were a rambunctious Italian family that lived next door to the De Francesco's, also Italian but from different regions; one Capri, the other Naples. They would regularly dis each other's cultural heritage, both of them telling the neighbourhood why the others' region bred degenerates. The women, Lucia and Francesca, constantly locked in competitiveness, adding new features to their homes - a dorma window, a porch, an extension; they were constantly rivalling each other's home improvements. They even competed when Italy won the world cup in 1982 even though they were on the same side.

The Patel's who owned the corner shop. She, the brains behind this thriving little business - it was like an Aladdin's den. There was everything in her shop; the first local store that started to stock authentic imported spices and everything that mum's generation had dearly missed. A genius idea given the demographics of our town. She was always overwhelmed with customers who would travel in from miles away to buy batches of authentic garam masala, that she made herself as well as kalonji, haldi, dal-chini, all with the same aromas that they had missed from back home.

The women of Shipley Road were a sisterhood. Bullet proof, cast iron. They would run to each other's aid if ever they heard one in trouble - casually knocking on a door with a fabricated pretext to interrupt whatever ominous noises they could hear - usually the sound of their neighbourhood sister being beaten at the hands of her husband. Sometimes one of them would come and stay with us, on the pretext of bringing their young children to play. But it was in fact, to escape for the night. They would return home when it was safe for them to do so. Domestic violence was dealt with in a very different way; women helped each other. No external agencies or police were ever called for the shame it would bring on their household, and on their husbands who, they all continued fiercely and bizarrely to protect. These women were each other's sanctuaries, and refuges - the only refuges available to support each other back then.

They even developed a way of communicating across the language barrier, a community vernacular in which they understood each other; through slang, coined words and phrases, gestures and intuition. A hybrid of English, Hindi, Urdu, Punjabi and Italian. A dialect that was so unique, they even invented their own phrases. One phrase I remember in particular, that they coined for their men, "They are all dirty - clever." What did that even mean? I used to wonder. They would all chat over the fences and nod in agreement, including the Italian women; it was the only time they concurred with one another. As I grew up, I realised it was a reference to their deviant husbands, pulling the wool over their eyes as they sneaked out of the house on an evening to 'work', but were most likely at the local men's club, drinking with other women.

The kids of Shipley Road

Away from the realm of the suitors, there was another world we grew up in. In between cooking and school, the summers were spent playing. Summer breaks back then were seemingly never ending. A time when we savoured simple things, even a piece of chalk would occupy us for hours. And most engaging of all activities - making bogies. Not the sticky green variety; bogies was the nickname for go-carts. Who on earth decided to call them that? If it were a competition, every United Nations child was represented here in the annual bogie event. The Italian kids crafted theirs like you would imagine; slick Italian design, they even painted them red. They were fast as hell and not much in the way of speed control. Stylish and well-proportioned with good wheels and steering that was more than a skipping rope connected to the front axle, unlike ours. They meticulously carved finger grooves on the wooden handle that functioned as brakes, pivoting perfectly to grip the back wheels. They might even have consulted Enzo himself, such was this masterpiece of design.

The Indians came a close second, as they had more manpower, obviously; there were more of them and they diligently worked through the night, churning out mass-produced bogies; they even started selling them in true

Indian enterprising spirit. We teamed up with Irish Johnny O'Sullivan. It was not our best move, we felt sorry for him as no one else wanted him. Johnny was badly coordinated, and he somehow got the back wheels muddled up with the front, which completely slowed down our bogie. As he tried to yank them off, one snapped. As punishment we sent him into the old German couples' garden to salvage more stuff that was in their open scrap heap, which we needed to 'balance the aerodynamics', so my brother said.

The German who we shamefully nicknamed Hitler (unfortunately the only reference we had to Germany at the time), and his wife must have been in their late '80s. They would sit in the middle window of their tall, terraced house opposite, looking out daily. She, with an ill-fitting toupee, was wedged in a wheelchair with a knitted woollen blanket over her legs. He, sitting beside her in stone cold silence, just staring out. We wondered if they were made of wax; their inert, emotionless faces looking out solemnly at the high spirited, energetic children running up and down the street. To us they really were the most frightening people on earth.

When Johnny did manage to hoist himself up over the stone wall, his foot accidentally crashed through a corrugated plastic sheet that was covering their vegetable patch. He was stuck; bits of plastic wrapped around his ankles. We actually thought Hitler would get his imaginary gun out and shoot him. All we could see from behind the wall was Johnny's mop of bright red hair, as he violently thrashed from one side to another trying to free himself. "RUUUNNNN!!" we screamed as we all scarpered. The street had never been so quiet. Just the sound of poor Johnny squealing like a piglet, as he tried to pull his way out of the scratchy plastic sheet cutting into his shins; peeing himself in the process, to add insult to injury to Hitler's vegetable patch. At least the vegetables got watered that day.

Vegetable patches were a must. The Germans grew cabbage, lettuce, carrots and white radishes - ingredients for saur kraut I imagine. The O'Sullivan's vegetable patch grew potatoes; they were Irish after all. The Indians grew hot birds eye chillies, coriander and other essential sabji, vegetables for their vegetarian diets. Mum grew whatever she could in the space we had - radishes, carrots and turnips. She definitely had the right touch when it came to nurturing any kind of greenery, plants and flowers. From her bounty, she made the most delicious buttery, sweet carrot and turnip curry - a kind of bubble and squeak with just a few Indian spices. It was delectable. My first food memories are of being fed by her practical working hands as she rolled small pieces of carrot and turnip in roti laced with butter known as 'chopri roti'. It was the most sumptuous and flavourful vegetable I had ever tasted. The red radish was a bonus vegetable - a kind of two in one as it sprouted another shoot that grew above the ground; its flower turned into a tasty little pocket rocket of flavour called mongray. Every kid on the street knew about our mongray and would snag handfuls from our garden. They looked like miniature green beans. Punchy, sharp, acidic in flavour with a wasabi-like heat. We enjoyed the burn on the tongue, often competing to see how many we could stuff in our mouths before they burnt like hell, whilst playing our summer games.

It was Noah who freed Johnny from the corrugated plastic that day. Hitlers unusually young son. The optics suggested that they had him later in life, especially considering how frail they looked next to this young boy. He could quite easily have passed as a grandson such was the incongruence in their appearance. Noah was never allowed to play out with the other children on the street. We used to imagine him locked in a cupboard. When he did surface, he looked and acted socially inept; his movements were jarred and rigid. There was no fluidity to him as he walked and when he turned, it was as if he was robotic, stopping and considering his direction for a few seconds. I also wondered whether being indoors was actually the cause of his quirkiness. Lack of vitamin D and rickets was rife back then. Behaviourally, he could have been on the spectrum. Spectral conditions were rare or not fully acknowledged in the 1970s. Poor Noah.

The bogie season would always end with one magnificent race akin to the popular whacky races that we used to love watching on TV. The race was organised carefully, by the Italians who seemed to set all the rules. They would mark the start line from the top of the street, where the poor-quality tarmac met the main road, to the end of the street approximately 250 yards down. A treacherous terrain which had seen all kinds of stresses placed on it, from the rag and bone man's horse and cart, heavy wagons delivering coal and salvaged goods that had been dragged on it, slicing chunks out of this cheap, brittle tarmac.

Many a bogie had been obliterated on this racetrack. This was not just about winning; it was about resourcefulness and early tribal instincts being played out in the bogie competitions. Was it the beginnings of socio-cultural dynamics in our childhood? Evolutionary cultural clashes in a survival of the fittest kind of go kart Olympics. We only had one opportunity in this race, there were no second chances. An elder was always assigned to watch over us, usually another neighbour - Raam Bhaskar. Noah would watch from the side lines, unable to take part as we trundled down the life-threatening bumpy street, banging into each other like dodgems, wheels flying off and brakes failing. Many of us rolling over the finish line with no bogie in sight. The Italians would always win; it was fait-accompli, but we all rejoiced at the finish line with a bag of sherbet pips from Nora's corner shop. It wasn't about being the best, it was about being part of that community. An era of simplicity with no expectations, other than invention, resourcefulness and fun wherever we could create it.

These were happy childhood memories, bathed in innocence, curiosity, appreciation and celebration of differences and food which we regularly sneaked into each other's homes to taste. My friend Anna's mum made the best pasta. We ignored the fact that there were bits of Italian sausage in there and swore oaths not to tell mum what we had eaten, when we returned home. Life was happy for the kids of Shipley Road, despite the hostile politically volatile world to which we were oblivious.

Only one event of our childhood that we all shared, scarred us for life. After the dark incident of that summer, no one took part in go-karting, football, or much else again. One afternoon, Noah climbed out of the attic window and beckoned us all to watch him, gesturing for us all to move closer. Perplexed and with a sense of foreboding that something sinister was about to ensue, the unthinkable happened. We didn't understand what he was saying to us; his speech was unfathomable. He climbed onto the ledge, at thirty-five-foot, from the cold concrete paving below. He stood ramrod straight, arms outstretched each side; rigid. For seconds that seemed endless, the world stood still, our mouths were wide open and bone dry as our collective breathing slowed to a stop. Without bending a limb, Noah leant forward, still in a perfectly formed T-shape, with a look of peace on his face, as if this had been preconceived, choreographed even. He proceeded to lean further away from the window, letting his body weight and gravity pull him, face forward, down. And down.

In that tiny window of time, Noah had leaned into his death. No jumping involved; he floated down four stories of dark stone, to land with a resounding thud on the cold grey paving below. It was a few horrific moments before we realised what had just happened. Raam came running, pulling us all away, trying to shield our eyes from what we had all just horrifically witnessed. Noah's parents, nowhere to be seen. Thank God they did not witness their son's demise but curse the fact that we just had. This split-second tragic event imprinted itself deeply on our minds; yet no one mentioned it until many years later. It was just a thing that had happened.

Back then there was no such thing as counselling for children like us. Only a brisk police interview to make basic statements. Mum and other parents were reluctant to let us out to play for years after this incident. By then, we were all too old for the whacky race style carefree summers that were spent being happy children. A space where we were innocent, unburdened by the drama of a chaotic world that was unjust, violent and politically incorrect. PC wasn't even a term that had any level of relevance or gravitas around it. In our childhood, our world was viewed through one set of eyes - we were all just a messy set of underprivileged children, making the most of our time to play and develop. In that space, we were all part of one culture, one religion and one colour - happy young people playing peacefully together.

Chapter 6

Nailah

The Brown Bombshell of 55 Elgon Road

They waited for her every morning to walk past the long line of offices on Elgon Road. The road where the law practices and other high-end offices were situated. She walked past them daily, flicking her shoulder length hair strategically, whilst hearing the cat calls from the Clerks, standing at the windows in their offices. The very un-PC heckling that, at the time, she quite enjoyed. It was harmless. She had known these boys for many years, they were all good friends, having grown up in their jobs together. This was her regular early morning salute; a daily ritual that was nothing but flirtatious fun. These young men were more akin to family - brothers, protectors and her biggest cheerleaders.

"You're welcome boys!" she would shout as she waved to them, whilst entering the office at Mills & Palmer.

It didn't start that way. Back track five years; at the tender age of sixteen, Nailah was jolted from a carefree life; dancing to the tunes of Bay City Rollers, Abba and Blondie into a life of duty and heavy responsibilities. Life changed for us all; but she and Laylah felt the sudden force of dad leaving like a shockwave, which reverberated across their entire existence. Their lives changed overnight. They took on the unforeseen burden of becoming guardians, protectors, replacement fathers and surrogate husbands. After Laylah was married, Nailah was left alone as the only breadwinner of the family. She knew her duty was to stay with mum, to help her physically, financially and emotionally.

Nailah took on many roles. Gravitating between being a daughter, to a carer, provider and lifeline to mum. A role that she hadn't anticipated when mum had been persuaded to banish dad from our lives forever. Neither of my two older sisters had foreseen the repercussions on them; the fallout of this life changing move. There was no plan, and no exit strategy. They hit the ground running; they had no choice. This immense burden and sudden responsibility shaped their characters in more ways than one.

As the only older daughter, left to carry the can, the dynamics of her strained relationship with mum were constantly swaying. One minute she was the decision maker for the family, the next, she was the daughter, the subordinate, taking orders from her. She forfeited many opportunities, albeit begrudgingly and she stayed for much longer than she needed to, supporting us through one of our darkest times. Was this one of the reasons she rejected so many eligible suitors? Mum put it down to her 'nakhra' - being picky, when in actual fact it was her fear. How would mum cope without her? She was the crutch that propped her up when she needed it, yet also surrendered to her controlling and oppressive demands. It was a serpentine mother-daughter relationship, that saw many tangled and convoluted generational clashes between them.

When mum buckled, as she did regularly, she was unable to see how she would cope. A fallen woman, in the eyes of the community, casting their judgemental aspersions over her. At these times, she would be reassured by Nailah, "I'm here for you… just don't forget that HE HAD TO GO," she said, referencing dad. "If he hadn't, I would have taken the younger ones and left." Those same words I had heard once before in the attic. What did she mean? Why was dad's exit so dramatic? We would never know; but it was evident that the decision to banish him was necessary. She continued, "I will be everything you need, you will never have to worry, I promise." That was all mum needed to hear to reaffirm her decision to have ousted him. Life was never going to be easy as a single mother in a judgemental world, but it was made bearable with the support of her daughter.

One of the only places mum was able to express herself and feel comfort was through food. She was determined that our food should not taste of sorrow. She instinctively knew what would uplift us from our deflated state and come to terms with our new reality. We were now free to cook whatever we wanted, and mealtimes became mini adventures. It saw us escape from the normal set meals; replacing them with foods that brought us joy. Mum remembered places where she had been at her happiest and there was always a particular food, usually from her childhood, that she knew she could elicit that same joy through its recreation.

Foods that she had loved as a carefree young girl. She somehow knew the taste would evoke the same emotion. And it did. One such joy came through Kulfi. Indian ice cream, that was not churned, and was made with only a few ingredients. A cup of evaporated milk, a cup of cream, mixed together with half a cup of condensed milk. Mum added a dash of rosewater to this to give it a floral, woody flavour that tasted like Pakistan. It was placed into a Pyrex dish and frozen. When it came out of the freezer, it was garnished with chopped nuts - usually pistachios and almonds. We would all huddle together and dip in our spoons; eating it straight out of the bowl. This was the taste of mum's childhood. It was pure comfort and joy.

For Nailah, it was extra chillies on everything; she had a penchant for heat, in fact she was kamikaze with it.

She made the tastiest chilli masala beans on toast. Made with a can of baked beans which she transformed, with just a small number of ingredients, into the fieriest concoction known to man. Even a vindaloo would hang its head in shame next to this. A few spices and a tin of baked beans; who knew the joy this simple dish could bring to us? South Asian people were good at appropriating food off the shelf; always turning it into a spicier, curried version. Everything needed a bit of spicing up to suit their palette. The baked beans straight out of the tin, were thrown into a pan of tempering onions with garlic and ginger all fried together in butter. A good hit of chilli powder and salt, the two ingredients that brought it to life, and garam masala for that spicy Indian twist. It bubbled up before more chillies were added, fresh ones this time, finely chopped. When cooked, this was served over hot buttered toast with fresh coriander. We would demolish a whole loaf of bread with these spicy beans, whilst sipping on hot chai to counteract the hot chilli. It may sound like madness, but that trick actually worked.

Her job at Mills & Palmer was not Nailah's first. She had worked in various places before that, trying to navigate her way through this foreign world of work. A world for which she was ill-equipped and unprepared. The objective was not to build a career, it was simply to bring home a wage. We needed it. There were hiccups along the way before she eventually found her feet. Her first job as an apprentice in a hair salon; the best of a bad bunch of opportunities, for someone of her age, having left school with just a handful of O-levels. It paid a pittance, but at least it was something. She soon realised it was not for her when she fell victim to an over-zealous trainee, who ruined her beautiful shiny long hair with perm solution, that saw it coil up so tightly, it sat rigid to her head and didn't move for weeks. It looked like an Afro, and it took several bottles of relaxer to gradually soften it. We mocked her for years afterwards.

Her next move was suggested by an old schoolteacher we knew, who lived a few doors up from us. "You need a skill that will open a few more doors dear," Mrs Caine suggested.

She even helped to enrol her at the local college. Typing was a skill that came naturally to her, and she picked it up quickly. It prepared her for a more stable job and unbeknown to her at the time, a path that saw her life experiences and world grow, in ways she could never have imagined possible. After completing her course, she was assigned as a temp in various offices until a more permanent opportunity came up. This was at the new offices of Mills & Palmer, a firm of solicitors based in town.

The course of her life soon changed, one day after we received a letter which threatened to see our family homeless. She took it to work and devised a plan to get it under the nose of one of the older, senior partners - Mr Mills. The partners at the law firm were like royalty; no one bar the senior members of staff were allowed to speak directly to them. Nailah had never stepped foot outside of the typing pool, let alone spoken to the royalty. Until that day, when she smuggled the letter in her bag. She knew that her supervisor Brenda, the gatekeeper, would never allow her access to an experienced solicitor; but she planned her moment. Somehow, she escaped from the typing pool and managed to grab the attention of Mr Mills as he stepped out of his office. Speaking hurriedly; she knew her window of time with him was tight as she asked, "'Scuse me Sir, I hope you don't mind, but please can you help me?" Then handed him the letter and continued, "I'm Nailah, I work in the typ…" "What is it?" he asked impatiently before she could finish her sentence. He looked at his watch and then over his spectacles at her, to get a better view. Suddenly Brenda appeared and interrupted, "Get back to your desk now Nailah!" My sister embarrassed, snatched the letter back, then looking disheartened, started to make her way back to her desk.

She had only taken a couple of steps when she heard him beckon, "Wait, bring it back; I'll look at this tonight," said Mr Mills. She turned and handed it back to him. That was when he paused to look at her properly. He noticed her for the first time; seeing a fragile, vulnerable young girl. Through experience he had developed a strong skill for reading people; it was part of his job. He sensed a young soul who was carrying heaviness, and a huge weight on her shoulders for someone so young. That night as promised, he took the letter home.

A few days later, she was called into his office. At first, she thought it was to be reprimanded. As she looked around the room feeling uncomfortable; she knew she was in the presence of someone from a completely different world to ours. He had an air of superiority; but not the kind that made her feel inferior; his eyes had kindness in them, and he was looking at her endearingly. He sat behind a beautiful dark, highly polished mahogany desk scattered with photographs in pewter frames of a beautiful woman - probably his wife. Leaning back into his comfortable leather chair, peering over his spectacles he calmly said, "I have dealt with the letter;

you have absolutely nothing to worry about. Please assure your mother that you will not lose your home. The deed and title have been transferred into her name."

Nailah was overwhelmed by emotion as she took a deep breath and then sighed with relief. She wanted to leap out of her chair and hug this regal man, but knew she had to remain composed. He continued to look at her endearingly and she wished he would stop. It was not helping, as she tried her hardest to hold back the tears; her lips trembled as the floodgates opened up. One small tear trickled down her cheek, leaving a trail as it washed away her make up. Seeing her boss still tenderly smiling at her from behind his desk, she was unable to control the tears that began to cascade down her face. Mr Mills handed her a handkerchief from his drawer and continued, "I hope you are all ok dear. Please let me know if I can help with anything else."

Sniffling and nodding her way out of his office, she was confronted once again by Brenda, her mean supervisor. She was fully expecting to be told to get back to her seat, but instead the opposite happened. Brenda stretched out her arms and pulled her tightly into her chest. She smelt of cheap musk and cigarettes but nevertheless my sister lingered for a moment. "It's ok love, we are all here for you; you don't need to worry about a thing, ever again," said Brenda, wiping Nailah's tears away with her hands.

That day, kindness had been shown in a place where my sister least expected it. The display of sympathy and humanity obliterated the resounding sense of shame she had been carrying for months, working in that austere environment. She was no longer the Pakistani girl from the typing pool who was expected to keep her head down and take home her weekly wage. She felt like a real person with real value for the first time in her life. And it did not stop there. The senior partner who had helped her that day, Edward Mills, and his wife Margaret, took Nailah under their wing. In effect, she became their protégé.

Her world opened up

Edward and Margaret were a wealthy middle-class couple who had never had children. An organic bond grew between them as they got to know my sister. This relationship felt natural for all of them. They opened up a whole new world of possibilities, starting with introducing her to the finer things in life. Fine dining in French restaurants; days out exploring the Lake district and welcoming her into their trusted circle of family and friends. In their world, she began to flourish. She never had the opportunity to finish formal education; the Mills were her 'finishing school'. They showed her new life experiences which empowered her and made her feel special. She was no longer an outsider. It was as if she was a sponge, soaking up every new encounter which broadened her horizons by the day. No longer embarrassed by her shabby migrant upbringing, they encouraged her to feel comfortable about that too. To look at it as the blueprint for who she was. It had defined her and given her the strength to evolve into the woman she was to become.

She was growing up, becoming more confident, her preferences, her decisions and her aspirations. And her 'academy' could not have been more compassionate and wholesome. Even mum approved of the influence this caring couple had over her daughter. They respected the boundaries, never overstepping the mark; knowing that there was another set of cultural values that had to be afforded respect. It was a symbiotic relationship; they too gleaned a lot from our world, our values, our rich culture and, most of all, our food. Mrs Mills had never tasted a pakora sandwich. Once she had tried it, she did everything in her power to recreate it, adding her own sophisticated twist. That was her ginger chutney, dolloped between the ketchup and green chilli sauce. She even introduced it to the Grassington Women's Institute. Our pakora sandwiches were becoming famous.

Nailah's induction into this new world of possibility was a blessing. But, in the world of the suitors, it was also a curse. The new woman of the world, who knew the difference between an hors d'oeuvre and an amuse bouche, had higher expectations of her suitor. The tables had turned, she was now in the driving seat; not easily surrendering to be the 'chosen one'. But more concerning for mum was the fact that the bar had just been raised; from mediocre to remarkable. And she would never settle for anyone or anything less than worthy. Nailah, now the most discerning of all the Rauf girls.

Chapter 7

Zainab the rebel

The chapatti-station huddles

She was a rebel. With two years between us, she was older than me; much savvier and street wise and we connected in our daily chapatti huddle.

Dad's departure affected us all differently. She was angry at him but wasn't sure why. She had known him better than I had and been able to establish enough of a bond that, when suddenly broken, caused her more anguish. She was heartbroken and secretly mourned him. For her, it felt like bereavement. Why didn't he even say goodbye to his beautiful *Zee Zee* - his nickname for her. The lack of any plausible explanation as to why it happened that way, made his departure more painful, more perplexing. Unresolved, like a murder mystery; she felt trapped in an abyss of emotions, that were neither as decisive as the older two sisters or reconciled as mine. She was ambushed; in the middle, still searching for answers.

These unresolved issues manifested in anger, bitterness and rebellion. She made no secret of her disdain for the mixed-up values of being Asian in Britain. She saw through much of its hypocrisy; double standards which she attributed to oppressive and controlling men. She translated it as misogyny and was determined, at all costs, to avoid marrying a Pakistani man. Zainab was the only one who ever blatantly questioned the boundaries imposed by mum. She was fearless and questioned the consequences of her actions if caught out by her. She even attempted to escape the life that did not fit or serve her at the age of seventeen.

"Always remember I love you," she said to me, out of the blue one morning, as she left the house for work. I found it odd as she was never one for overly emotional declarations. When she didn't return home that night, mum went to look in her room to see if there were any clues as to where she might be hiding. When she opened her wardrobe to see empty hangers, all her clothes gone, she fell to her knees in shock, crying; "Hai Rabba!" Oh, Dear Lord, what will people say? She knew her daughter was capable of looking after herself but was more fearful of the repercussions on her if anyone in the community was to find out that one of her daughters was a 'runaway'. A term assigned to the ones who fled their homes, even when they were old enough to leave plausibly. What was more concerning to their parents; other than their safety and wellbeing, was the lingering sense of shame and dishonour they brought to the entire household. Everyone therein would be tarnished by their selfish act.

The runaways were often the ones who were savvier like Zainab and brave enough to stand up for themselves, seeing through the glibness of mixed-up cultural values. They were the true vanguards of change, trailblazers in their own ways. Seeking truth in a place of duplicity, where fake piety was used to control and subjugate them. It was not an uncommon scenario amongst Pakistani girls of that generation. Some were found and dragged back, but others had fled so far away that their absence was often shrouded in secrecy; their families inventing elaborate tales of their whereabouts, not too dissimilar to how mum covered dad's absence. One of our childhood friends Nusa had done an overnight runner of great magnitude. We were secretly in awe of her. She had legged it as far away as possible - to Perth Australia. Zainab on the other hand, only made it down the road to the next village - Baildon.

Weeks later, when she was discovered, she was coaxed and cajoled, to come back; no heavy-handed force deployed or required as did happen to others in some instances. We were not that type of family. It was Zainab herself that made the choice to return home; eventually. "Please Zainab, come home; we will work something out; this will affect everyone's life if you stay away." Begged mum: her passive-aggressive rationale, used to force her daughter back. We all knew her veiled emotionally blackmailing techniques well now, but Zainab was clever enough to know how to turn them back on mum and make them work for her. "Ok, I'll come back, but on my terms," she argued with mum.

She, the only one who possessed the ability to negotiate with her. The terms and conditions of her return had been well thought out in advance. Her bargaining afforded her more say in how her suitor would be found. She wanted to assist in the search. "I'll find someone myself and they will fit with what you want," she insisted. 'Fit with' defined loosely, in line with mum's tighter definition. Reluctantly, mum agreed if it meant she was still living at home, under her watchful eye. It also meant turning a blind eye to many of her rebellious antics. The stricter parameters of the suitor credentials were still very much aligned to mum's rigid guidelines. They had to be Muslim, Pakistani and brown.

Her return did not stop her from getting herself entangled in situations that would always end the same way. She was caught up in a ceaseless pattern that only she understood. A danger button that was pressed and was on repeat. She continued to chase pointless liaisons, knowing there was a threshold, a boundary that could not be crossed. She played with fire and often got burned. Perhaps this was her way of dealing with the trauma of losing dad? Her unresolved emotions being played out regularly. She fearlessly smashed the rules; those arbitrary perimeters which made no sense, just as much as dad's truancy made no sense. She was exposing the bigotry, the hypocrisy of it all. The collateral damage would always be heartbreak, hers and someone else's. I would hear all about it over our daily meet ups at the chapatti station; the place in the kitchen where we would stand for an hour daily, making roti for the family.

"Not again! you're always playing with fire and you're always gonna get burned!" I scolded her, shaking my head as she told me about her latest escapade whilst we made chapatti together. "I always get burned from this bloody smoke off the tava - griddle for a start," her curt response to me. Chapatti making was our daily ritual. My job was to 'ghun' or knead the flour to make the dough. It was always the same amount to cater for enough chapattis for our family - twelve in total. It took around half a kilo of chapatti flour, a dash of salt and cold water. Bringing the dough together for me varied from one day to the next and usually depended on my mood. If I was distracted, adding too much water too quickly, the dough turned a little soggy. I would have to then sneak to the 'atta' flour bin to retrieve an extra cup to restore the dryness. If mum caught me; I was in trouble because it meant that there would be too much leftover dough which would usually mean waste. The trick in getting the right balance of water to dough was to add it in increments, which allowed you to bring the dough together gently; slowly. This part was messy. Eventually, when you did collect it all into a rough ball, the sticky bits on your hands would start to disperse into the body of the dough. Then, you would dip your hands in water from a bowl placed next to your mixing station, to create a smooth blend.

Kneading the atta was a fine art. First with two fists facing downwards, punching it slowly, leaving knuckle prints as you went along. Then folding it in half, back onto itself and collecting it. This ensured that air trapped in small pockets which gave rise to a light and airy roti once the dough was rolled into a chapatti. Air gathered in the kneading process was a substitute for yeast. Kneading had to take at least ten to twelve minutes, to ensure the dough had enough air incorporated and the texture smooth. It was covered and left to one side to rest, allowing it to gently rise. This dough did not rise like bread dough, it had a more subtle rise but needed a necessary resting period. An hour was ample. Enough time to sit and watch an episode of my favourite cookery show on TV - Madhur Jaffrey.

When it was time to make this dough into roti; that was when our daily huddle at the chapatti station took place. Zainab at the griddle, ready to cook whilst I rolled out twelve individual dough balls into small rounds. Hands greased with butter to stop it sticking. The dough rolled into the palms of my hand creating a small ball - about the size of a tennis ball. The ball was dusted amply with flour, before being flattened, by patting it down, half prepping it to be rolled out. Rolling was an art too. I learned intuitively that by putting pressure on one side of the rolling pin, it would naturally allow the dough to rotate clockwise. At intervals of about ten of these movements, it was lifted and slapped between the hands a few times to help stretch it outwards. Mum used to tease us on the credentials of a round roti equating to securing a good suitor. I never bought into her round-roti superstition, it was a skill I perfected for myself and no one else.

Mum also insisted on making sure the edges were nice and thin. She hated uneven or what she called 'fat edges'.

Some days we would get so distracted in our conversations, that I would lose concentration and end up with an inconsistently fat edge. "Kandaay!" Edges! I would hear a shrill scream from mum forcing me to re-roll it, to ensure her quality control and exacting standards were being observed. Zainab's job was to cook these round, flat roti's on the hot griddle. They took anything between three to five minutes per roti. She drew the short straw, as hers was not the best job. She would complain, "I hate this bloody smoke in my eyes." The latter stages of cooking the roti involved throwing it directly onto the gas flame. This was followed by an explosion of steam that burst out of the puffed-up airy chapatti, always finding its way into poor Zainab's eyes. It didn't matter how much she attempted to avoid it, it would always get her, and her eyes would stream. But despite this, we bonded over our daily chore. The only 'sister -time' we got together, to gossip, snigger and I, to listen with great intrigue and amusement to her latest escapades. It was our very own private huddle.

Some days we made paratha, the buttery version of chapati which involved sandwiching chunks of butter between two thin rotis and rolling it as normal. The same process would also be deployed to make aloo paratha, which were stuffed with seasoned spicy potatoes. These took longer to make, giving us more time to catch up and chat. We would strategically plan to make aloo paratha on certain days, to ensure extra huddle time, to discuss something important - usually associated with a plot or a decoy to hide something from mum. That or navigate another tricky situation that Zainab was embroiled in. The chapatti station witnessed every emotion; from tears and laughter to fear and frustration. We laughed and wept here. It was our non-judgemental corner of the kitchen. Our hush-hush place which held countless secrets, exciting news, and sadness. I was trusted with many, if not all of her secrets. Assigned as Zainab's faithful confidante, I would never utter a word of her dalliances to a soul.

But there was one secret she brought to me that I wished she hadn't. It left me divided and helpless. I wanted to help her, I wanted her to have happiness more than anything, but I knew it would never be in our lifetime, under these circumstances. 'He' could have even been the one. He loved her, he was impressed and overwhelmed by her, and she felt the same. But he was not willing to change anything about himself, which for mum to agree to, would be a prerequisite for this to move forward and happen. Zainab respected that. Why should he change? He was a handsome Mancunian biker after all. She was delusional to think anything could ever come of it, let alone entertain the thought of mum giving her blessing.

"You know mum will love him. He'd be like another son to her, he's so helpful and he's always asking after her," she announced. To which I replied, "And in which fairy-tale world would mum be meeting him? Have you lost your marbles?" As quick as a flash she jumped to her regular injustice spiel. "It's so unfair, so stupid that so many of these Paki-confidence-tricksters slip through the net and make it through our front door." I would listen, as always, knowing what the next few lines would be. She continued.

"They come here as so-called Muslims, but an honest person with real values, real morals, scruples and integrity, would be barred simply for their extraction - not even religious, is it?" She was right; she continued her diatribe as I would continue to nod along. "Mum would overlook a good human being with good values and morals that does not hide behind some fake pretence of a religion - he is more of a Muslim than the ones born into it!" Once again, she was right. The incongruences could have had a steam train driven through them.

'Muslim by extraction' always prevailing. Whether they practiced or not, it was more agreeable to be of Muslim extraction than to be someone with a good moral compass, irrespective of religion. We had seen some morally corrupt characters pass through our front door on a few occasions. That itself summed up her point and she would always quote it, knowing it would fall on deaf ears.

Why were we still going along with the charade? What was it that kept us there and held us hostage for so long? It wasn't fear, it wasn't obedience because we argued back even though it didn't serve us. Her love of Mancunian Mark went from pure, to strained and then eventually messy. Mum knew of it, but turned a blind eye, for fear of losing her daughter again. It felt as if she knew it wouldn't last; that it would fizzle out. It drove an irreparable wedge between Zainab and mum. She knew she was being manipulated; emotionally taunted to believe she would be ostracised, cut out of the family fold, if she chose to go down this lonely road. Mancunian Mark stood his ground. He did not tolerate it. He argued that his love should have been enough for her to leave; enough for him to be her home. Was he worth that gamble?

Chapter 8

Farah

Food and love ~ Our panacea

Food was our love language, the panacea to make the world around us feel better. The only vocabulary required for us to feel connected. It was a natural and effortless bond. Unconditional love.

Mum was my earliest influencer, my exemplar. My earliest memories involve food and mum. I followed her every move around the basement kitchen as she cooked. I recall tugging at her dark purple velvet shawl, which she eventually would unwrap and gently place over me. I would clutch it tightly, suck and gnaw at it, smelling her scent, as I fell asleep to the aromas of her and the food she prepared.

She would create the most delicious, simple bowls of food, with vegetables she had harvested from the garden. Always multi-tasking. Cooking was something she sandwiched in between her other jobs. Even feeding me was something she slotted in, her outstretched hand, supplying my small open mouth with whatever she had created from very little resources. But somehow it embodied her careful consideration each time. The correct amount of spice; the combination of two, sometimes three elements and always cooked to the right degree, never overdone or underdone.

She was connected to the process in a way that it felt as if the ingredients sensed her instruction, knowing exactly what was expected of them; they obeyed her command. Our meals tasted of her emotions and feelings. Some days, as much as she fought against it, her sadness was evident in the food on our plates, and we sensed her misery. Other days, joy would prevail in whatever dish she had created, whilst feeling jubilant. I watched her move around the kitchen effortlessly and confidently, preparing, tasting and delivering her bounty to us daily.

Something as simple as turnip from the garden, would be chopped and tossed in butter and spices - turmeric, ground coriander, salt and chilli powder, then wrapped in 'pulki' - fluffy roti, laced with butter and it would taste divine. My palette was weaned on these simple, but complex flavours which I learned to recognise early on. Whilst feeding me with one hand, she would be carefully and precisely working on something else with the other. That too would be afforded enough attention to make sure it was nothing less than perfect. She made her talent to deliver delicious food seem effortless. She normalised it. Whilst my siblings played together, making mischief around the house, staying clear of the kitchen, I would be perched on a work surface somewhere, absorbing the meticulous process behind her every creation and concoction. I was her appendage. Glued to her; watching and learning; absorbing it all. I don't recall her ever teaching me anything, it was all diffused through simply watching her. Our bond was cemented through our mutual passion for food.

As I got old enough to handle tools in the kitchen, mainly sharp knives, without fear, I would await her instructions, "Peel the onions, garlic, ginger..." "Ok, what for?" would be my only question in response. It was all I needed to ask rather than 'how much?' I intuitively knew quantities required of each element, for each dish. Always less for vegetable dishes and dal, more for meaty dishes. If it were for a suitor banquet, then everything would have extra of each element, giving them more richness and exuberance – a display of generosity and abundance. The hardest part for me, physically was peeling and chopping onions in the freezing cold basement. It was especially punishing during the winter months when my fingers would freeze, standing next to the open cellar door, the only source of ventilation that let strong aromas leave the room, but welcome freezing cold air back in. Chopping as finely as my small hands would allow me to. There were no food processors back then, each onion had to be cut into tiny pieces. We often shared one knife between us, that mum would sharpen on the stone step outside. It would come back like a samurai sword which she trusted me to handle. She would always tell me I was her bravest child; I knew she was humouring me. Thankfully, I never lost a digit to onion chopping.

By the age of eight, I was surprisingly adept enough to prepare almost every masala - a generic term that pertained to anything spicy or sauce based required for most of our dishes. It became second nature for me to prepare this sauce or paste in advance of each suitor visit. For most curries, the masala was eighty percent of the job, and it gave us less to feel anxious about. One generic base would provide the foundation, on which many dishes could be crafted, with the addition of other spices required for a particular flavour or regional variation of a dish.

For a typical masala, I would finely chop two large or medium sized onions. Before vegetable oils came on the market readily, butter or ghee was always the preferred fat used for curries. Our onions were always fried in ghee - which mum would make from Adams butter. I used enough to cover the onions and allow them to brown, before adding a good tablespoon of cumin seeds. Garlic and ginger came next. Our 'no restrictions on garlic' policy meant that there was always a fresh batch, peeled and kept on a shelf in the coolest part of the adjoining basement cellar. The garlic shelf could easily be detected, sniffed out blindfolded, by the strong stench emanating from it. A good handful consisted of eight to ten cloves that would be roughly chopped and dropped into the browning onions. Then a fresh lump of ginger, whose skin would be scraped away; never peeled as it took away too much of this expensive root. It would be finely grated into the onions and garlic.

The right shade of brown onion came about once they were verging on golden; that was when they would be removed from the heat. They continued to cook in the residual heat of the oil, turning them a deeper shade of golden brown. Then, freshly chopped tomatoes or a whole tin of tomatoes were added to make a thick paste. Our standard spices come next - turmeric, ground coriander seeds and garam masala in equal quantities - a tablespoon would suffice for this recipe. Salt always added at this point, in increments; tasting it to check the levels. The masala was then returned to a gentle simmer, allowing the onions to break down and create a smooth paste. This masala would be divvied up to create separate dishes. Any other elements such as whole spices: cinnamon, cardamom and cloves, for more fragrant dishes, could be added later.

The kitchen was the only playground I needed, as bizarre as that sounded. When I wasn't cooking, I was organising the spice cupboard, adding whatever new spice mum would excitedly bring home from Mrs Patels corner shop. They would be emptied out of the brown paper bag into washed out jam jars, with no labels. They were easily identifiable to us, especially the whole spices: cloves, peppercorns, cinnamon bark, coriander seeds, cumin, and fennel. The spice cupboard looked like an apothecary cabinet by the time I had finished shuffling the jars around.

Mum would make blends that pertained to specific dishes, by grinding them with a homemade pestle and mortar. A marble door handle that she had salvaged became a crushing device and an old steel pot, the vessel. I would be enlisted to stand and bash the living daylights out of her combinations, until they were reduced to a fine powder. Identifiable by aroma alone; no labels required for either of us. Time spent in the kitchen with mum was our bonding; we could be pottering around there for hours, just the two of us, chatting or quietly lost in our own worlds. Food was our love language and our panacea to make the world around us feel better. The only vocabulary required for us to feel connected. It was a natural and effortless bond. Unconditional love.

Even her pet names for me pertained to food - 'makhan' butter. I never fully understood why it was a term of endearment. Perhaps because butter was soft? And if she saw me vexed or angry, I would be a 'laal mirach' - red chilli. Hot headed obviously. She would also refer to me as 'tandee hava' - a cool breeze. On certain days that I sensed her anguish, I would make her a cup of masala chai; a comforting concoction of loose-leaf tea, simmered gently in milk and whole spices - cardamom, cinnamon, cloves and peppercorns, which I knew she loved. It would be served sweet, alongside my chilli cheese toast. A snack we both loved, made with only three ingredients: green chillies, Wensleydale cheese, and white bread. Everything melted under the grill. We would sit together on the stone doorstep outside the kitchen and sip this calming elixir, then bite into the chilli cheese toast. The chilli, burning our mouths, as she poured her out woes to me. I would sit, quietly listening, never complaining; knowing I was her sounding board. The only daughter she could rely on to vent, without fear of retort or judgement.

I thrived on mum's approval; to her I was an exemplar of 'naik' or pure goodliness as she would regularly refer to me. Usually whilst berating her other rebellious daughters. I enjoyed this comparison, in fact I pandered to it. It was a source of validation which I needed at the time, to justify my hard toil and endeavours. I would also seek her favour through perfecting recipes or adding something different to them; a new element or technique to impress her. Mum celebrated me in everything I created for her, even when it tasted slightly off the mark. She was my biggest cheerleader, championing me daily.

Until one day, when everything changed.

Sullied

"Is this Nailah? She's beautiful... How old is she?" Asked a suitor's mother as I served her tea before my sister Nailah entered the room. "No! screeched mum, she's my youngest daughter Farah." Her curt response. "In fact, she's too young, she's only twelve years old," mum continued, to my complete chagrin. I was sixteen at the time.

As I got older, I began to be mistaken for my sisters by the suitors and their mothers. That was when mum suddenly changed towards me. She began to see me as a threat. From that day onwards, I was forbidden from entering the room in case I was preferred, over one of them. For the first time

I felt a sense of shame around me. Not about the fact that I could have passed for being older or likened to my sisters; that I was flattered about. The shame stemmed from mum's incommensurate reaction. It equated to disgust when she saw them looking at me in a certain way. She would turn to look at me disapprovingly and that was when I felt sullied. I was already feeling awkward during these tense teenage years, but when my changing body became the reason for me being prohibited from the room and the gaze, of others. I felt all wrong.

"You stay away from the room from now on," I was told. I was unceremoniously barred and hidden away; allowed only to pass food that I had prepared, to the door, where it would be handed to mum. She would snatch it and usher me away quickly to make sure I wasn't seen. I was Cinderella. Hiding a small person in a house isn't as easy as you might imagine it to be. There were instances where I would have to sneak in between rooms, forced to hide from a prying guest, who decided to take a stroll. Some days, I was even rumbled.

On one particularly traumatic occasion, I remember being shoved head-first into the bathroom airing cupboard. After hearing an entire family making their way up to the only toilet in the house, there hadn't been enough time for me to make the dash from the bathroom to hide. So instead, a panic-stricken mum thought it better to wedge me into the narrow airing cupboard, situated between the bath and the door. It would have been too embarrassing for her to admit the lie she had just invented, moments earlier about my absence. The shame of it backfiring, was not an option.

I tightly gripped the venetian doors, holding them closed from the inside. The doors refused to connect to the lock, because of the extra inch my body occupied in this space. As I stood there, deathly quiet and still, there was no avoiding what unfolded before me. There was enough of a gap between each wooden slat, that allowed me to look through. So, I did the only thing I could. I clenched my eyes firmly shut. Had I not, I would have been privy to the entire family's toilet habits that day. But that was the least of my fears. I prayed no one to be curious enough to look in the cupboard as I was inclined to do when visiting other peoples' bathrooms. The fallout would have been more than my rigid body from the cupboard, had this actually happened. I traumatically replayed this imaginary scenario over and over again in my head for years afterwards. It would never have ended well; for anyone.

It didn't stop at bathroom-gate. On another occasion, I was caught in the kitchen by an intrusive suitor's mum. I pretended to be hired help that day; it was the only excuse I could muster up on the spot. Then, there were the days that my sisters were 'no-shows'. Both of them refusing to entertain the suitor if they had seen something unfavourable from the upstairs window as they entered the house. 'The window of judgement,' I called it. It would decide whether it was worth making an appearance or not. If not, that would be the only time that I would be called in to serve the food. Mum's fierce instructions to me were to, 'look as dishevelled and unkempt as possible.' I would be made to wear something very unbecoming, usually oversized, to hide all my curves and contours. It was harder to dress down than dress up. If mum had her way, she would have wrapped my head in a balaclava to fend off the stares of which she was so afraid.

I would wonder whether her irrational fear was based on the thought of anyone gazing inappropriately at me - her baby, or whether she did not want to disrupt the order; the sequence, that she had put in place for us. A sequence that she herself had once disrupted, that saw her marriage fail and my aunt Zohra remain a spinster. Mum's superstitions, always dictating the way she went about things in her world. One thing I did know; neither of my sisters would have taken half the crap I did. I was the only one that ever listened to her without defiance or confrontation. Maybe I shouldn't have been so submissive. Should I too have kicked back more? She never spoke to me about when it would be my turn - the time when I would be the subject of the suitors and their families. She didn't make any reference to it, despite the fact that we had lived and breathed this bizarre ritual together. Travelled this unpredictable terrain; a journey that spanned more than a decade of our lives, experiencing the highs and lows and the after-effects.

For this reason, I began to call it Suitorland.

Suitorland was an existential journey. A window to the world and my life-skill academy. A conduit for me to find myself, through my passion for food and the quest to help mum find 'the one'. This odyssey opened my eyes to personalities and characters from the quirky and closeted to the corrupt and hilarious. It was also the mirror that was needed for us all to see ourselves. It was a tunnel through which we witnessed mum's alter ego, her white-lies, blatant lies and magnificent embellishments. I was a spectator, quietly sitting back and taking it all in, remaining unperturbed. I would eventually discover my power as I began to carve my own path through creativity of a different kind. The kind that enabled me to question the world around me; the conventions, the traditions, and even Suitorland itself.

And when 'my turn' finally did come around, it would be so far removed from what anyone was expecting.

Chapter 9

"H"

'The chosen one'

He was lost, but I found him

She put him first. A shadow in amongst five strong female figures, with an obstinate matriarch of a mum

It was bad enough for him, navigating his way through a house of females, but on top of that he was flanked either side. There were two sets of them - two older sisters and two younger. Would he ever find himself in this situation?

Hamzah's story

His character was moulded and nurtured by mum from day one. She placed him in the highest rank, as sons often are, by their Pakistani parents. My brother Hamzah or "H" as we called him was the chosen one.

The long-awaited son, sunshine boy; brown, but blue-eyed boy. He was the third child, and he was the prize that mum had been waiting for. Finally, a boy! Greeted with jubilation by mum and dad, two older sisters and the entire neighbourhood. A special boy, who will inherit the family name, propagate the lineage; look after aging parents - the latter, the only downside of this role which was always assigned to the sons. There was an unspoken power afforded to boys. They would never be considered a burden to their parents unlike the girls, their daughters.

When girls were born, they were seen as a responsibility. A burden to raise them and to marry them off; such was the heaviness of this burden on their parents. But H would never be that. From the minute he was born, he was stamped with, 'The superior one,' something the patriarchy nurtured and reinforced in this generation, which we, the girls and women, simply had to accept. When dad left abruptly, H was immediately assigned the role of man of the house, without consultation, explanation, or a job description. At eight years old, I don't recall anyone asking him , 'was he ok?' In his newly appointed role, he was left to find his own way. He was also the only one who was spoiled, over indulged with toys, affection and attention. None of which was asked for; he just wanted his father back.

"He had to go, we had no choice puttar, son," I recall mum saying, wiping away the tears coursing down the face of her confused little boy, as he looked up at her, defiantly stomping, "Why why why? I want my dad, I want my dad, give him back!" I remember feeling the same, but no one asked Zainab or myself. Were we not important enough to have opinions or feelings? He was lavished with things to appease him, gifts to comfort him and to help him heal. The sudden void was papered over with what mum thought was a reward. The reward - the gift of importance, power, control and superiority over the girls. This bigotry served only to add to his confusion. Perpetuating the generational values of an archaic patriarchy, embedded in mum's own DNA. "Now you're the man of the house," she comforted him. But this was not an honour, it was a burden, an unwanted responsibility that weighed heavy on his young shoulders. What did that even mean to an eight-year-old boy? He was conflicted when told the same day, that he would never be able to see his father again.

With no male role model, his trauma played out very differently from ours. His search for a father figure would not be objectified into a future suitor, a companion that embodied the pieces that were missing, as it did for us. His search for dad was more tumultuous and being played out in the present tense. A daily narrative of uncertainty and insecurities that manifested in his character and encumbered his evolution into a man. This was never going to be an easy journey.

As women and young girls, it was easier to comfort each other through our loss. We came together through our interests; activities such as making food, creating things and making 'stuff'. We were able to connect and comfort each other during these activities; it was our therapy. As a boy, his interests were not the same, he had no interest in cooking or sewing - these were our nesting instincts that naturally saw the women huddling together. He was left alone with memories of a figurehead who he had only ever seen as a caring, kind and a nurturing father. A man who had spent hours with his young son, walking along the railway line that ran parallel to the house, chatting, playing cricket and returning home with a head full of stories and a giant bag of sweets. It came as no surprise that, years later, he would discover a way of finding him. It was inevitable. He was desperate for a resolution, closure, answers, even a relationship with the man that had vanished into thin air.

I was always dismayed by the privileges of his overnight elevation to the 'man of the house'. A position which afforded him to escape the drudgery of all chores; he was never expected to lift a finger. In fact, he may well have been given a clip board as he stood on the side lines. Acting like some kind of supervisor, inspecting my work and enjoying his authority; sometimes deliberately creating more chores for me as he saw fit, just to see me run around for his amusement. Grinning, whilst pointing and mocking me. "Spoilt shit head," I would whisper under my breath, visualising ways to make him cry which, on occasion, I did. I stamped on his action figures and models of planes that had taken him hours, if not days to painstakingly assemble. I left them for dead. He never knew how they had made their way under the rugs; smashed to smithereens. That was my revenge, my counterblow and the only source of satisfaction I had in getting him back.

His elevated status enabled him to do everything that was forbidden to us. Through this archaic value system and unjust elevation of him, our house was divided into 'one rule for you and one rule for your brother'. These twisted generational values did nothing but make us feel belligerent toward him; seeing it as wrong but unable to speak up against it. Pakistani mothers of boys had suffered the same discrimination themselves, but were now reinforcing those same values, which saw them subjugate their daughters and elevate their sons. Not only were they keeping the rusty wheel of patriarchy turning, they were now compounding it.

The only one who openly questioned it and did not pander to him was Zainab. There was only a year between them; she was his closest sibling, and she wasn't afraid to speak her mind. But their clashes only served to add more duties to my plate after she point-blank refused to do them. As the youngest, I was more fearful; if not afraid of him and the repercussions, if mum was to intervene, appeasing him, reinforcing his power and giving him the whip hand. It was her way of over-compensating and distracting him from the absence of dad.

Of his many other privileges, he would also be spared Suitorland. Mum's rule book, incongruent once again, this time, exposing the huge disparity between brother and sisters. He was allowed to socialise in a way that was forbidden to us. He even got to frequent the local social scene and the only one-night club in Shipley at the time known as Neon Nights. It was a popular place to meet and socialise for young people in our town. "He is a man… its different for him," mum would say, shrugging her shoulders, her inequitable justification. "Wish I was a bloody man," Zainab's response to these gross inequities.

"My 'beta'- son will look after me," she would say to anyone who asked who she would live with in her older years. Eventually, he would be assigned as carer to mum as she aged. Maybe that was the reason she gave him such a wide birth; she knew the road ahead would be more difficult for him. She even imagined living with him as an old woman, him caring for her when she was too old to care for herself. Would he feed her, dress her, make sure she was comfortable and warm? It was for this reason, that she had to do everything to make him feel she deserved his care in her later years. Mum was pre-empting his favour. That too, the reason he was never restricted, as we were. An advance reward for the years she saw ahead of him. And on this premise, she trusted him to find a wife for himself, who would be equally committed to looking after her.

"Oi, what's for dinner?" he would bellow, poking his head out from his bedroom door. I would run to reply, "Aloo gosht and roti," meat and potato curry and chapatti. Unimpressed by this perfectly delicious meal, he would consider for a moment before continuing. "Make me a masala omelette with a side of spicy tomatoes and fried bread."

I was also assigned to be his personal chef - to prepare food 'off menu' if he wasn't willing to eat what we did. Had it been anything else he requested of me, I would have reacted differently, but food - I welcomed this commission and that was the only reason I obliged. At whatever the time of day the request was made, it was fulfilled. Masala omelette, an utterly delicious spin on a regular omelette, which saw spices added in small quantities relative to the ratio of eggs. For two eggs, I would use a quarter teaspoon of garam masala, chilli powder and cumin seeds. Salt and fresh chillies (to taste) with a small bunch of coriander, a quarter onion and a small tomato all chopped finely and mixed together. Quantities of spice were down to your palette; my brother liked it spicy, so I made sure to add extra fresh chillies.

The mixture, tipped into a frying pan with a good tablespoon of hot, sizzling butter. The butter had to be spitting on the heat, otherwise you didn't get the inward curl from the outer edges of the omelette. Holding the pan up into the air, I swirled the omelette around to make sure all the liquid dried up, leaving a glossy top layer. I would always flip it, not fold it in half; we liked our omelette served flat, well cooked, and crispy on the edges. Always served with a side of fried bread made by spreading butter over bread then letting it sizzle on the griddle on both sides. This entire dish was pure joy; all washed down with hot chai.

Mum should have stepped in sooner, but she never did discourage his entitled behaviour. She enabled and excused it. Unaware, if not ignorant of the potential repercussions this would have on our brother-sister relationship in later life. A pernicious pattern was setting in. He would never understand strength and resourcefulness in the same way the girls did. Everything was handed to him on a plate. Mum was creating a rod for her own back. As women and young girls, we had spent years searching for a father figure but somehow, we managed to find a way of dealing with it. Introspection allowed us to deal with what we didn't have. It came through our own inner resources, which replaced the sense of loss we all felt. It was how we dealt with it; we wouldn't let dad's desertion from the past, encumber our future. We had to overcome his vacancy using every tool we had within ourselves.

H's angst-ridden teenage years saw him get angrier and more aggressive. It was inevitable. He was acting out. With no guidance, no male role model and no one to pull him into shape when he stepped out of line, his outbursts were a cry for help. His desperate yearning and search for our absent father was more tumultuous than we could ever have imagined; overindulging him had served only to emasculate and render him helpless. He would never know the resourcefulness that came from a challenge or a struggle in the way we did. Our survival instincts were on high alert at all times and our struggles had defined us as women. Nothing came to us easily. Our challenges gave us strength and ultimately helped us to map the missing parts we needed in our suitors. The right elements - just like a recipe; a blend that suited our individuality. Getting to this point required complex emotions, analysis and digging deep.

H's assumed man of the house status was an imaginary

concept with nothing to validate it other than privileges and favour from mum. He rejected it as he grew more resentful. He needed a father to bring sense back into his world and give him the closure for which he was so desperate. The question was, could a relationship ever be salvaged with dad after all these torturous years?

He found him...

He was fifteen when he found dad. The teenage years had mentally taken their toll and he was drained. Mum too had reached her threshold. She was ill-equipped to deal with his chaotic and turbulent barrage of emotions, which were constant; unyielding and intolerable, for everyone. The mother-son relationship was splintered and fracturing further. She was walking on eggshells around the only man in her life that she had ever truly loved.

How he found dad we would never know but it was always on the cards. I remember the day that he announced. "I saw dad." The three words rolled easily off his tongue. He delivered his message in a way that felt as if he had already accepted mum's reaction. He was reconciled, at ease for the first time. The words felt like a blow to mum's stomach even though, for years, she had been expecting them. They still cut deep into her. It was the first time I had seen a look of disdain on her face towards her precious son, her pride and joy. I sensed her feelings of betrayal in her sharp intake of breath as she replied, "And what?" lifting her eyes from behind her reading glasses. She was feigning calmness; acting. I sensed that too. Desperately trying to remain composed, she was cornered; ambushed and wondering what was coming next. What had been said to him? Why was his expression so cold, and so full of contempt?

H continued, "And I will see him again, that's what." With those words, he left the room, leaving mum to contemplate the impact, the blow that had been dealt and the repercussions that would follow. She knew that it would affect our lives moving forward in one of two ways; it would either unite us or divide us. The only certainty in this situation was, that life would never be the same again, for any of us. She could handle the betrayal, but what she couldn't handle was allowing that man to infiltrate our lives ever again. Hamzah was now a conduit for that to happen. The thought of him even within our sphere of existence was repugnant to her. She braced herself, defeated and still in shock, knowing something was broken and irreparable. She shrugged her shoulders and sighed deeply, looking upwards as she did when beckoning strength form the Almighty. "Hey Rabba... *Please God*, help me."

As predicted, my brother began to see dad regularly. Whilst we never knew the exact days it happened, we read it through his behaviour and body language. He always returned home sombre, deflated and pensive. It was evident that he needed dad, but he needed mum more, hence his return home. As much as I wanted desperately to know about dad; everything about him, I could never bring myself to ask; that would have simply added to mum's sense of betrayal. I would never do that to her. It was apparent that this rekindled relationship would have been anything but joyous. There were too many unanswered questions for it to have started on a high note. What did they talk about I wondered?

Mum knew that his relationship was built on a house of cards; she knew dad would have been lying or worse still turning her son against her. Whilst he was banished from us, mum never uttered a word that would have seen us hate or turn against him. Was he doing the opposite? What was his spin, that saw H returning to him again and again? Whatever it was, it divided our family. My brother had not been fully present or engaged with us for years, but now, any involvement in our day to day lives was kaput. He had always supported mum at the suitor meetings, but now that too had stopped.

Mum's new lies to the suitors and their families would see her boasting, "My son and his father are both away on business today, selling goods in Turkey; they need leather goods there you know?" or "They are in Singapore selling spices, they need spices there you know." Her cover-ups were becoming even more desperate and far-fetched. What she didn't realise was how ludicrous and implausible her lies were becoming. Turkey was one of the biggest manufacturing countries; why would they need leather goods from the UK?

And Singapore, had its own spice industry.

It was also glaringly obvious, that H resented mum. He was broken and emotionally stunted after years of her pandering to him. She had crippled him. He had grown to hate our world and everything it represented - especially the world of the suitors. He resented all of us. The Rauf women to him symbolised the absence of his dad, the lost years and what could have been. Everything about *us* to him, was flawed, tainted, and ugly. But he would never know the truth. As painful as the rejection and betrayal felt, mum also knew that she had to protect her son from the truth. When H found dad, he wanted to believe the fantasy that he had constructed in his own mind. Mum bizarrely enabled that too. She felt he was owed recompense for the unrequited love of his father. She surrendered, knowing that he needed it in order to find his peace; to find himself. It was the closure she thought he needed. Did he ever find what he had been searching for?

I found him, in the kitchen...

It took a long time to happen, but H eventually evolved for the better. It was a slow process that started with him showing appreciation for my efforts in feeding him. His once angry barking demands dissolved into requests. He would take an interest in how effortlessly his food was created to order. This was his only way of showing remorse for his younger self bullying me and a turning point which saw a loving brother-sister relationship begin to emerge. He would sit and watch me make his meals and eventually start to practice making them himself. Finally, I had an apprentice. A student to whom I could pass my skills, albeit the most unlikely sibling in the house.

I never asked him about dad, but he volunteered something one day, unexpectedly that made me sob uncontrollably, as we sat eating pakora sandwiches. It turned out that for all the years we had been separated, dad had been living only streets away. HOW? How was this possible? How had we never seen him? How had he hidden from us? Had he bought a house so close by to spy on us? His house was on route to the bus stop, where we caught the B45 to school daily. He must have watched us pass by each day. He had seen us all growing up, from afar. How did that make him feel... What did he see... How often? All these questions and more were swimming around in my head, making me feel dizzy. My brother consoled me as the tears welled up and rolled down my cheeks.

He also conceded that he had envied me growing up. My calmness, my resolve and my ability to put my head down and just get on with life. "You were the only one with no ego, no agenda, and no axe to grind," he said. In return I admitted that it was me who had crushed his action figures and model planes over the years. From then on, we had a newfound respect for each other. I may have lost years of knowing a father figure, but that day I found my brother.

Chapter 10

Letters and Lies

The Daily Jang Classifieds

First came the letter, then came the lies.

Everyone from the Indian subcontinent knew it. It was the oldest Urdu newspaper, printed in Karachi, distributed in the UK and read by the entire Pakistani population in Yorkshire - The Daily Jang. It was first published during World War II - its name 'Jang', translating to 'War'.

In Shipley, you had to reserve a copy with your news agent, for fear of it selling out fast. Its contents were pretty irrelevant to our lives in England, as it shared news from Pakistan; mostly politics, sport (cricket) and other sections pertaining to the subcontinent. The only section that was of interest to mum, however, was the classifieds, more specifically the matrimonial pages.

When it opened up its marital ads section in the UK; it was a game changer. Many Pakistani families listed their prospective suitors, both male and female. The listings were pretty impressive. Credentials ranged from doctors - highly desirable, lawyers, - also desirable, engineers - impressive, scientists, and more. The format of each listing was standard. I'm not quite sure who devised it, or why it was so rigid. It was usually written by or on behalf of parents referencing their sons / daughters' particulars, in the most clinical and unimaginative way. It always began with their profession, followed by several lines referencing their physical attributes which again, I always found pretty insipid. The descriptions related to height, complexion, age and in some instances, even weight. Embellishment and misrepresentation featured often, as we discovered over wasted spreads of food that had been laid out for the subsequent meetings.

We had heard of some highly successful marriages, resulting from this matrimonial service, so of course, without hesitation, mum subscribed to it, hoping that it would bring in the right suitors for us. A typical Suitor *ad* looked something like this:

Our son, Jangir, is an Oxford Graduate. A neuroscientist with a degree in Biochemical science and a postgraduate in Biomedical studies. He is currently working with Shell Oil.

He is 5 foot 11 (which usually meant a good few inches shorter) He is of good character (not always) slim and smart (whatever that meant). His interests are hiking, playing cricket and travel (not always the case).

We are looking for a degree educated young woman. Height: must be no shorter than 5ft (yes, that direct). Must be fair skinned (yes, that racist). Slim and smart (whatever that meant).

No time wasters appreciated (the audacity of it!)

If you are interested, please enquire to the PO box given.

That was it - a classified ad in the matrimonial section.

Interests were usually a complete fabrication by parents. Many suitors were stumped when they were raised in conversation at the meetings. They would look to their parents as if to say, 'You could have warned me in advance, I would have prepared for this lie.'

Mum spent long hours scouring these ads, enlisting me to help her read through them, then marking the ones of interest. I saw it as another mundane task and a millstone around my neck, all part of the suitor search. We then had to devise our own ads, hoping they would not elicit the same cynicism we felt from reading theirs. Mum made me write each of the ads neatly by hand, to my complete contempt.

Our advert read:

Our daughter is 20 years old. (Lie: Actual age 23)

She is a Legal Executive at a prestigious law firm. (Lie: actual job, legal secretary in a Solicitors office in Shipley)

She is 5ft 6. (Lie 5ft 3)

Slim and smart. (True, but still flummoxed as to why this was even a credential?)

Fair skinned. (I didn't see the point of this racist attribute either).

Her interests range from, reading literature, walking in nature and baking. (All lies). This is where I had to step in and engineer interests, to make them both look more appealing as potential 'homely' wives. It went on...

We are looking for a professional young man, no older than 25 years of age. Must be educated to Degree level.

Must be working in a stable job and ideally own his own property. Please enquire via the details provided.

Regards

We waited for the replies to come flooding in, but to our bemusement, our ad received no responses. It indicated that we were either asking for too much or our credentials were not as desirable or commensurate to what we were asking for in return. So, it was redrafted, after I encouraged mum to be more honest. This time, its tone was pitched differently. It was more realistic and relevant to Nailah's credentials and attributes; ones that actually mattered. It read:

Our daughter is 23 (her actual age) She is a legal secretary; PA to a partner (her actual job). She is slim and smart (mum insisted I keep this line). She is 5ft 3" (actual height). She is bright, well mannered, cooks well and her hobbies are gardening and reading (still slightly embellished but plausible).

We are looking for a young man (no height or age specified) who is a professional, looking to settle down and eventually buy a home of his own, together with our daughter. If you feel we are the right match for you, please feel free to get in touch via the details given.

We look forward to hearing from you.

Mrs Rauf

After this ad was posted, we were inundated with responses. Enough to last months of introductory meetings. It seemed to hit all the right notes and we learned a lot from that. We gleaned that in Suitorland, honesty and humility were the only desirable credentials that mattered.

Chapter 11

The only power couple we knew

Diya Malhotra ~ She was both in this relationship

When life and the search became too arduous for her, mum would enlist the help of her only sibling in the UK, her youngest brother - our maternal uncle. He had moved to England a few years after she had settled here. Uncle Raad was a handsome young man. He lived in Wessex Gardens, a wealthy borough of London. He oozed style, charisma and was married to the most glamorous woman we had ever laid eyes on, Diya Malhotra. Even her name was alluring. When they visited us in Yorkshire, we swooned at this shining example of a truly avant-garde duo - a power couple of their time. Diya was not like any other Pakistani woman we knew. She was the opposite in fact of everything mum represented in values and culture.

They had met, not long after Raad arrived in London from Lahore to study medicine. She was the daughter of his landlord. They began secretly courting when she came to collect the rent one day. It wasn't too long after that, they got married. Mum tried everything to stop him marrying her. She judged her for being too 'modern' for her brother. It would have been his first relationship and mum was worried that he was still too immature to cope emotionally. That and the fact that Diya posed an obvious threat to her; mum was afraid that she would destabilise their close sibling bond. She did her best to see her off, trying to convince Raad to, "Have a fling instead. She isn't one of us, she's different; it won't last."

This was mum's duplicitous side coming out. Encouraging her own brother to have love affairs; breaking all the rules that she enforced on us. There was always a different set of rules for men. But frighteningly, it was being enabled by women; pitching them against each other, through casting aspersions and passing judgement. Diya was bait. She was ahead of the curve in so many ways, a far cry from anything mum or her younger brother had ever been exposed to, let alone experienced growing up in their conservative life in Pakistan.

It was a whirlwind romance and they married in a stylish wedding in central London, paid for by her affluent father, who, we were told was related to The Aga Khan. We all attended, wearing our matching homemade purple velour dresses, looking like the Von trap family. This was the one and only time Mum had her hair dressed properly by a real hairdresser in London. It was sculpted it into a beehive, and it was the most glamorous I had ever seen her look.

After they were married, Diya and Raad visited us regularly. They were a stylish couple and the only positive role models, who in our eyes, represented wholesome values. Values and words that were not even spoken of in our home referencing relationships; those being 'love and respect'. When they came to see us, they bought an air of fun, positivity and something we had never seen or felt between our own parents - sensuality. They even coordinated their outfits. Matching trench coats and jeans; every minute detail of their image was carefully choreographed by Diya. This was also the only time we saw a man acquiesce to a woman. Raad worshipped her.

She was truly magnificent. She was much taller than the average height south Asian woman. She had smooth, flawless dark skin and unusual but striking features. A slender, hooked nose and wide deep brown oriental eyes. A thick main of heavy, ebony black hair that hung loosely around her shoulders. She wasn't afraid of showing off her long slender bare legs, that stretched out before her from under her mini skirt, to mum's disapproval. She was a law unto herself and did not conform to the pseudo-religious values that were imposed on us. Gazing suggestively at Raad, whilst sharing her silk cut cigarette, she was defiantly unperturbed by mum's disparaging glances. Diya was an aberration and not afraid to voice her opinions, often making overt statements about the archaic way our religion was practiced in the UK.

"We follow the religious teachings very differently where I grew up; not some re-interpretation by ill-informed and controlling men," she would challenge mum. An obvious reference to the patriarchy that dis-empowered women, which she was intelligent enough to unravel and dissect. We listened intently as she sat before us, eating a plate of food that was prepared especially for her. She ate lightly, often voicing her disdain for conventional curries that she deemed 'too oily'. She even changed Raad's eating habits, replacing them with her own preferences.

Stuffed bitter gourd; also known as Karela, she told us, was one of the healthiest vegetables we could eat. It tasted rank, but mum found a way of getting rid of the bitterness of the outer crimped and bumpy skin. She soaked it in salt overnight and it did the trick. The next day she opened it up and stuffed it with spicy mince keema, then tied it together with string, to keep the mince inside the skin as it cooked slowly for a few hours. I always thought it looked like burnt dead rats when cooked. But it was always on the menu when they visited. Dessert would be equally healthy, made with vegetables oddly enough. Carrot halwa; another one of their favourites. Carrots simmered slowly in milk, sugar and cardamom until reduced down to a rice pudding like texture.

Mum never argued with Diya, even though she wanted to pull her up, when she felt judged and patronised. Instead, she dutifully carried on tight-lipped. She was the paradigm of righteousness and sanctimony, even though she was painfully oppressed by those very things. Misogyny and patriarchy were not in her vocabulary. She had many strengths, but standing up to oppression wasn't one of them. She tiptoed her way through it, like many others of her generation. Unlike Diya, who was quick to hold up a mirror to these flawed decrepit values and defend her rights and the rights of all women for that matter. She was a strong role model for us. We were impressed and mesmerised by her; she represented the opposite of everything we were being conditioned to believe to mum's dismay. Over time, and understandably, mum began to distance her impressionable daughters from our beautiful, strong, avant-garde aunt.

It was only through Diya and Raad that we caught a glimpse of an exciting and different reality. A world where we could stay true to our values but be free from unnecessary and otiose restrictions that made no sense to us. An alternate reality of 'what could be' and so far removed from the drab and stagnant life we were fumbling our way through, living in Yorkshire.

Chapter 12

Coming out of the closet - He was gay.

The 'business' of finding a suitor was rife amongst the Pakistani community of 1985.

asood Majeed was nicknamed 'Magic' by us. He worked as cabin crew for British Airways. Where his sexual preferences lay, we were uncertain but could possibly guess.

Suitor Sunday had become a weekend ritual akin to a sport. It followed a consistent format. The search, the anticipation, the feeding, vetting and the cross-examination of each suitor. They were mostly still being found through the Daily Jang newspaper, but also in other more inventive ways. Communication networks were growing. Some suitors were coming to us through the vast matrix of Pakistani women who were now connected by a venous system-like thread, that ran through the region and even stretched across the country. I imagined charts on their walls, plotted with red string, linking this expansive nexus of all the suitors in the land. These industrious women had forged in-roads into the many families of prospective suitors. Some even made an occupation of sharing their 'lists' with mum in exchange for a small fee - an informal, under the radar matrimonial service. The business of finding a suitor was rife amongst the Pakistani community of 1985.

Masood and his family were introduced to mum through this network. They travelled up from the outskirts of London, a community not as parochial as Bradford at the time. His mother, Naheed, was as described by mum as 'modernised'. She had uncommonly short, cropped hair, which was worn tucked behind her ears; no dupatta veil on her head which was also uncommon. Her sharp decisive dress sense mirrored her overall manner. She was direct and brusque with an air of superiority about her. She peered down her nose through the large gold rimmed glasses perched at the end of it to vet Nailah. Up and down, with her unsubtle head movements, as if she was eyeing up a piece of furniture or another inanimate object. She circled around a vexed looking Nailah.

'Who the hell does she imagine she is? I sensed my sister thinking... Have you even seen the state of yourself?' I gleaned from her almost tangible and disgusted expression. Naheed finally stopped circling my sister and declared in Urdu, "Betee achee hey, aap ki - Your daughter is good." I could still read Nailah's facial expressions, and she was even more irritated. After her vetting, came the predicted small talk. Masood threw a few flirtatious glances over Nailah's way, and she reciprocated; finding him worthy and handsome, despite his offensive mother.

"So, beta daughter, vot is your job?" Inquired his mum in her thick Pinglish - Pakistani-English accent. "I'm a legal secretary auntie," came Nailah's swift reply. "Sec-re-tary? Oh, I thought you were more than a sec-re-tary?"

his mum mouthed, breaking the word into syllables, with her eyebrows now raised above her glasses. "I am auntie," Nailah replied with a look that said, 'more than you'll ever flippin' know'. She continued, "I work for a senior partner, I do a lot of his casework as well as secretarial… I'm more what you would call a Legal Executive auntie." Naheed announced, "Sharbaash," - bravo! clasping her heavily bejewelled hands together and then continuing. "So, then you are like a lawyer?"

"Err not quite." Again, Nailah's irritated face read - 'if she doesn't shut her trap soon, I may put my fist in it'. Her pained expression was so obvious that I almost spilled the tea as I poured it. Masood suddenly interjected to stop his mother from continuing her irritating and judgemental questions. "I really like your turquoise," he announced with his head tilted. We all swiftly turned to look his way. The tilt of the head and the hand that rose up toward his face, made a peculiar but very definitive pawing gesture. I didn't quite know there was a word for it, so I assumed it was a quirk.

The turquoise he was referring to eccentrically was the colour of Nailah's dress. Her expression, however, was more perceptive, as she detected something in him that was more than a quirk. Being a decade older than me and more worldly-wise, she beamed from ear to ear. The widest toothy smile I had ever seen her flash at a suitor meeting. A smile that was on the brink of a laugh. She was expressing a genuine curiosity to learn more of what Masood had to offer this day. He continued, "I've always had a penchant for turquoise, since those beads I played with as a child," he said looking over at his mother, indicating that it was her beads he was referring to.

That word 'penchant', I had never heard before; could it be French? It was said with a flamboyancy that I assumed came with the phonetic of the word. And the other word that wasn't yet in our vocabulary to describe him was 'camp'. Masood was undeniably, camp. His mum interjected, her hands fidgeting as she straightened her cashmere shawl as a form of distraction. Her shrill high-pitched laugh dominated the room, as she attempted to downplay and distract from what had struck us already as unconventional expression from her son.

She interjected before he could continue further. "Oh, you know how boys are alvays remembering things; colours of their childhood." We didn't know what she meant but humoured her with our contrived laughter. Mum too feigned a laugh but couldn't help herself from nervously squinting in bemusement. She too had picked up on the irregular tone in her son's voice and flamboyant mannerisms, which she brushed off as a southern thing. "In fact," Majid continued. "That's enough Beta, bas stop!" his mum aggressively interrupted him; cutting him dead.

"Oh, this samosa is just soooo yummy," she declared, putting an entire half samosa into her mouth. A Punjabi samosa today; these were larger in size than my usual bite sized ones and the result of an experiment. A Punjabi samosa was constructed to stand upright because of its flattened bottom, which distinguished it from our regular, triangular shaped versions. They were a work in progress. I followed a new Madhur Jaffrey recipe, where she demonstrated folding pastry in a way that created a much larger pocket for the filling. I was hoping that Naheed would savour it more slowly, as each samosa had taken time for me to construct.

This, her first genuinely positive comment was followed by, "Did you make it beta," looking at Nailah. "No, she did" Nailah replied, pointing at me as I took a small bite out of my own samosa. On noticing me, sitting quietly out of the way, his mum once again ran her eyes up and down me before announcing, "Oh, isn't she soo cute? *soo Healthy!*" I was jarred by this phrase.

Both my sisters giggled as they bit into their samosas, knowing I would not enjoy the rest of mine. The word healthy, whilst it had a positive connotation, was a trigger for me. In the Asian community *healthy* was another word for slightly rotund or overweight and in my case, signified that I had enjoyed too many samosas over the years and leftovers in fact, from the suitor banquets. I was feeling unsettled by all the eyes analysing me, sizing me up; literally. I subtly pulled my clothes tighter around me, squeezing my arms inwards, hoping it would make me look less 'healthy'. The years of preparing these delicious banquet-style meals and enjoying the leftovers had obviously added extra pounds, but it didn't bother me. I was comfortable, enjoying my food, never paying attention to how it translated onto my waistline. Until it was pointed out so ineptly and then reinforced by my mocking and much more slender sisters, who mum described as 'slim and smart'. I knew that I didn't fit that category, but again, I was unperturbed by it. I wasn't on offer yet, so there was no need for me to care how I appeared, so I went back to scoffing my samosa, savouring each tasty bite.

After the guests had left, things took an interesting turn. I had assumed Masood's idiosyncrasies and abrupt exit, after being dragged away by his mother, had seen the end of him. "That was quite funny! he was so odd!" I said to Nailah, to which she replied, "I quite liked him," then turned to mum and asked, "can I see him again?" Mum looked clearly puzzled and taken aback but nevertheless, agreed to a second meeting. He was a charming man, there was no doubt about that. He definitely had a warmth and friendliness that drew us all in and despite his idiosyncrasies, had made us laugh. He lightened the mood of the meeting, in stark contrast to the other more austere suitors who had visited us over the years.

Mum looked sprightlier now as we cleared the plates. Every time a second meeting was requested, it sent her into a frenzy, as she imagined a happy ending on the horizon for her daughter. We were all hoping and praying for that happy ending to come soon for Nailah. With each unsuccessful suitor outcome, she was growing more weary; more defeated.

Laylah her sidekick, now married, was getting on with her life in another country, moving forward, making babies, making her own family. She didn't want to be left on the proverbial shelf; her shelf-life soon to expire, if measured by Pakistani standards of the time. She was fast approaching spinster-dom. But worse than that, the prospect of looking after mum and her younger siblings was taking more chunks out of her mentally than we imagined. She could be stuck with us for the rest of her life if she didn't get a move on and that to her, was a grim prospect.

Ironically, as much as I wanted her to make haste, I didn't want her to just settle either, to follow that same acquiescence as her older sister. I wanted her to hold out for the right man. He was out there somewhere, and I would keep the laborious banquets going until we found him, however long that took. Sometimes I did wonder whether she was deliberately slowing the process down. There was more complexity to her rejection of eligible men than we realised. Whilst she hated the idea of being burdened with mum; there was a conflicting sense of duty still very much prevalent. A fear that was fuelled by her sense of obligation and her angst for 'what would happen to mum if I left her?'

The next visit was unchaperoned. Masood ditched his mum, arriving on his own. Mum allowed him to sit with Nailah in the living room and for them to chat unhindered. I made pink tea for him, subconsciously wondering whether he might be drawn to the colour of it, as he had her turquoise dress. Pink or Kashmiri tea; a beautiful milky concoction, scented with dried, edible rose petals which also imparted their colour into it, turning it a deep, rich pink. Made with loose Kashmiri tea leaves, cloves, cinnamon, cardamom pods, star anise and dried edible rose petals. Everything brought gently to the boil in a ratio of half milk and half water. The trick was to simmer it slowly over a gentle heat so that the tea and the spices fused together, fully absorbing into each other and reducing to a creamy consistency. It was served with crushed pistachios and more dried rose petals to garnish.

As I anticipated, Masood spent a few minutes staring at the tea, swilling it around mum's china cup, marvelling and commenting on the contrast between the green pistachio and pink petals, before slowly sipping and savouring it. Today he had come to see my sister, as she had requested, but also to make an unexpected announcement and a request of his own. As he sat back on the settee with his legs crossed, Nailah noticed his heavily glossed lips catching the light. He slowly began to speak, opening the conversation.

"Well, you know, I do want to get married and do what we're meant to do?" He said, raising his well-manicured hands in the air. Unsure of whether this was a rhetorical statement or a question, Nailah interrupted. "And what's that then?" He replied, "You know, have children, propagate, *pleeease* the parents," extending the word please and continuing to sip his pink tea. "Well, I don't see it like that; otherwise, I would be married by now," Nailah replied intently. He sighed, then fidgeted on his seat before continuing. "Well, my situation is more complicated, I like women, but you know, I kind of prefer men more," he revealed, without even flinching.

He was edging closer to the crux of his announcement, which was already obvious from all the signs. Nailah responded, premeditatedly saying, "I know. So, what do you want from me?" This was the first time anyone had 'seen' him, even before he had a chance to finish. It took him by surprise, and it begged the question - why had he been invited back? It was looking like there might be an agenda on the cards for both of them. Feeling more at ease now, Masood continued, "Well, if you know, then this could work for both of us?" "I'm all ears," said Nailah, as she reached for the teapot and poured him another cup of the pink elixir.

Deny and dupe

She wasn't perturbed by the revelation of him being gay, if anything she respected him for coming out to her. She had seen through the pretence in that first meeting, even seeing through his mother's vain attempts to conceal what she also knew about her son, but unlike him, would never accept or acknowledge it. She was the one in denial and her agenda was far more sinister than his. In her refusal to accept the truth about him, she was frequenting the homes of other prospectives and 'unsuspectives' with a view to emotionally defraud someone into marrying him. Her duplicitous plan -

was to deny and dupe.

Masood was trapped. Nailah knew that it must have taken an incredible leap of faith for him to concede his true sexuality. She knew the implications of how this could easily backfire and the consequences for him, but more importantly his duplicitous mother. Would she be able to handle the shockwave that would reverberate through the tight knit suitor nexus, a direct result of his exposure? Nailah had made Masood feel comfortable enough to speak openly with her, to confide in her. He had sensed something in her, that he knew would help him traverse the rocky terrain of being a closeted gay man in a Muslim world and now in Suitorland.

"I will never be able to come out to them you know," he went on to reveal. That too she had guessed, but what did he want from her? other than support which she was willing to give him, but only to a certain extent. As well as the revelation, there was a proposition that he had devised and, he was also bringing that to our table. "This could work for both of us," he repeated. Nailah sat quietly and listened, as he went on to describe in detail, the dynamics of his proposal which had been carefully mapped out. It involved more dishonesty and fraud as she had guessed. There was a look of desperation on his face; Nailah could not help but feel sorry for him.

Homosexuality was not accepted in Islam, which did not mean to say that it didn't exist. It existed and was more prevalent than we imagined, in the clandestine niches, which were known only to gay men and women from the south Asian community. They had their own underground closed society; a hush hush network. Nailah, unbeknown to us had a gay male friend called Armi, who had already told her all about this sequestered community.

She knew what was coming next but continued to listen to him without reaction or judgement. Masood raced through the dynamics of his proposition. "If it suits you, we get married and it will be an 'open marriage' where you and I will have the freedom to do as we please. It can't be easy for you either, being trapped in this house with your family at your age; don't you want to live a little too?" She flinched at his assumptions but allowed him to continue into the details, which were now becoming too far-fetched and swaying too much in his favour. "We will live in our own house and do our own thing; no one will be the wiser." He paused, pouting and leaning forward, placing both elbows on his knees. A double-life scenario was his proposition and now, it was time for her to say her part.

"First off, I'm not trapped. I choose to be here; I'm not looking for a get-out and certainly not one that will see me flitting from one man to the next to 'live a little' as you put it; that is not my thing. And I am not here to judge you either Masood, I sense your pain, but there is another way. I asked you back today to try and convince you to come out, not to me, but to your parents, to your family. I have other gay friends like you and can introduce you to them; they will help you I promise." She paused, to gauge a reaction; hoping to convince him that his preposterous proposition would serve only to entrench him and his accomplice (if he were to ever find one) so deeply in a web of deceit, that it would eventually be to his own demise. No one would be 'free' as he had fantasised, in this cloak and dagger world that he was proposing. She wanted him to see sense, to 'come out', even if that meant being cut off, ostracised by his loved ones; at least he would be living his truth. But was he brave enough to do that?

His posture became rigid as he leant backwards into the chair. He stretched out his legs, which was when she noticed his bright pink painted toenails. That too didn't unsettle her. She was more unsettled by the prospect of him peddling his scheme to other; more unsuspecting women, but eventually, she knew he would come undone. That would have far graver consequences on him and his family. If he went with her plan today, he could quietly live his life; neither he nor his family be the subject of negative aspersions that were forever being cast by the vicious gossip, rife in the Asian community; a heinous prospect. As much as she hadn't warmed to his mother's judgemental observations of her, Nailah's wisdom and compassion had risen above that too. She had the interests of his mother at heart. "I will help you Masood, you will always have a friend in me. Don't do it, don't live a lie," were her closing words to him.

He left without finishing his tea; his open toed chappal -

flip flops concealed under his carefully pressed cabin crew trousers.

A few weeks later, we learnt that Masood and his mum had frequented other houses with a view to finding another token bride. His mother, his co-conspirator had been knowingly trying to dupe others into his befuddled web. If we learned anything from this encounter, it was that there were many kinds of enablers out there. She, another symptom of the messy intergenerational east-meets-west values being navigated, played out, and dumped on our generation. Denial was easier than confrontation. For many, it was more acceptable to lie, knowingly hide behind a sham façade. And they were both out there, knowingly and shamelessly duping others.

Chapter 13

Yusuf-Uddin the Political Asylum seeker

We all fell in love with him

He was an extremely handsome man. The term 'political asylum' was not a familiar one to us, until he showed up to the house alone one day to tell us more. His name was Yusuf - Uddin.

He cowered down to bow, as mum reached up to place her hand on his head, gently stroking his ample thick black wavy hair - an old-fashioned religious greeting that had a rustic and endearing charm to it. Mum was genuinely charmed by him. He had unconventionally long hair for a man, which fell in perfect loose, ringlet like curls around his shoulders. He reminded me of the then famous Pakistani cricketer Imran Khan, on who we all had an overt crush. We all took it in turns to have a furtive look at him through the slit between the door and wall, as he sat alone in the living room. One by one, we greeted him before excitedly running out to let the other sister know exactly what to expect.

"He's fit," Nailah gushed, who was first in. She blew into the air, raised her brows in a comical fashion, before announcing, "but a bit too young for me - you can have him," looking directly at Zainab, who had no intention of entertaining anyone today; she was about to pull a 'no show'. But on seeing him, she made an exception. She swiftly ran upstairs to make herself look more presentable. On returning, she was wearing one of her favourite royal blue silk kurta dresses which she coupled with a soft dusky rose scarf, casually draped over one shoulder. She looked elegant and demure. It always intrigued me how, despite her impetuous nature, poised to catapult out of control when affronted, she could easily present the opposite image of calmness and serenity.

There was a tranquillity around her as she entered the room where Yusuf was waiting. As she walked in, he promptly stood up, bowing his head once again, displaying an etiquette that belonged to another era. He lifted his eyes briefly as she greeted him with the customary, "Asalam alaikum." He responded, "Wa laikum salaam." The room fell quiet for a few moments before mum announced, with a look of pride, "Yusuf-Uddin is from the same part of Lahore where I grew up Zainab." It was rare that anyone from the same city as mum visit our house. Ordinarily any reference to it was made when mum used it, to boast of her regional heritage, which gave her a supercilious upper hand, if she felt the need to draw on it. Lahore, Pakistan's cultural capital, was steeped in rich history, which to her symbolised hierarchy, pedigree and good breeding. The city of gardens, historic buildings and treasures where the more educated middle-class people lived. There wasn't a huge Lahori demographic in Yorkshire, so when anyone did turn up, mum entertained them as she would her own family.

They had already chatted about landmarks, places and people they had known, even though there was a good thirty-year age gap between them. The conversation sparked up mum's early memories, that caused the tip of her nose to turn deep pink, which happened usually when she felt emotional, on the verge of crying. They had been so deeply engaged in conversation that the usual formalities of the suitor meeting were forgotten. "Oh, good mum that's nice," interjected Zainab, the only words that she could muster up to look genuinely interested and enter into the dialogue which mum had hijacked thus far. The truth be known, *she* did not care one iota for mum's cultural roots.

Pakistan was a vague representation of our heritage; a faraway place, with very little relevance to us. A place we had only ever heard about, in mum's romanticised anecdotes, and seen in the black and white photographs pasted in an album that we flicked through from time to time. It was the only album with early photos of dad and her together. Their wedding photo, where they were sitting together on the 'chat -kohta rooftop, mum smiling as dad looked to be teasing her about something. I wondered what he was saying to make her smile so much. That and other photos were the only visual connection we had to the place mum referred to as 'back home.'

The conversation continued when Yusuf turned towards Zainab and asked, "Have you ever visited Paakhistaan," he pronounced that from his throat, in a way we had never heard before; it sounded poetic, otherworldly and enticing. She responded politely, "No but I'd like to one day." That was a lie. "You must, he continued, it is truly beautiful." She turned to look at him, whilst studying the angles of his face. His sharp cheekbones and strong jawline met perfectly with the outline of his long neck. His flawless complexion had a golden tinge to it, and was unusual for a Pakistani skin tone.

The only imperfection she could see was a scar to the side of his temple that cut into his eyebrow. It looked as if he had been gashed with something sharp. This was the first time she had found a Pakistani man attractive. Ordinarily she dismissed them; blocking them out mentally, having associated them with values that repelled her from a very young age. Values that she linked to control, oppression, and misogyny. Then there was abandonment. That residual, lingering emotion connected with the only Pakistani man she had ever truly loved - dad. South Asian men triggered a visceral response that would instinctively elicit a sense of foreboding, an inner voice in her that screamed - RUN!

But not Yusuf. His energy was different. He displayed a humility, a gentleness, a self-assurance that was warm and genuine. It was beginning to draw her in. She wanted to know more about him and what had made him leave his beautiful Pakistan behind. She asked facetiously, "So, why did you come to England when Pakistan is such a wonderful place to live?" Mum looked over at her in a way that signalled annoyance. She too had come to England from that same beautiful city; everyone's circumstances were different. This question felt offensive to her, but at the same time, she was also intrigued to hear his answer.

She knew that one of the reasons there wasn't a significant Lahori community here in Yorkshire, was because this beautiful city, was probably one of the most desirable places to live in Pakistan. The city that the politicians, the artists and highly educated chose to inhabit. It was hugely cosmopolitan and so much more sophisticated than the culturally bereft Yorkshire of that time. Why would anyone leave? After she returned from Laylah's wedding, mum recounted, how the people in Lahore and Islamabad were 'ahead of us', so much more forward thinking and progressive. Yusuf smiled, he didn't feel affronted by the question, in fact he welcomed it. His explanation would open up a dialogue so profound, so enlightening and so engaging that it would take place over several visits, over the next few weeks.

Life in his homeland and home city, was idyllic. Yusuf had left for a reason that we had never heard of before known as asylum, from a home and a country he had loved. What did this mean and why did it sound so ominous to us? He explained the reasons to us carefully, over the next few visits. During that time, his audience expanded as we would all gather around him to learn more about his plight and his compelling story. It started in the years when Yusuf began his basic military training in the Pakistani army. He was stationed in the north west region of Pakistan which, for decades, had been affected by military insurgencies. After months of serving, he quickly realised that his allegiances were not in line with the regime under which he was enlisted, and he wanted out. Being discharged was not as easy as he had imagined, especially in one of the most politically volatile regions of Pakistan. He was told it would take months, if not years for him to be released. His only option was escape, which he knew posed serious consequences, at worst death, if he were ever caught.

It took months of being smuggled dangerously across several borders, where he was captured, detained, and tortured in the Middle East; suspected of being a spy. Whilst there, he had been subjected to horrific acts of violence, starvation, and protracted periods of isolation. He bore scars where he had been physically assaulted, the scar above his eye was one. We all listened intently, as he described the extraordinarily complex and oblique political state of the country he had fled and with each sentence we learned something new. He had been passed through many detention centres and camps over a period of five years before he reached Europe and eventually Greece where he finally sought 'political asylum' for reasons of persecution and his life being threatened.

It had taken years for him to prove his position which also saw him thrown into prison. His agonising journey had seen him held in limbo for years, until finally he made it out, transported to the UK, where he was granted political asylum. He described his meals as sparse and frugal over the entire time he spent running and in captivity. Whilst in Afghanistan, he described an old Bedouin lady who, daily, surreptitiously passed him a soupy dish known as Khichdi that was made with lentils and rice, simmered together. He savoured that meal; it was a staple and one that we too knew very well.

England had allowed him to pass through the system with others like him, fleeing a country and its oppressors, seeking a better life and more importantly a safer one. He was still campaigning from the UK for the rights of some of his fellow citizens trying to flee similar oppressive circumstances, which also posed a threat. If discovered he knew he could be deported, at any moment, yet he still had strength of conviction, and was prepared to fight, even if it meant facing grave consequences.

We had never met anyone like him before and he was welcomed into our family, in a way we had never imagined possible for a relative stranger. We all loved him, but an obvious question needed to be asked and Zainab asked it without mincing her words, "Is this the right time to be seeking a British wife?" It took him a while to respond but finally he conceded, "I will not lie, marriage will give me stability, a home, a family, one that I have lost back in Pakistan. But most of all, it will give me rights." We all knew what 'rights' meant. "So, you want citizenship? - the right to stay here in this country and a British born wife will give you that? Zainab probed directly, to which he replied, "Yes."

We were all invested in Yusuf now, emotionally enmeshed in his traumatic journey. He had a cause, a battle to fight which he would continue to fight from here in Britain, his new home. Paradoxically, he sought refuge here, even though he believed that the western world had caused much of the unrest in his homeland. Would there ever be peace in the war-torn countries he escaped? What he needed was stability and he needed a place to call home. Yusuf needed our help. What would we do? His time with us was special. As we sat listening to him, we ate Khichdi that mum made for him and drank Roo afza, a middle eastern cordial that reminded him of his time spent in hiding.

Zainab opened her heart to a Pakistani man for the first time in her life. It was inevitable. It was a deep affection that she did not know she had in her. But could she love him meaningfully enough she wondered. Could that love be sustained for someone who represented everything that repelled her growing up? There was long, considered period of deep contemplation. Not just for Zainab but for all of us. Yusuf had come to teach us something. He imparted wisdom and knowledge that we would never have encountered in our simple lives in Yorkshire, adding another dimension to our emotional repertoire.

After much soul searching and many heart-wrenching conversations, it was not a decision that was taken lightly. Zainab followed her gut instincts. She had recognised the kind of love she felt for him and with that, realised that it would not be enough for the journey ahead. Certainly not enough to sustain a marriage in the long run. I was impressed with her understanding of herself, and it confirmed that she, out of all of us was the most in tune with her emotional intelligence.

Mum was left to tell Yusuf. She did it as tenderly and as gently, as only a mother could. As he stood at the doorway, on the day he left us, he bowed his head for the final time. Mum, reaching up, ran her hand over his hair and down his face and gently whispered a prayer in his ear, "Allah Hafiz Yusuf Uddin - God be with you."

Chapter 14

Grandad, Stacey and the baked Alaska

Mum met Stacey Hussain in the back garden. She was a pretty young woman in her late teens who had recently run away from Grimsby, to live in Bradford and marry Zulfi, the love of her life. He was a Pakistani comedian and they lived in the house opposite. Pakistani comedian, two words I would never have put together in the same sentence. They met at one of his performances and had fallen in love. Her white parents were mortified, not just at the prospect of a Muslim son in law, but at his unconventional career choice. Stacey did a midnight runner to escape Grimsby, a town where the only real diversity was to be found in the Taj Mahal Bengali restaurant.

Mum and Stacey hit it off immediately and she took this young, disenfranchised couple under her wing. Both of them had been ostracised by their racist parents. Zulfi disowned for marrying a white woman, Stacey for marrying a brown man. Prejudice on each side. Racism clearly worked both ways. "Don't worry we will be like your family," mum reassured them. How contradictory, I thought, to see mum interacting so positively with this young couple. They were of our generation but had defied convention and broken free. The same conventions that she so rigidly imposed on us. It was hypocritical in fact. We would never be supported by her for doing this.

Magic Baked Alaska

Zulfi would tour the country with his show, Stacey by his side, his glamorous young wife. On many occasions we would all somehow squeeze into his Ford Cortina and be driven to watch him perform his act in another town. They bought a lightness and element of fun to our lives. There were also many new culinary insights and lessons to be learned in this newfound friendship. Mum taught Stacey the art of cooking a classic chicken biryani and in exchange, Stacey taught mum the art of baking cakes. The only culinary skill mum lacked, by virtue of not being in the least bit interested in baking. One day, Stacey introduced us to the best cake we had ever tasted known as Baked Alaska. Our oven was finally commissioned, to do more than act as another cupboard. Baked Alaska was enough of a reason to find new storage spaces for the bulk sized bags of Elephant Atta chapatti flour and Tilda basmati rice.

Eating this cake for the first time was truly a revelation; an epiphany. We had never known a cake so heavenly. Working our way through the textured layers, each one tasted different, some were baked, some were whipped and some even frozen. It felt like alchemy, that these layers coexisted and held themselves together in perfect harmony. As each fine layer hit our palettes, we watched each other's expressions in amazement. I don't think we had ever been as quiet or united, as a family, enjoying the same food, together in sync. This cake was truly an event, a masterpiece juxtaposition of flavour and texture. We savoured every mouthful.

After a few lessons from mum, Stacey walked away having mastered the art of a perfectly layered Biryani, which mum assured her would help her 'keep hold of her Pakistani husband' of whom she said, "needs to eat 'apna' - our food regularly. Asian men don't like to eat boiled food every day you know," she advised a perplexed Stacey. Sadly, she was not as good a teacher as mum, who was unable to fully grasp her baked Alaska. Stacey continued to make it for us regularly and was commissioned to create it for one of our most special visitors - our maternal grandfather.

Grandad Abbas, or 'Baba-jaan' as we knew him, spent two weeks with us one summer. He was in his late seventies at the time. A tall, strong man who had been extremely handsome in his youth. He and Grandma, 'Nani jaan', were married at a young age. They had a strong, loving relationship and together raised a family of nine children. Married life for them was good. He was a successful businessman, an entrepreneur of his time, juggling enterprises which included an ice cream factory and a few apartment buildings. He was generous and provided well for his entire extended family and workers, even paying for the weddings of his staff when they needed his help.

Life was simple, easy and abundant back then. Each of their nine children were married in succession apart from mum. She jumped the queue. None of them had a huge amount of say or choice in their suitors, but nevertheless remained married, bar mum. Shortly after mum was married, the unthinkable happened, which left grandad heartbroken. Nani jaan died suddenly, prematurely and cruelly. It was tragic and unfair. It happened in a flash, on a day of heavy rain which saturated the open flat rooftops or 'chat-kotay' as they were known. The chat-kotay were a place where the family would regularly gather in the height of summer, to eat, socialise, entertain and even sleep under the stars. "The stars were so bright, vivid like a shimmering blanket," mum recalled to us fondly. The family would all lay under the night sky, chatting, telling jokes and stories and then falling asleep.

One day, when it rained particularly heavily, the rooftop had become swamped with water that collected in puddles under Nani jaan's feet. She trudged through in the torrential rain that bounced heavily around her, as she attempted to recover an electric cable, which had been left outside the night before. She was alone, surrounded by a pool of water, reflecting the dark grey angry skies above her and feeling the splash of heavy rain droplets against her bare ankles. As she wrapped the cable around her arm, a loose wire pierced her, stabbing her arm and sending 500kw of electricity through her body. She was killed instantly.

It happened only a matter of months into mum's newly married life and it robbed the joy from those early days of conjugal bliss. Mum even said it had felt like an omen. From that day onwards bad luck, she said, had cursed her life. She told us how Lahore had come to a complete standstill on the day of the janaza - funeral; such was the impact of her loss on the city and community who had loved her. Grandad was inconsolable for years afterwards. Life was never the same; he became reclusive, introspective and spent his days and years in prayer; restricted to his masallah - prayer mat. A vigil that never ended.

It had been at least twenty years since her loss, when we met him. I was intrigued by this man and followed him around the house; everywhere. He was a man of very few words. Slouching, but still tall, he had hard leathery skin on his face and hands, weathered from the intense heat he had worked in throughout most of his life. He wore a long neutral kurta shirt, a traditional outfit for a man of prayer. I could see mum in his face, there was a clear resemblance. I watched him intently, as he flicked his rosary beads between his fingers and mouthed his prayers, Ayat-e-kareema and others silently.

Everywhere he walked, he left a trail of scent behind him which was a combination of sandalwood and musk. It was heady and beautiful. I would sit next to him as he prayed and began to mimic his actions. When he tripped over my shoes one day, it was the only time I heard him speak curtly, "This is not a mosque!" I was terrified as he stretched his long arm towards me and without thinking, I instinctively held out my hand. He took it and we walked down the stairs together, gently holding hands. He extended more words to me along the way, expressing warmth and a tenderness that can only be experienced from a kind old soul. That day, I felt the love of my granddad, which I knew I would carry with me through my life.

An English Rose for Grandad

He had travelled to England with my aunt Zohra, who he had instructed to ask mum to help him find an 'an English rose' to marry. When mum heard this instruction, she was understandably appalled and disgusted by her father's request. "Where's his 'sharam' shame gone?" she asked her sister. He was too old to be thinking about this, but too young to be suffering delusional behaviour. Was she really being enlisted to find a suitor for her father too? And where exactly would she be expected to find an English rose to suit his needs? Had he completely lost his marbles? No. He was serious. He was intent on taking an English bride back home to Lahore.

On the same day mum found out about his kinky desire for an English Rose, Stacey was on her way over with the baked Alaska, for granddad. But now, mum was feeling uneasy about her meeting him, in case he got any deranged ideas about this particular English rose. She tried calling her to cancel, but it was too late. She had quietly let herself in through the back door and entered the room with her usual joyous expression. Stacey would often turn up to our house wearing little in the way of modest clothing, which didn't bother us. She could wear what she wanted in front of us, it made no difference. But today was probably not the right day for this attire. We could see behind the huge cake she was carrying, that she was wearing a figure-hugging strapless top, her shoulders fully bare and on show.

"Helloh babbajaaan!" she bellowed in her thick Grimsby accent, "I've heard so much about you!" Her beautiful smooth shoulders were now on full display. If it weren't for the cake, she had held in front of her chest, her entire cleavage would have taken centre stage. "I bought you a cake, it's a baked Alask…" Before she could finish, mum interrupted, "Yes, we know… thank you, she continued; pulling off her 'dupatta' scarf and wrapping it around Stacey, who continued to carefully place the cake in front of grandad. As she bent forward, she revealed more than her bare shoulders. "Oooh this is gorgeous, is it for me?" She innocently inquired about mum's scarf. Grandad did not lower his gaze, as instructed by the Holy scriptures. He did the opposite in fact and took in every bit of this English Rose's ample cleavage, which was now on full show.

"I hope you like the cake; I made it especially for you today," she continued as she served him slice after slice, leaning over the table each time to pour him more tea. He quickly savoured each plateful, beckoning her to continue serving, so he continued to grab another eyeful. Mum attempted several times to throw her veil over Stacey's chest, without success. At one point Stacey held it up, giggling; thinking it was a game. She danced around the room emulating the moves of a belly dancer, to grandad's sheer delight. I could see that mum was completely repulsed as we all howled with laughter. We had never seen grandad smile as much as we did that day. He left England a much happier man than he had arrived. Without his English rose of a bride, but a vision of one that I was sure would stay with him forever.

Chapter 15

Moving up in the world

A house move saw one of many well needed changes for us in the early 1990's. Our new semi-detached house was considered moving up in the world, upgrading from our old stone terraced house. Shipley road was changing, all the original neighbours had moved away. The house no longer served us; it was tired and incongruent with mum's desire for better surroundings. New families also began moving into the street which meant starting new relationships, which was not mum's strength. Our move was born out of disdain, as she began to hate the house, the memories that haunted her and the new neighbours. It was easier to leave and start afresh somewhere new.

We moved further out, away from the old parochial community that mum was hoping to flee. She couldn't be bothered to make any more excuses about dad. The rumour mill was already rife with speculation that ranged from: 'he was an alcoholic' and 'had another family'; to 'he was in prison for fraud and mum was covering up for him'. He was even 'dead - killed by mum' in some rumours. As much as she wanted that to be true, it wasn't the case. "It is easier to leave than argue with idiots," was mum's rationale. The only justification we needed to get out. No one had her back anymore, as in the early days of the sisterhood. They had all moved away. The new breed was of a different ilk; a different generation that mum had nothing in common with or more to the point, the patience to cope with.

Our upgraded house, also saw entertaining the suitors differently. In our new home, the kitchen was much better equipped, thankfully for me. We had a gas stove, which felt like a fresh start. We convinced ourselves that gas was better, even though it took time to get used to cooking on it and early on, many a dish got ruined and burned. It cooked way too quickly, because of the sudden intensity of heat, as opposed to the more controlled, slower heat from the electric rings we were used to. Our chapattis were however much better. Electric cookers did not make roti the same way as gas. With a gas flame, air was pumped into the rolled-out chapatti dough, creating a balloon known as a 'pulki'. When you patted this pulki down, it turned into the softest pillowy chapatti you could ever eat.

The new house was more modern, compact but most of all cleaner. The dust, the damp and the mice in the old Victorian terrace was not something we needed to worry about, ever again. We thought the views on Shipley Road were good, but in our new home, they were spectacular - the entire Aire Valley was visible to us. I would stand and analyse it for hours, then slowly, began to make drawings in my sketchbook. When I wasn't cooking, I was painting with whatever materials I could get my hands on. It was here that my other passion for art was born.

Life was good on Oakley Drive.

Chapter 16

The munching moaning medic Dr Greg

We struggled to pronounce his name, Ghazumfar, and so we called him Greg instead. He also reminded us of the old actor Gregory Peck, tall slender and a very mild-mannered English gentleman. He came to the house on his own, in between a shift at the local infirmary. Today the food was to be wheeled in on the new trolley-dolly. A multi-layered set of trays on wheels that mum had picked up at the second-hand market. It made the passage of food so much easier for me - wheeled all in one go as opposed to several trips back and forth to and from the kitchen. It was just as well for this particular insatiable suitor.

He made himself comfortable within minutes and without hesitation, dived straight into the plate of shami-kebabs, that had taken me hours to prepare the day before. Mum watched him in astonishment as he munched his way through eight kebabs, showing no signs of stopping or any other sign in fact to warrant his being here as a potential suitor. An irritated Nailah, also sat watching him, wondering why she had bothered making the effort to come out for this voracious man. Mum attempted to make conversation, thinking that perhaps he was nervous. So far, we had gleaned only two facts about him, he was a surgeon, and he loved my shami kebabs.

"So, 'beta' - son you work at the infirmary, that must be a very fulfilling job?" He grunted, barely lifting his head, or making eye contact as he grabbed the large ladle reserved for the chai, dipping it instead, straight into the lamb nihari - slow cooked lamb shank in a spicy, peppery gravy. Another dish that had taken me hours to cook especially for him. The banquets were always prepared and matched suitably to suitor credentials. Doctors were high up on the list of being afforded exuberant dishes, whilst lawyers came a close second. 'Professionals,' whose jobs were vague or ambiguous, were served snacks and sundries such as samosa or pakora, until we established whether another meeting would be on the cards.

Greg fell into the five-star treatment category, but we were beginning to reconsider that decision. He was a surgeon with an obviously insatiable appetite, and a man of few words, or so we thought. After polishing off his third plate of the lamb, he took the cloth napkin and wiped away the sauce from the outer edges of his mouth leaving a deep yellow 'haldi'- turmeric stain on it. It would need a good soak to get rid of that I grimaced. "Oh, my days, auntie. This is so good, so good... I haven't eaten 'upna' - our food in ages." Finally, the surgeon spoke. In a thick Midlands accent, which made the word apna (our) sound distorted to our ears. This was followed by a sharp belch as he leant back and rubbed his protruding stomach, looking comfortably replete.

"You are very welcome beta, son... I am glad you

enjoyed it, you must be hungr…" before mum could finish the sentence he cut in. "I've just come out of a ten-hour procedure…" That explained his ravenousness, but not his impudence. He still didn't appear interested in Nailah, who was still sitting opposite him, now scowling, unimpressed and on the brink of leaving the room. He continued, "I hate the bloody NHS, it's a right con you know." We didn't know, but we were about to learn more.

He leant forward and continued delivering his, what would become, a long oration, with a mixture of conviction and passion "We work like dogs, and we're expected to be grateful. This is not what we signed up for." This too was also a revelation to us, having assumed his profession carried far more prestige and respectability than he was angrily recounting. "I mean, how unfair is it, that the lifesaving doctors and surgeons like us are given so little respect? Just like our parents; forced to work long hours in the mills; it's no different, is it?" Mum was nodding rapidly now in agreement, "Yes beta, you are right, we never knew this… would you like some water?" As he tore a piece of roti and dipped it straight into the lamb nihari dish, he didn't notice Nailah leave the room. I stayed and listened with mum.

He was evidently a frustrated surgeon and angry at the politics surrounding his profession; the injustices of working long hours for the lack of esteem afforded to 'life savers' as he referred to himself. We continued to sit through his protracted rant, fuelled by his contempt of 'greedy corporates.' Mum attempted to interject, but he was not here to listen, each time interrupting with more eye-opening revelations. "This current government rewards the rich businessmen," he said rolling his eyes, "the man who turns over millions is hailed a hero and guess what? he doesn't even pay his taxes in this country." His limitless diatribe was a snapshot of the discontent that he and most likely others like him were experiencing.

When mum attempted to ask him anything that could have elicited a positive response, she may as well have been throwing him a clay pigeon, ready for his next round of vitriolic gunshot. "But beta, don't you feel privileged that you were able to study this degree in this country and be given the opportunities you have – able to become a doctor?" PULL! "I don't owe these corrupt scoundrels anything!" He barked, to a bewildered mum. "Oh, ok but would your parents have been able to afford…" she began before I nudged her. This question was certainly not going to help stop his tirade.

Dr Greg did make some valid points, but had the context been different, it would have resonated more meaningfully. He had either forgotten that he was here as a suitor or had blatantly ignored it. Mum dared not ask what his intentions were toward Nailah, for fear of the fallout it could bring with it. So, we quietly listened. As he stood up to leave, he walked over towards mum, who nervously, wondered what was coming next. Maybe another never-ending rant? Instead, another uncustomary gesture as he kissed her cheek and said, "Thanks for dinner auntie... same again next week?" Dumbfounded, mum walked him to the door and mustered the courage to ask, "Are you even interested in 'shaadi' marriage beta? He smiled as he dashed to his car. "Love ya daughter's shami's auntie." He was referring to the kebabs. Mum's eyes lit up. "Oh, 'Mehr bani!' - thanks Beta!"

Nailah was standing at the top of the stairs watching him leave, when she shouted down, "Are you serious mum? What a self-absorbed narcissist!" Mum, looking perplexed, turned to her and said, "Didn't you just hear what he said?" She had mistaken the word shami for 'shaadi' - marriage, thinking he had said he would love to get married to her daughter. No one corrected her, such was our disdain in her desperation.

He turned up unannounced the following week, this time, to our astonishment, wearing scrubs. He had just finished another long shift. Mum did allow him in out of pity; he looked hungry. No one bothered going into the room apart from her. She offered him a plate of leftover kebabs and asked, "Are you even here to see my daughter?" "I'll be honest auntie, I really love your kebabs."

These were *my* kebabs not mum's. I had perfected that recipe over many years and now, had got them just right. A combination of finely ground lamb mince with chana-dal (split lentil) and spices: garam masala, cloves, cinnamon, ginger, garlic and dried chillies; all mixed together then rolled to create small patties. These were wrapped around a punchy layer of finely chopped coriander, mint and green chillies, then dipped in a thin layer of beaten egg-wash before being shallow fried. The proportions of each ingredient were the key to perfection in these kebabs. Mum shamefully took the compliment that day from Greg. He planted another kiss on her face before leaving again.

He continued to show up for months; sporadically and randomly, based on his shift pattern. For whatever reason, mum had a soft spot for him and kept a plate of frozen kebabs in the freezer, on standby. He would be left to sit in the living room on his own, munching through the kebabs and muttering to himself, "Just a set of money grabbing brutes! We are the true hero's not you... Wake up world!"

Chapter 17

Shazad, the barrister who tried
to swindle us - twice

In Suitorland, we were beginning to see our fair share of quirky characters. Every type in fact, from the highly entertaining to the dubious. We had come to expect a certain level of deviant, but not the downright shady, that were the dowry swindling duo - Shazad and his sister Shakeela.

Slime. Stringy, snotty, sliminess that comes off okra before it is cooked. I always gagged a little preparing this dish; it was not my favourite, because of this stomach-churning aspect to it. He claimed to be one of the top barristers in the country. Why on earth did he need help finding a wife? Surely there would be a queue for someone of his ilk, I thought to myself whilst prepping the slimy okra that day. Once the okra or ladies' fingers as they were also known, had been topped and tailed (the tip and end removed) I would run them under cold water to try and remove some of the slime. It usually disappeared within minutes of throwing them into a rich tomatoey masala; as it did today. But a different kind of slime was about to descend on us. Was the okra an omen?

Sharply dressed, Shezad wore a bespoke suit that was obviously tailored to fit. Mum recognised the loom-spun woollen weft; the expensive kind she had worked on many years ago for the mills, plucking out imperfections. Those textiles were destined for Saville Row to create suits like his. He even smelt expensive. Everything about him oozed style, panache; perfection. What was he looking for in Bradford? My brother, a car fanatic was suitably impressed as we took a closer look at his car from the upstairs window. It was a 1975 Jaguar. Shezad came to visit us with his sister. She too was equally well turned out, wearing an Indian cut, Nero-style jacket, with hand stitched zardozi embroidery, that again mum recognised instantly and complimented her, "Beautiful 'khadhai' - embroidery betee" - daughter.

"Thanks Auntie. My Ami, mum, picked this one up in Delhi Haat," she boasted, holding her face upwards, her eyes looking down her sharp nose at us all. Deli Haat was the famous artisan market in Delhi, India where the wealthy and often entitled people could afford to shop.

"Arkari kutti - stuck up bitch, " Zainab whispered in my ear. She was right in her observations. Shakeela had an air of entitlement around her as she touched her neck, drawing attention to the expensive Rajasthani choker. "Ami also bought me the real Kashmiri shawls," she continued, looking insolently at mum's shawl, which she had made herself from an off-cut of fabric and embroidered with a running stitch along the edge. She spoke in a haughty, semi-hybridised accent, which was hard for me to fathom. There were hints of a 'twang' that we associated with someone who was not born in the UK, mixed with a southern accent.

This duo fell into a category we called, 'posh paki's'.

The kind that often looked down on working class families like ours. She had already displayed traits of that personality type in the hallway within minutes of their greeting. What were they looking for here? continued to beg the question in my head. Who do they think they are, but more to the point, who do they think we are? What had mum said to them, that made them think we might be a suitable match? My adverts in the matrimonial section were surely not that impressive. They had come through the Daily Jang channel; their mother had pre-empted their visit, over the phone telling mum that her son and daughter would be coming up to see us, as she was indisposed that day; whatever that meant. And here they were, Shezad and Shakeela, brother and sister who came on a mission, but not of the kind we were expecting.

I was also wondering what mum's excuses for dad's absence would be on this day, but before the question came up; as she sat down, slowly and judgementally looking around the room Shakeela announced, "So Mr Rauf is with the British consul in Paakhistaan?" Mum had already pre-empted the 'dad-lie.' "U- hum," was mum's coy reply. What could she follow that with? Did she even know what this prestigious job entailed? We were all looking at mum now, wondering what she would say next. "Chai? You must be so thirsty after your drive from…?"

"Winds-fordshire," they both said in tandem. Was there even such a place I thought? It was the result of their both answering in sync, Shakeela had said Windsor whilst

Shazad said Hertfordshire. "Well which one is it?" asked Nailah. She had sensed something about these two that didn't quite sit right with her. "Oh, ha ha, I meant, erm, we meant Windsor, it was Hertfordshire yesterday... that's what happens when you have a portfolio of houses everywhere!" Shakeela laughed, trying to brush off their faux pas, with a combination of humour and boastfulness. It translated as uncouth, as Zainab leant over towards me once again whispering in my ear, "Shoday" - classless show-offs.

Unable to mask her suspicion, Nailah raised her brows, poised to ask yet another question looking at Shezad. "So, you are a Barrister? What chambers?" He straightened his posture, unbuttoning his jacket as if to allow him to breath out, as he said, "Manchester, yes Manchester." Unsure of why he needed to affirm it twice, she continued to probe, "We have dealings there with a large family law firm; you might know it?" His head tilted to the side and his eyes moved suddenly as if trying to search for a reply. Nailah sensed that there was a lot more here that didn't quite add up. Even his accent was incongruous to that of his sister, he had a northern twang and less affectation than her.

Shakeela interjected as she began to sip the tea I had served for her. Blowing the milky skin that collects on the surface of the 'dud patti' - milky chai she continued, "We have a portfolio of houses in England and Sindh Pakhistaan." I couldn't help jarring each time she said Pakistan that way; I too detected something pretentious in her delivery. I had also never heard the term portfolio applied to houses, for me it meant a folder in which I carried my artwork to college. Their many homes were purported to be in Islamabad and Sindh Hyderabad.

"I know Islamabad well; what Province," mum asked with genuine curiosity. "Close to the airport auntie," replied Shakeela. "Any particular part?" mum continued to probe. "Well, erm actually, I'm not the right person to ask, 'ami': mum knows more," continued Shakeela, looking flustered. This pair were beginning to look less plausible by the second. Thus far, neither of them had asked a single question of our family and of Nailah, who they had come to meet. What did they want from us? As they finished the first course; the okra I had made for them, Shezad reached down to the floor, to pick up a small folder he had carried in with him. We assumed it contained something pertaining to his work and would not have been surprised if it were another thing for them to flaunt at us. He was allegedly one of the most successful Barristers in the country according to his mother. He opened the folder which had a small gold logo that I could just about make out. It read 'Sharia finance HQ'. He looked over to Shakeela who glanced at him in return and nodded as she wiped her slender fingers with a napkin, then pulled her sleeves back strategically over her wrists. Her Rolex was clearly visible as she gulped down her water and cleared her throat.

"Mahr is such an important part of our custom don't you

think auntie?" asked Shakeela. Mum shrugged nonchalantly. It was the first time the subject of 'mahr', or dowry had cropped up at a suitor meeting. Ordinarily, it was discussed much further down the line when a betrothal had been cemented. 'Haq-mahr' was an obligatory payment of money promised by the husband to the bride as a form of insurance in case the unforeseen happened during her married life. In some cases, daughters were given property by their parents to ensure they would be financially independent; again, if the unthinkable such as divorce or death of their spouse was ever to happen. For us, it had never been enough of a subject to warrant a discussion, certainly not at the first meeting.

It made mum feel a sense of unease as she said, "It is important for the daughter's security in the event of things not working out as planned, Allah reham karray - God forbid." Shakeela continued to press by saying, "Like what?" Mum looked around her, puzzled at her questions. She was superstitious and would never refer to anything specifically foreboding for fear of it manifesting. She kept her comment vague, "Like things not going to plan. May God protect us…"

"Well, we think so too," said Shezad, interjecting. "More so for families like yours auntie, where the head of the house is, well… absent. And that is why we set up our own special 'Mehr fund scheme'. It is different to the usual conventions expected of the groom." Scheme? Mum thought. The mehr, was traditionally the obligation of the groom; a kind of prenuptial agreement that could easily be dealt with without any new-fangled scheme. Ordinarily it was around a few thousand pounds, but always relative to what a family's circumstances could afford. What and why were they making such a fuss about it at this stage?

Shezad pulled out a sheet of paper from the folder headed 'Mehr Saving Fund'. Dowry fund. 'How bizarre' I thought to myself. "We're offering an insurance scheme, for families with mostly daughters like yourself auntie." It appeared they knew more about us than we had assumed. Mum had not mentioned anything about her four daughters to their mother. How did they know this, and that dad was, as he had just mentioned, 'absent.' It felt like a swindle of some kind was being unravelled. They had done their research on our family well before they set foot through the door.

Shezad, looking directly now at Nailah, began reading some of the words on the 'agreement' he had in his hand. "If you sign up with us today, we are asking just a small percentage of your obligatory payment that you wou…" Nailah cut in before he could finish, "There is no such thing as obligatory payment for the girl's family on a 'mehr'; do you think we don't know how this works? And furthermore, it appears you know an awful lot more about us than we thought; how do you know that our father is absent?" Mum stood up and walked over to Nailah, perching on the arm of her chair, as if to present a united front. Shakeela looked uneasy as she flicked crumbs off her dress and turned to

Shezad beckoning him with a turn of her head. She looked down at her Rolex. "Goodness is that the time?" We have another appointment." Nailah was not finished quite yet as she continued, "And I asked my senior partner to look you up; there's no record of you anywhere Shezad, you're not listed in any chambers we know of. Can you explain that?"

As they abruptly exited, we were left to process and untangle their fraudulent entrance into our lives and a potential swindle. We wondered how many had fallen prey to these confidence tricksters and how much money they had cheated out of unsuspecting families. Mum turned to Nailah and asked, "How come you didn't mention that you had already done your background checks?" Nailah looking smug, crossed her arms, holding up the folder they had forgotten to pick up in their haste as they left swiftly. "So, I could rumble them and have the evidence to show for it." She flicked through the papers shaking her head in disbelief at the fraudulent income they had been gaining of out of their dubious dowry scheme.

These fraudsters were not deterred by being caught out by us. A few months later, after mum responded to another advert in the Daily Jang, she called the number to hear the same woman on the phone who had claimed to be their mother. It confirmed a frightening trend of opportunists and fraudsters entering the introductory marriage scene. Suitorland was now rife with con artists and confidence tricksters. It was no longer the virtuous place we had known from a time gone by. It appeared that careful due diligence was now required before anyone entered our home. That day mum insisted I pen another letter to the Daily Jang. This time, a letter of complaint. It was shared in their Classifieds as a disclaimer and read:

Dear Readers,

Please be aware and mindful of anyone entering your homes making false claims or requesting any form of money / payment at introductory meetings. Anyone found doing this must be reported to the authorities with immediate effect. This is against the law, our policies and everything we stand for as a newspaper.

It was printed in the classifieds of all editions of the Daily Jang that followed. We had done our part in making people more cautious as well as rumble the dowry swindlers and any other potential tricksters.

I had thought about making Hyderabadi dum biryani for them that day. It was a good job I hadn't wasted my time on that exquisite dish for this set of dubious swindlers.

Chapter 18

The long train ride to Inverness

When someone is suddenly wrenched from your life, you can spend an eternity searching for them. The void was palpable, tangible and painful. Denial only carries you so far in life.

Did we ever find him?

The trip

I remember what I was wearing that day; a beautiful lemon-yellow kurta dress that mum had made for me. It was decorated with ornate silver buttons and a silver trim piping around the cuffs. As the train pulled out from Leeds station, heading north to York for us to board the Pullman to Inverness, I remember feeling very self-conscious. A little too conspicuous for my awkward teenage self. I imagined the eyes of everyone in the station staring at mum and I, dressed in our colourful Pakistani attire; we must have stood out a mile. It would have been unusual to see a Pakistani girl on a train travelling anywhere north of Leeds let alone all the way up Scotland. Having said that, the looks and stares that we encountered were not in any way hostile. They were quite endearing in fact, many of them from older folk; curious but complimentary as they glanced our way, smiling. Even the young men who boarded at different stops looked over and grinned at me. I remember feeling special.

It was quite a trek - nine hours in total, with changes of train at stops on the way but there was no journey more beautiful than this long ride to Inverness, with spectacular coastal views almost all the way. This was a quite different type of suitor visit. His name was Tarik, and he had turned the tables on us today, requesting that we visit him in his beautiful home, situated in the furthest climes of the Scottish Highlands. Nailah, being her usual prima-donna self was not prepared to make the trip all the way north, so instead, I got roped in to do it. My job was to vet his suitability for her - a testament to how much my opinion was trusted. "Well at least you don't have to cook today ha," she joked as she dropped mum and I at the station.

Whilst annoyed at her, I would not have missed this ride for anything. We experienced breath-taking scenery stretching for miles for the first time in our life. This was a completely different world, which was a far cry away from grim Bradford. I would have happily taken this train ride over cooking any day. I was obsessed with nature, landscapes, the sky. Mum and I chatted all the way up the coast on the train. It was easy being with her on occasions like this. We were both nature lovers and would regularly spend time outdoors, whether it was walking to the green grocers via the scenic route, through the glen or planting vegetables and flowers together.

We both loved the same plants and flowers, with hydrangea being one of our favourites. We carefully nurtured ours into a magnificent flowering shrub from a small cutting given to us by a neighbour. It blossomed each year into the most resplendent bluish pink colours, spreading from a corner of the garden to the front door. We had a beautiful intuitive connection through food and nature and could read each other's thoughts, while sitting quietly, looking out at the world passing by, as we did today.

We took a packed lunch of pakora sandwiches with us on this long trip. It was the perfect east-meets-west sandwich, if ever there was one. A simple deep-fried dumpling made with sliced onions and spices: chilli powder, garam masala, ginger, fresh chillies, and cumin; all bound together with gram flour - besan. The batter dumplings were spooned carefully into hot oil and deep fried until crisp and golden. On their own with chutney or sandwiched in bread, this was unequivocally, one of the best deep-fried snacks, especially when wrapped in sliced Sunblest bread with a big dollop of tomato ketchup. The obvious aromas of Indian food infiltrated the entire carriage. I remember looking around and feeling embarrassed but unapologetic, as I savoured each bite.

We arrived in Inverness in the late afternoon to be collected by Tarik at the station. He drove us to his house, through a long winding path, high up over the hills, where you could feel a distinct Scottish chill in the air, even in the height of summer. Situated in its own land surrounded by a lake; there it was, a beautiful white building on an ample sized plot with varied features that could be seen even from a distance. A white picket fence enclosed an acre or more of well-maintained lawn, that was striped to suggest it had been mowed with precision and care. Well-coordinated flower beds ran on one side, shrubs along the other with a variety of beautiful pine and conifer trees, some that I had never seen before. It was like a small-scale Capability Brown landscape; a surreal picturesque haven. Captivated by the breath-taking scenery alone, a thought crossed my mind, 'if she doesn't want him, I'll have him'.

You could even see The North Sea in the distance; this was truly a dream house, where you would imagine bringing up a family. Children adding the only missing link, to make this beautiful house a home or, as mum called it add 'ronak' - the joy that comes from family life. I soaked it all up, every single detail. Tarik was an architect and had built this house from scratch. It was obvious that he was as talented, as he was discerning and precise. As he showed us around each room, I could see he understood space, scale and light, making the most of all aspects of the land and its distinctive features. The landscape complimented the rooms; windows facing certain directions that he had cut out to maximise the views. It was an impressive house and felt like a completely new world to us.

We chatted as we ate a delicious meal that he had cooked for us. Tandoori chicken in an actual tandoor (outdoor oven) which, of course he had built himself. Nothing about this brilliant man surprised us - he was without doubt a Renaissance man. Had we found 'The one?' He could quite easily have been just that, with everything we had seen so far. He was an impressive over-achiever. It was almost too good to be true. I had a feeling though, that somehow it was a little too good to be true. It was an intuitive feeling that got stronger, the more I thought about it. Even with all his plus points, he bizarrely just wasn't enough or *right*. Unpacking why it felt this way, was an epiphany.

With all the comings and goings over the years, I knew Nailah in a way that she probably didn't even know herself. I knew what she needed, what in fact we all needed. She had a habit of always picking on the most minuscule detail or fault against a good suitor and seeing them off. There was a pattern emerging and I realised on this day, what it was all about. It wasn't about them; it was about us. A message was being whispered to me through the cool highland breeze. It felt like an oracle, telling me something and that put my senses on high alert; listening to what it had to say. It was an insight that unravelled a convoluted set of values that plagued us all. The Rauf girls were more complex than I thought.

At the moment of realisation, I knew intuitively that there were too many factors that stood against poor Tarik. As remarkable a human being that he was, he just wasn't for us. What we were searching for, was far more complex. And it came from dad's absence. A role model that only a father can give you, to recognise values and characteristics in a life partner, was missing for us. There was an obvious void and with that void, there came struggle, hardship and a resourcefulness that we had created for ourselves, in order to survive in our world. It was our primal instinct to fight. We were not equipped to accept anything that we hadn't fought for, or that was handed too easily to us on a plate. Tarik was flawless and in that, he was 'too easy' for us. There was no challenge. And this was not his fault.

Were we all looking for dad? When someone is suddenly wrenched from your life and that someone is THE most important person up to that point, you can spend a lifetime searching for him. We were all still looking for dad. The void was palpable, tangible, painful. Denial only carries you so far in life. We had never had the role model in him, so we also were looking for someone or something we had never fully experienced. It was intricate and messed up. I knew that we needed to address this knotty, mixed-up set of values for our own reasons, in order to heal and in order to find the 'right' man to bring us home.

Not many people understood hardship in the same way that our family did and how we overcompensated for it. Having lived through the hardship, physical, emotional and material, it raised the bar of expectations for us. It was like a drug in the system, the fight or flight instinct changed our wiring. We had arrived at this point having spent our lives pushing through barriers that restricted us in a society that judged us. Nailah had pushed through so much more, including trauma from a young age that only she knew of. It had hardened her to the world and to men. She he had no choice but to be her own strength. But she needed someone stronger, with enough backbone to be able to brave her. I knew my sister and Tarik was not the man for her.

I had a strong feeling that mum saw it too. I could detect it in her eyes, it was like an awakening for us both. Inverness had turned out to be the retreat we needed away from Bradford to realise this. Tarik was everything on paper, but he was missing a crucial element; the substance we knew he needed to keep someone like Nailah happy, settled, secure and balanced. And we were all cut form the same cloth.

Seeing it this way, recognising it with such clarity, I felt we were on the way to healing ourselves from trauma and from the damage that had been inadvertently inflicted on us, both with and without a father. And I saw it in the most beautiful place I had ever visited. As we travelled the long journey home through the dusk, watching the sun set over Bewick on sea, mum and I hardly said a word to one another. It had been an ethereal and enlightening day, and we were soaking it all in. There was no doubt in our minds that Tarik was a good man, solid and dependable, but just not the man that we, as a family needed. What kept us going? The search, the fear, the anticipation, the longing? Whatever it was, it was obvious that we were all travelling our own train ride, each one of us; on our individual journey of self-discovery.

Chapter 19

Where in Suitorland was he?

...the most unlikeliest of all suitors

At the age of twenty-eight, and considered past her shelf life in the Pakistani community, Nailah was still living at home. With every unsuccessful suitor outcome, the tension grew between her and mum. It felt as if we were living in a combat zone, as they launched their vitriolic verbal missiles and grenades at each other on a daily basis. Even in silence, there was conflict. I remember walking on eggshells trying to mediate between them. Passing messages back and forth - dates, times, availability. I, their personal assistant, ensuring smooth coordination of the suitor days.

Why could she not just be more compliant? It was already hard enough for us all, as the queue was backing up and there were three more siblings behind her, including me. Until she was married, mum would not focus properly on the rest of us. It had now become an obsession, an infatuation to find 'the one'. Nailah had either resigned herself to a life of spinsterdom or she was just going through the motions for her own reasons. Why she didn't use her initiative and look for her own suitor, that too baffled me. She had enough about her to find someone who ticked all her discerning boxes, before getting to that point of settling for anyone, like her older sister. At this rate, that was looking more likely to happen. But she continued to reject them. Where in Suitorland was he? - the most sought after of all suitors.

Nothing was suitable about him

The day that he came to visit, nothing was going according to plan; almost everything about that day was wrong, including him. Usually, the meetings were carefully coordinated and plotted with precision. But, on this particular day, the plan went completely out of the window as he got his days mixed up, arriving a day too early. It was Saturday, he was scheduled to come on Sunday.

The doorbell rang, just as I'd started to peel and chop a batch of onions to prepare the dishes for the following day's feast. As I glanced out of the window, I could see the profile of what appeared to be a middle-aged man. He was dishevelled, standing by the door, scratching his head. His car, parked outside our gate - a white Ford fiesta, looked as though it had seen better days. It was rusted in places, a wheel trim was missing, a wing mirror broken and it had several dents across the bodywork.

Mum came running into the kitchen to look out of the window, as she did whenever anyone knocked on the door. "Who is this?" she asked me anxiously, as if I knew. "I dunno?" I shrugged as I continued to chop; my eyes streaming with onion tears. I looked again, wiping my eyes to get a better view. This is when I noticed his crooked tie which was ill-matched with the rest of his outfit. "I do not know mum" I repeated; irritated. Mum grabbed her dupatta scarf, wrapping it loosely around her and shuffled to the door wearing her old house slippers. As she tentatively opened it, I listened in. "Salaam Mrs Rauf?" I heard the man say. "Yes, I am her," mum replied. "It's Numan," he continued. There was a long pause. "Erm Salaam," mum continued, sounding puzzled. There was another pause before she went on to quickly say, "But, but, but…" I rolled my eyes, in disgust, thinking this is precisely the reason the British took the mickey out of us.

"But you're not supposed to be here today." She finally finished her sentence. "Really? oh," he said with concern. I ran over to peek through the tiny slit between the door and the frame, to see the man reach into his pocket and pull out a crumpled piece of paper. He opened it, whilst putting on his glasses to read it carefully. He suddenly looked up, open mouthed, clearly shocked as he said in a deflated tone. "I'm so sorry, I'm so sorry you're right, I got my days completely mixed up; so very sorry." He put the paper back into his pocket and began to turn away, to walk back to his car.

I was beginning to rethink the feast I was working on, after seeing him and wondering to myself, was he even worth it? Definitely not suitable suitor material, given his shabby appearance. Maybe it was a blessing that he showed up by mistake. He had done me a favour and saved me hours of prepping. He won't be invited back I thought. As he was about to leave, mum did an unexpected thing. She reached out her hand, touched his shoulder in a kind, maternal way, and gently whispered.

"Puttar, son, you're here now, you've driven all the way from Salford, please just come in and have tea at least."

I wasn't sure whether it was kindness or pity that motivated this gesture. But I was quite glad though, realising that over a simple chai and a plate of custard creams, mum could let him down gently; telling him not to bother making the trip tomorrow as planned. It was a great plan to save me from another gigantic cook - genius mum! I ran to switch on the kettle thinking, 'poor man, he didn't stand a chance in any case'. Everything about him, from first appearances warranted a 'no-show' from Nailah. 'No-shows' were the days she didn't even bother coming downstairs, when she had seen something unfavourable about a 'prospective', from the window of judgement. Sometimes it was as minor as the colour of their socks. Today, this poor man was riddled with 'no-show' qualities.

I used to be able to identify them too as time went by. My verbal translation of a no-show would be muttering, "You're toast!" I nicknamed those particular suitors 'Toast' for that reason. Numan was toast, or so I thought. I didn't even bother running upstairs to let her know what was going on, she was probably engrossed in one of her latest romance novels. So, I left it.

As I tipped custard creams and ginger nut biscuits onto

a small plate and poured two cups of tea, the door opened. Thinking it was mum who was coming to collect it, I was surprised to see Nailah. She was dressed in her usual home attire, a plain old kurta dress, the print on which had faded. Under the dress, she was wearing her comfy house joggers. She held out her arms to take the tray, as I excitedly announced, "It's ok sis, you don't have to go in. He's toast!" She looked at me expressionless and undeterred, still stretching her arms out in front of her, gesturing for me to hand her the tray.

'What is she about to do?' I thought to myself, worried she was about to go into the room to do something stupid. This was unlike her. Was she about to give him a dressing down? scold him for showing up having made zero effort and expecting her to even entertain him? She would often comment on appearances after the suitors had left, when we would sit together laughing and gossiping whilst munching on the leftovers. Maybe today she was feeling brave enough tell him to his face. As I put the tray in her hand, I giggled, "Be gentle, he came with good intentions, he just needs some fashion ad…" She left before I could finish the sentence.

I heard her kick open the door to the living room. I quickly followed her. She kicked the door shut behind her, equally as fast, shutting me out. I was looking forward to seeing her expression as she served Toast his tea. That wasn't possible now that I was locked out. "Charming!" I sighed walking away. A few minutes later mum followed, straightening her scarf. As she shuffled back into the kitchen, she shrugged her shoulders, pulling her lips down at the sides as if to say, 'no, I don't know either'.

Assuming he would be leaving shortly, I started to pack away the onions and spices. I felt a real sense of reprieve, in the knowledge that I could relax, or better still, go and finish one of the paintings I had been working on.

Suddenly there was a high-pitched giggle which came from the living room, that stopped me in my tracks. Poor feller, she's really ripping into him, probably laughing at his clapped-out car. I looked across at mum, whose expression suggested she wasn't happy with her daughter behaving so spitefully to someone who had come with good intentions. She was poised to walk back in and stop her from continuing with her unacceptable behaviour, until the sound of a man's laughter followed. Obviously, this was him. 'Well at least he is taking her roasting in good spirit, I thought; or maybe he's giving her a taste of her own medicine? She wasn't looking her best, he must have been laughing at the old joggers she was wearing. Without warning there came a resounding roar, from both of them this time, laughing in tandem. A bemused looking mum grabbed my hand, as I attempted to slide the chilli powder back into the cupboard.

"Kya Mazak hai? What on earth are they laughing at?" she whispered, tilting her head, listening with intent. "She's grilling him mum!" I replied. "Chup karr! Shhhh!" mum whispered heading to the door to get a closer listen. She stayed there for a moment, while I stood still, also trying to listen. She returned moments later and grabbed my hands, as I was wrapping the peeled onions to save for another day. "Bas. Stop; Not so fast dear," she calmly uttered. "Not so fast what?" I replied. As far as I was concerned, my duties were done for the day. 'I'm out of here' was all I could think. But to my utter dismay, that was not the case. The laughter continued intermittently, interspersed with conversation. Now, I needed to hear what they were talking about. He, the unlikeliest suitor and my sister in deep conversation. I tiptoed to the living room door and pressed my ear firmly to it, trying to grasp exactly what were they laughing about. I needed to hear what was keeping them both in that room longer than we had expected.

I heard him say with persuasion, "Yes, I was struck off, but I went to the Supreme Court and fought like a bloody crusader to make my point. I held a mirror up to the insidious racism, and exposed the flaws that the so-called professionals haven't got a clue about." It appeared there was a serious conversation taking place. I was intrigued to hear more about it myself. He continued, "You know they don't even know the difference between statutory and mandatory laws." "EXACTLY!" Nailah said with equal conviction. Although I wasn't fully sure about the context, I gleaned that after the laughter, there was a profound conversation taking place between them. They continued to exchange their thoughts and views on the judicial system in the UK, something they both understood well. I heard Nailah once again, "It's about time someone did expose it; do you know how frustrating it is for me? I see it, I hear it daily in my job, but my hands are tied, I'm just a minion, a cog in the rusty old wheel."

I was taken aback. I had never heard her speak so honestly, so passionately, so truthfully about her work; it felt like I was listening to a stranger. This was a side of her I had never seen or heard before. It was refreshing to hear her speak so candidly, voicing her opinions and her woes. She was fighting her own battle in a realm of her life to which we were not privy. Here was another woman, another Nailah and 'Toast' was bringing that out of her. 'Should I start again on the onions?' I was thinking. He might be here for some time. I made my way back into the kitchen, half excited at the thought of a connection between the two of them, and half deflated at the prospect of cooking again.

Mum had already made a start on the onions; it looked like a simple tempering was being prepared. A buttery base made of a good dollop or two of butter with the only onion I had peeled and chopped finely. A few cloves of crushed garlic too. The onion, flash fried, the opposite to sautéing, as it was fried with speed on the highest heat setting that darkens it within minutes. You had to be vigilant and precise about the moment you turned off the heat. By catching it at the right moment, it cooked in the residual heat of the hot butter and crisped up. Basically, crispy fried onions and garlic.

This simple, standard tempering or tarka was thrown over the top of boiled lentils - dal. A few cups of split lentils known as masoor dal, boiled with a small grabful of salt, chilli powder, garam masala, ground coriander and turmeric. Once soft, it was ready for the splatter that is made by throwing the tarka or tempering over the top of it. Watching it sizzle, seeping down into the lentils as they soaked up all the buttery glossy coating was always satisfying. Mum had made the dal in less than twelve minutes. That equated to the time I had been standing, listening in to my sister and the unlikeliest suitor chatting away.

Beautiful dal. A rustic, comforting, salt of the earth dish. Everyone loved dal; it was a leveller of a dish that broke down walls between classes, regions and religions. Dal embodied calm, kindness, comfort and love. "The heart is not complete until dal," my uncle Raad proclaimed one day. That saying resonated and stuck with me. He was right, you can eat the most lavish meal, but nothing satisfies the soul quite like dal. Best served with buttery roti or basmati rice, as it was today. Mum calmly looked up and quietly said with a smile, "Batcha - child, go do what you want to, I'll take care of the food today."

It turned out that Toast, Numan was a Human Rights Lawyer. He fought daily for the rights of those seeking nationality in Britain, for reasons of political exile and asylum; refugees, much like our beloved Yusuf Uddin. He was fighting at the highest level for their rights, to a better life, to be treated humanely, or to be repatriated to escape their own troubled countries. "Well, the western world did play a big part in destabilising their homeland," he uttered disdainfully, as they sat talking deeply, enjoying the humble dish of dal and roti that mum had prepared. There seemed to be no end to their easy flowing dialogue. There was an obvious tangible connection between the two. He was clearly passionate, strong and tenacious. Unafraid to defend his values and principles, even if it meant being thrown into the slammer for short stints, then fiercely bouncing back. He had fire, integrity, ethics, and strength. He was a truth seeker, unafraid to put his neck on the line, to defend his cause and the basic human rights of others. There was a solid foundation here. He would not be deterred by anything or anyone in making a stand for his principles and for humanity.

I walked in and out of the room a few times, under the pretext of collecting dishes and supplying water. I noticed my sister looking relaxed, there was no pretence as there usually was in these first meetings. Sitting on the floor, legs crossed, leaning against the settee in her old joggers, wearing not a scrap of make-up; she was beaming and looking truly alive for the first in a long time. I saw and felt an indescribable sense of relief on her face and in the air around her. Was he the one she had been looking for all these years? Could we finally stop the search? Had we found THE one? I sensed that he was. I also sensed that he was a strong, compassionate man and she needed that. As mum and I stood in the kitchen together clearing away dishes, we didn't say a word. We didn't need to. It was as if, lost in our own thoughts, we were savouring a moment of stillness, resolution and an overwhelming sense of peace.

Who could have thought it? Here we were after over a decade of the most exuberant feasts and fights that had defined our household. An era that engulfed and consumed mum with finding her daughter precisely what she needed. It felt like this era was now coming to an end. And all it took to clinch this deal was a plate of custard creams and ginger nuts (slightly past their shelf life), followed by dal. Glorious dal. To this day, I have no idea what enticed Nailah out of her bedroom for him. After six hours - the longest ever suitor meeting, Numan finally left. As I was tidying up, I found the crumpled paper from his pocket next to where he had been sitting. I opened it up to see that it was one of my ads to the Daily Jang Newspaper. After the irony of everything else that happened that day, this did not surprise me. He had responded to one of my begrudgingly written adverts to the classifieds. This was one of many adverts that I cursed, as I painstakingly wrote it out for mum. Finally, even that arduous task had paid off.

It would be the last letter I would ever write to the newspaper. I felt overcome with emotion. Tears of both elation and sadness trickled down my face. No more words on paper to secure a suitor ever again. The gates of Suitorland were closing. And Nailah never thanked me once, for any of it. What a bitch.

Chapter 20

The Secret Millionaire

No one expected what was on the menu that day

Another meeting was imminent. Mum and Nailah were invited to Numan's home in Salford. I tagged along, curious to see whether his humble home would be enough for her. She had settled for a lot less when it came to his unkempt appearance and dilapidated car, the very things that would have rendered any other suitor inadmissible. In fact, they wouldn't have even made it over the threshold.

It was an unexpectedly gruelling drive to his home, over the Pennines. A sharp slip road veered us off the M62 motorway, over the most secluded part of Saddleworth moor. An area where you see nothing for miles, but mossy hills and dark sombre clouds moving slowly across the moors. Eventually, the slip road led us through to a long winding path, through to an area of unlit woodland. This was not on the map. I wondered whether he was a bohemian hippy that lived in the woods. That would be fitting with his shabby appearance and clapped-out car. We were all beginning to feel nervous driving through the uneven terrain, that was now taking us off-road. Nailah was driving and enlisted me to navigate, with the help of an old AA road map. Not my strongest skill, but I did my best fathom it and guide her.

"Are we close?" Nailah asked, squinting to see where this dubious looking path was taking us. "I'm really sorry, I don't know… this isn't on the map," I conceded. It was obvious now that we were lost. "I can't see a bloomin' thing!" she continued, vexed. Day was fast becoming night, as the trees began to turn a homogeneous shade of dark emerald green. The light between the leaves was dimming, which made it even more difficult to see the road ahead. She stopped the car and briskly grabbed the map from me, rotating it as if that would have helped make sense of it. There were no signs of roads on this area of the map, just a blob of green with nothing to suggest houses, tracks or anything else for that matter. A vacant space. She continued to drive up the path that now turned into a dirt track. We had no idea where it was leading but carried on, nevertheless. I was hoping to see something - a hut, a caravan or worst-case scenario, a tent pitched in the middle of this uninhabited stretch of eerie looking land. I even wondered whether she liked him enough to live in a caravan.

Then suddenly, it appeared. The white Ford fiesta, looking as if it had been dumped at the side of the track. "Shukkar - Allah!" Thank God I heard mum say with relief. Her first words throughout this entire journey. She had been terrified, sitting in the back seat as we drove through the dim woodland. "Ar - gaye - are we here?" she sighed, unbuckling her seatbelt. "Where? there's no houses here mum?" I said, bemused. It was just the car and a spotlight, precariously positioned on a wooden post above it. We could see more lights leading to what looked like a clearer road. It gave us hope as we continued driving.

Then, without warning, a concertina of bright lights came on in succession. They were intently positioned to light up, theatrically, and purposefully leading us somewhere. But still, we were not fully sure where. In the distance, we were able to make out a halo of lights that appeared to be coming from several small houses or dwellings, positioned around another dwelling in the centre. Finally, signs of life. I could hear mum whispering prayers. "Shukarr, alhumdulila," - Thank God, again and again. "That had to be one of the creepiest drives I've ever taken," snapped Nailah. I was just hoping that he was still worth it.

As we drove closer, we could see that the small houses were all connected around what appeared to be a larger building, but it was obvious they were in fact annexes to the building - a large manor house. "I wonder which one of these little houses is his," Nailah said, as we tried to fathom signage, house numbers, anything to suggest it belonged to Numan. As we slowly edged past each one, still unsure, I noticed the silhouette of a man standing in the doorway of the manor house. I could only just make him out in the glare of the headlights as we edged closer. He was wearing a deep red smoking jacket and matching cravat around his neck. His posture was rigid as he stood bolt upright. "Shall I run out and ask him if he knows which one belongs to Numan?

I said opening the car door. "Let's just park up here, it can't be far, we'll all walk together," Nailah replied.

She pulled the car up next to a tall oak tree. We stretched our limbs in relief and took deep breaths as we climbed out of the vehicle. Mum wrapped her heavy embroidered Benares shawl around her. We locked arms as we walked unsteadily on the gravel, which was crunching under our feet. We passed a turning circle, which hosted one of my favourite trees - monkey puzzle. As we approached the beautiful looking manor house, we could see the man was still standing there, poised as if he was waiting for us.

"Hai hai," *Oh dear God*, mum whispered, a sign that usually meant she was anxious, or nervous about something. The gentleman in the doorway was now waving, as if to beckon us over. I was just hoping he knew which one of these annexes belonged to Numan. We could also see that he was smiling, his head tilted to the side. We all tilted our heads in tandem to get a better view of his face, as we edged closer. I noticed his shiny clean-shaven skin and his sharp chiselled cheek bones defined by the light bouncing off them. Tidy slicked back hair, fitting in with his all-over sharp appearance. This man looked familiar.

It was him; Numan. But what was he doing standing in the doorway of this manor house? Then the penny dropped, it was his doorway, his house. And he was The Lord of the Manor.

"What the hell?" I caught Nailah whisper under her

breath. Numan stretched his hand towards a bewildered looking mum. She took it, followed by Nailah who took his other hand as he led them both inside.

They walked into the hallway through a monumental carved wooden door, whilst I was left to make my own way in. Too distracted by the beautiful entrance to notice the extra step, I fell, face first into the doormat. If there was ever a more fitting metaphor for my existence, this was surely it. Nailah looked back at me, unimpressed, frowning and mouthed, "Get up you clumsy cow; don't embarrass me." That was typical of her, ungrateful, entitled sister, I thought. Did she even know that it was one of MY letter's that landed her here in the first place? I had it stuffed in my bag; I put it there as a souvenir. It could even be used as ammunition to whip her with if she became too cocksure of herself. But not quite yet; it was enough to have it lying dormant; part of my arsenal if needed.

A diversion

The clapped-out car, the shabby clothes, his unkempt appearance; it was all a diversion, and we were about to learn more that evening, over dinner.

An exuberant dinner had been prepared for us. This beautiful house was a sensory experience. From the moment we entered, my senses were heightened. The scent of bergamot incense infused the air in the lobby. It smelt clean and expensive. My sharp sense of smell picked up on the hints of spices used in the food, that was coming from the direction of what I assumed to be the kitchen. They were deliberately masked and not as pungent as the aromas of spices that filled our entire household on a cook day. My eyes were drawn up the panelled walls to the high ceilings, with original architraves; all beautifully preserved. The panelling that divided the long walls, continued up a huge staircase, which was half covered in an expensive woven Persian carpet. The edges of the original oak wooden stairs poking out each side. This was more than a manor house; it was a stately home.

There were people milling around, who appeared, from their aloof body language and lack of eye contact, to be workers - his staff. A house of this stature warranted staff. A housekeeper, a cook, a groundsman and most important of all, a right hand man, whose name was Jalal. I guessed this from the way he had been beckoned over to us with a shrill call from Numan, "Laal!" and he came scurrying over; he clearly knew the drill. He took our coats, without making any eye contact. Numan handed him Nailah's car keys and instructed him to move it closer to the house. Jalal was also one of his closest and most trusted confidantes.

A private chef had been enlisted for today's spread of food. This was obvious from looking at the printed menu, which had been placed at the side of the carefully arranged Spode plates. This was Pakistani fine dining - the kind you would only find in a high-end restaurant or a private dining experience. A truly ample feast awaited us.

Starters

Cauliflower bhajia

Tandoori sea bass served with Bombay potatoes

Mains

Slow cooked traditional Goat korma

Guinea Fowl biryani

Sabzi

Dessert

Kheer

Kulfi

Gulab Jamun

Each dish had been carefully crafted by Chef. We had not expected or prepared ourselves for this. I was desperate to sneak behind the scenes to see who and how - who had created it and how this had come into being. Was it a small team I wondered. The menu was impressive; even the wording elevated the status of each dish from standard to exquisite. The cauliflower bhajia was basically a posh pakora. It sounded like something Madhur Jaffrey would craft in one of her cookery shows.

Finally, we had made it into the same sophisticated ranks as Madhur. The carefully separated cauliflower florets, almost all identical in size, were dipped in a light batter akin to a tempura, made of delicately spiced gram flour. It was much lighter than the one I used to make a pakora. Also airier, with the addition of soda water - a trick I had seen on an episode of Madhur. Instead of onion, asofeteda was used to give the taste of it; very clever. The finely ground spices added to the batter, included chilli powder, cumin and coriander. When flash fried, these little pocket rockets were light and crispy and packed with flavour; not too dense in texture or overbearing in spice. They had to be eaten within minutes of being removed from the hot oil, so they were served to us promptly, still sizzling on the plate. I couldn't help myself grinning at mum, knowing she too had clocked the complexity of this delectable starter. I could not imagine ever recreating these. Even if I tried, mine would surely die a soggy death before they reached the table, given the haphazard timing and unpredictability of our suitor meetings.

The fish, sea bass, I had never heard of, let alone tasted. The tandoori marinade, I could recreate easily, but who knew it could be used on fish? This too was a revelation for me. I watched mum peer through her reading glasses, to look at the menu in more detail. On seeing the goat curry, she excitedly announced, "Vadda gosht!" - BIG MEAT. This was an archaic, bordering on Neanderthal term, that referenced the size of goat in comparison to our usual meat source - mutton or lamb; both significantly smaller. Goat was not only rare to get hold of, but it was also pricey. Nailah cast a sharp disapproving glance mum's way, signalling her to shush her crudeness and to remind her that we were in the presence of a Lord.

Guinea fowl biryani. Another opulent sounding dish. But what on earth was a Guinea fowl? Was I about to see a small furry animal cooked in amongst the rice? I was slightly repulsed at the thought. None of us, brave enough to ask the question for fear of appearing more ignorant than we probably already looked. It was in fact another rare bird, akin to duck or pigeon -neither of which I had ever tasted. Apparently, it was all the rage; served in classy, upmarket restaurants in London and Lahore. It was delicious. A side of delicately spiced, al dente style, mixed vegetables - all intact, perfectly cooked, no fuzzy edges from being overdone.

The desserts were classic, if not vintage in comparison to the rest of the menu. Kheer, a thick-set rice pudding, which was delicately flavoured with rosewater and garnished beautifully with dried rose petals. The Kulfi, Indian ice cream was probably my favourite part of the banquet. It was served cleverly on small wooden sticks, like small popsicles; genius. Finally miniature gulab jamuns infused in syrup. I always found these little syrupy dough balls to be sickly sweet if the balance of sugar wasn't right. But of course, these were flawless.

We quietly savoured each course. Occasionally, I tapped mum's feet under the table to communicate our shared delight and multitude of culinary epiphanies. I also made mental notes; knowing that I would be plagiarising some of these opulent dishes myself one day. It felt like good karma had finally prevailed on several counts. Not just for Nailah, but for me too. Finally, someone had taken the trouble to cook the most splendid banquet for me. I was already imagining their wedding menu.

But looking across the table at Nailah, I sensed that she was not as jubilant as I would have expected her to be. I sensed an austere aura around her as she sat back in her seat after finishing her meal. I worked out very quickly that there was an obvious elephant in the room. Why had he felt the need to deploy all the shabby deflections at the first meeting? The clapped out car and his unkempt appearance being the obvious. This, the reason behind Nailah's obvious irritation. She looked directly at him, as if poised to challenge him. As the dinner table was being cleared, she looked across the table and said with a mixture of conviction, annoyance and sarcasm, "You have a beautiful house Lord; you live well Lord, we can see that." Numan nodded nervously; he too it seemed expected some kind of rebuttal from her, sensing her sarcasm and irritation through her tone and her body language.

"But you don't take stuff with you when you go," she continued, "it's just stuff, things, fluff," pointing to all the beautiful things in the room. She was referring to his obvious materialistic side; the only way she could deliver her message as if to say she was neither overly impressed nor in awe of it. She placed her hands on the table in front of her, signalling that she had said her piece. Now it was his turn. "I know, you are right. It is just stuff, but it's stuff that has taken me over three decades of slogging my guts…" he didn't finish his sentence before she cut in. "Even if you had shown up to our house dressed as you are now, with your driver, do you honestly think I'd be shallow enough to fall for you; just for that? I have turned away many a 'rishta' - suitor who thought that would be the hook to get me all excited."

She had made her point as succinctly as she could; specifying the obvious, and I was proud of her for making her opinions known. She continued; elaborating her point further, as I tucked into my third kulfi on a stick. "Not everyone is a gold digger you know. Is that what you really think of women? Because if you do, then it's clear that you're the one with the problem and insecurities!" Another good point but I did however want her to slow down a little. I was still basking in the excitement of the food which I wasn't quite yet ready to give up. She continued, "And if you think I'm impressed by a grotesque display of wealth..." She was cut short, by mum who threw her a sharp look, as if to signal stop now, enough, he's got the point!

There was more to the story. "You're right, he conceded. You're absolutely right, everything you have said is spot on," he said with a look of embarrassment and concern. His voice began to waver. "But there is something else you need to know." 'Oh no. What else? could this be a deal breaker?' I thought. That cursed letter, in my bag was a bad idea;

had I just jinxed the situation? We were all poised for what was to follow, as he beckoned his confidante Jalal over. It looked as if this part of the discussion had been rehearsed. He handed a frame to Numan, who turned it around to face us and dropped his head down. There was a photograph of a family in the frame. We could just make out that he was also in the photograph with two small children and a woman. They all looked to be happy, smiling, enjoying themselves in what appeared to be an exotic location, with palm trees in the background - obviously a holiday snap. He went onto explain, "This is my family…"

Mum's horrified expression screamed: 'What kind of hideous game is this?' She didn't hold back as she asked curtly, "Who is the woman in the photo?" "The mother of my children," Numan replied swiftly. Mum pushed her hands against the table forcing her chair back, then pulled herself up to her feet as she grabbed her Benares scarf. "Challo! Let's go!" she called out to Nailah and myself dramatically. "Please auntie, wait!" begged Numan, "Let me explain. We met at university, and she fell pregnant, so we were forced to marry by our parents. It was all wrong and we are no longer together; we have been separated for two years." This, was his brisk explanation of this situation.

Mum was unable to conceal her contempt; she looked him up and down in disgust, shamefully reducing him, as only mothers are capable of, when defending their children. Numan repeated, "She is the mother of my children and that is as far as it goes. The children are with her tonight," he continued. Nailah, at this point, seemed less shocked than mum. As much as she liked him, she wasn't invested enough to be shattered by this revelation. Calmly she said, "So how come you didn't mention that too when you came to see us last week?" I was on the brink of pulling out the crumpled advert, stuffed in my bag to cut in with, 'didn't you read where it says - no lying time wasters need apply', before realising that those words were not actually written in my ad.

"I wanted to tell you, but I was so impressed with you Nailah," he went on to explain. "I just wanted to see you one more time, explain it in person" Her expression was unfathomable. Normally I could read Nailah well, but she was poker faced; expressionless. What was she thinking? "So, you thought you would lure us here first to try and hook me in?" she replied. He dropped his head, facing downwards. His sense of shame, almost tangible. It was an uncomfortable exchange. I wanted to get out of there, as fast as I could. Leaving this delicious meal behind was the only thing I would have been sad about at this point.

There was a painfully long protracted few minutes of silence. We didn't leave. Nailah sat back in her chair, dropping her shoulders and her stiff posture, with a look of empathy. We had not altogether been truthful ourselves. There was dishonesty on our part too that needed to be shared with him. Mum had told another gargantuan lie about dad earlier, who she claimed was working for the BBC in the Middle East. That and other secrets, that only Nailah knew she would have to reveal to him in time. If this was as bad as it got, then it wasn't bad enough to walk away; just yet. He was vulnerable and she could see that. The children in the photograph didn't unsettle her; she loved children. They would never be a burden or encumbrance, as they were innocent in all of this and only added to his character, his strength and sense of duty. He understood, parenthood and responsibility; the kind she herself had been burdened with, looking after us after dad had left. Whilst we were not her children, we depended on her to support the family. She sensed and felt his turmoil and was prepared to listen and give him another chance. It was obvious, she was falling for him.

Will you be my second wife?

We left that evening with mixed emotions. Mixed in the sense that Nailah was unusually calm, mum was unsure, if not perturbed and I was still puzzled that he had replied to my advert, knowing his situation was unresolved. But I had a strong feeling that this was not the end. And I was also left wondering when would I eat another delicious meal at his house again?

Mum was prepared to accept a divorcee if that was her daughter's choice. But a divorce was not on the cards. It was much more complicated. A tumultuous few months ensued as they began meeting secretly, spending as much time together as they could, unbeknown to mum. It was a convoluted situation where a clean break was not an option, but another marriage was. An Islamic marriage was permissible under these unusual circumstances, as long as Numan was able to provide equally for each wife. Equal; in every way.

I asked Nailah one day after she confided in me that they were seeing each other secretly. "Are you up for that? Why can't he just end it, I don't understand? He loves you; he should make you officially his wife."

"It's not that simple Farah!" she snapped. Numan and his ex-wife were intrinsically linked in so many ways. Divorce in his situation would mean walking away from everything, including his children and this was the sticking point. They were being used as bait; weapons to emotionally blackmail and crush him. He was torn. There was only one option if Nailah wanted to be with him and that was to be his second wife, until all matters were resolved.

"Marry me," he begged her, "it's only an 'arrangement' with her and it means nothing, other than continuing to be a father to my children." This was his proposal. As ludicrous as this proposition sounded, Nailah thought deeply about it, she too was torn. There was no doubt that they loved each other and desperately wanted to be together, but the circumstances were not right. Mum was certainly not entertaining her unmarried daughter being involved with a married man, no matter how his proposal was being packaged. As the months went by, both of them were increasingly crushed under the pressure, and no one was winning.

She could not be the 'other woman', no matter how it was presented. It just did not sit right, as much she turned it around in her head, or loved him, she would not compromise on this. So, she made the only decision she could in this tangled situation. She set him free, giving him time to work things out and come back for her when everything was resolved. She also made it clear that she would only wait a certain amount of time for him. If he didn't come through in that time, she would move on with her life.

Time went by and after months of no communication from him, her world began to cave in. It felt like the end. She confined herself to her bedroom for weeks, allowing only bowls of food to pass in and out as she slid into a deep, dark depression.

Chapter 21

The 'in-betweener'

Khalil the singing dentist
"There ain't no use in hiding your lying eyes"

He was by far one of the most entertaining of all suitors. He brought lightness at a time that we all needed it. More importantly, he brought a glimmer of hope back to Nailah. He was a dentist, with his own private clinic and a private number plate on his open-top sports car.

It was a jovial entrance that day. He was beaming an extra-white, shining wide smile. It was the first thing we all noticed as he greeted us, open mouthed and grinning confidently. "Asalaaaam everyone! Greetings!" He sounded like Aladdin, and I could tell he couldn't speak Urdu very well; that was the most contrived, forced 'Asalaam' I had ever heard. What a 'coconut' I thought to myself. But a lovely set of gnashers - he was a dentist after all and was bound to have good teeth. He looked older than his actual age, despite his perfect smile. Nailah had agreed to meeting him, after mum pulled his details up from another introductory marriage site in a new Asian supplement newspaper specific to Yorkshire - 'The Asian Target.' Yet another kooky name for an ethnic newspaper, but back then, anything that represented the Asian community was better than nothing. The best part of this introductory service was, no letters were required.

Interested applicants connected by phone call only.

As he began casually chatting to us all, he looked at ease. I noticed his greying sideburns that were quite distinctive looking. I was glad that he hadn't attempted to colour his hair, as many Asian men did, which to me always looked too severe and obvious. Khalil was pleasant, a confident man, who didn't beat around the bush. He was direct; even complimenting Nailah on the colour of her dress, but not in the same manner as our gay friend Masood. Khalil was distinctly more alpha male. "You look lovely," he said with his expanded smile. Nailah graciously accepted the compliment, "Thank you," she beamed back.

This was always the most awkward part of the meeting; those first few minutes. We learnt a lot about people on first impressions; it was a skill we acquired in Suitorland. We could glean someone's personality in those first few moments, even before they opened their mouths, much like Khalil. We had become experts in reading peoples body language, facial expressions and overall comportment. Khalil was personable. His language, and his mannerisms, all displayed the traits of an honest, well-adjusted person. He was self-made and industrious. A grafter, who was proud of his achievements and not ashamed to boast about the fact he had recently been interviewed for a news feature about Paediatric Dentistry on TV. I knew he looked familiar. I recognised him, having seen that feature only a few weeks beforehand.

"I believe high quality dentistry should be available to all, from the cradle to the grave." I even recalled one of his lines on the TV interview which he reiterated for us. He was endearing, upbeat and positive, which was refreshing. Mum nodded in agreement, as if she was following the conversation, but in reality, she wasn't. Khalil was a divorcee; he had been married many years before. Unlike Numan, he had been honest an open about that fact before he came to visit. He had also been 'properly' divorced for years; again, unlike Numan. I could see that mum was more curious about why his first marriage had failed, than his views on dentistry. As she attempted to pry into his personal life, he didn't elaborate on anything in too much detail, other than tell us he had married young and things hadn't worked out; which was plausible. Now, he said looking directly at Nailah, "I'm ready to settle down, for good, hopefully with someone who is at the same point in their life as me."

As always, I had carefully planned the menu for that day, with a dentist in mind. Nothing too sweet, to cause tooth decay and nothing too coloured, in case it stained his teeth. So, sugar and turmeric were definitely off the menu. I made Lamb Pilau. This was a full meal in itself, and it was relatively easy to make from scratch. No need to make a heavy masala for a curry. It involved boiling a good batch, usually anything from twelve to fifteen solid lamb chops in a pan (more if you felt the urge to snag a few before the dish is ready), with whole spices and a large onion, chopped roughly. No precision was required at this point, which was a bonus. A teaspoon of each spice was ample - whole peppercorns, coriander seeds, cloves, black cardamom - two of the latter and a stick of cinnamon. Salt to taste. All the elements would boil in the water until a foamy looking froth came to the surface, then dissipated to leave a clear liquid surrounding the boiled chops, much like a consommé. The liquid - 'yakhni' or broth, mum would often make for us as a comforting soup if we were feeling under the weather. "It's good for your bones," she would insist as she forced us to slurp it down in big mouthfuls.

After the stock was drained and set to one side, the leftover spices, onions and chops stayed in the pan. Ghee added, enough to coat them and then the heat cranked up whilst briskly stir-frying the meat. This was the part where I would always snag one or two of the chops, tempted by their delicious crisp outer edge and golden-brown colour. The stock poured back in, followed by washed, drained and soaked basmati rice. The ratio of stock to rice was always 2:1, respectively. As it boiled down, I was instructed to listen carefully to the sounds that indicated sizzling was happening on the base of the pan. This was the sound of water being boiled off. Mum once described that sound to me as 'sarr-sarr-sarr' which I found quite useful as it was onomatopoeically precise. I could actually hear it 'sarr-ing!' Recipe books definitely needed to include the phonetic sounds that food should be making as it cooks. Wouldn't that have be a novel idea I thought.

Once the liquid evaporated from around the surface of the rice, a dampened cloth was spread over the top of the pan. This trapped in the moisture and allowed it to continue to cook gently in the steam. The house would always absorb the distinct aroma of pilau spices and emit the smell for days. A side dish of mint yogurt raita was enough to serve with this robust meaty rice dish. Perfectly hearty, tasty and nothing a dentist could complain about.

For dessert, I made another dentist approved dish, Fruit chaat. This was made with plenty of finely chopped apples and other seasonal fruits, all tossed in a special blend known as chaat masala. Fruit chaat was definitely an acquired taste. It was never on my list of favourites as a child; it grew on me later, as my palette evolved. The battle between opposing flavours on my tongue would eventually develop and appreciate this harmonious play between sweet and sour. A good dessert option, if entertaining a health freak like Khalil, who loved it. He complimented mum on it, who as always, took the credit for all my hard work.

As the meeting progressed, I detected a sense of ease; it was a pleasant dynamic. Nailah was in a stronger place and open to finding someone new after an almost six-month suitor sabbatical. She had accepted that Numan was not coming back for her. That episode had taught her many things. Most of all, for her to become even more discerning, about what she was and was *not* prepared to settle for. As we sat down for tea after the meal, Khalil excused himself for a few minutes to 'get something from his car' he explained, "Excuse me auntie, I'll be back in a minute," he said as he left the room. I tidied up the plates and used those minutes to turn to Nailah and ask, "So what do you think?" "He's alright, he's quite fun actually," she responded. He was fun; that was evident, but probably a bit more fun than we had expected or could have in fact imagined.

As he strolled back into the hallway, he was clutching something tightly to his chest. I briefly glimpsed it as he passed the kitchen window. He walked into the hallway, where we could all hear a distinctive strumming. Looking at each other in bewilderment, we could hear that it was the strumming of a guitar that was coming from the hallway, and it was definitely getting closer. "Are you serious," Nailah winced, pulling her head into her shoulders, looking as if she wanted to hide into her kurta dress. The door flung open and there he stood, with his wide mouthed smile, doing something we would never have expected. He belted out at the top of his voice, "YOU CAN'T HIIIDE YOUR LYING EYEESS."

I bolted, as fast as I could, without hesitation; unable to contain my laughter, the tears streaming down my eyes, whilst trying desperately to find a place to hide in the kitchen. This was beyond cringe-worthy. I could see Nailah's face from behind the cupboard, starting to change colour, blushing as he continued to sing; now staring directly at her. My brother didn't make any pretence of it, he let rip; there was no disguising it with him. He laughed so loudly and with intent, throughout the whole performance. Mum was stunned; trying her hardest to remain composed and desperately shush my brother's laughter. She didn't want to offend Khalil, but at the same time, she too wanted him desperately to shut up. This was a first for us, which brought not only laughter but years of recounting and living through what had to be, one of the funniest suitor scenarios we had ever witnessed.

Khalil certainly had confidence, balls even, to perform this classic Eagles track, without any sign of nerves, or any signs of slowing down for that matter. His strumming got faster as he raced through two more verses, raising his head to the ceiling; eyes pressed together tightly as he belted out the last line, "There ain't no use in hiding your lying eyes…" Strummmmmm. Pause.

I wanted to throw an egg at him. Were we expected to clap? Not sure, but Nailah started the applause gleefully, as we all politely joined in; relieved that the painful performance had come to an end. What a strange choice of song I thought? His voice wasn't bad, he could definitely hold a note; he also had enough power and melody behind it too. But the element of surprise and being caught off-guard hadn't allowed us to fully enjoy it. I wished we had known what to expect in advance. But now, as we applauded him, he beamed an even wider smile if that was possible. He must have interpreted this as encouragement, as he started again. There was that dreaded strum again. 'NOOOOOO!' I could hear us all silently thinking. He went on to give us three more songs including 'Hound Dog, Unforgettable and I got you babe'; pausing only to tune the strings of his guitar.

He struck more than the chords on his guitar that day. Whether it was his dulcet tones or the ballads that turned her on, Nailah agreed to meet him a week later, then on several occasions thereafter. There was a distinct connection between them. When they began to speak candidly about their 'exes' the kinship between them became evident for what it was. It was in fact all Khalil spoke about, non-stop. He talked only about his ex-wife, who he admitted, was the 'only' love of his life. It was obvious that he still had unresolved feelings for her, conceding that he wasn't sure whether moving forward at this moment was a good idea.

Fully expecting Nailah to be angry, the opposite happened. She consoled him. It was too early in the relationship for her to have developed any feelings for him. She empathised with him, realising that she too was emotionally stuck in the same place. It was obvious that she hadn't fully resolved her own feelings for Numan. She missed him in the same way Khalil missed his ex-wife. There was a reason she had met Khalil the singing dentist; they both needed this encounter, in order come to their own realisations; dig deep about what they truly wanted moving forward. As he walked her back to the train station, he held her hand, kissed it gently, and didn't say a word. They both knew that after this, there would be no more meetings between them.

Nailah was tired, weary from all her feelings of denial. Still yearning desperately for Numan, she knew that he was the only one who had ever made her feel this way. She missed him and felt lost without him. She only felt at peace with him in her life and needed to feel complete again. And she knew what she had to do next.

Chapter 22

Marry her or Bugger off!

If this was a romantic movie where love conquers all, Nailah and Numan would be meeting on a bridge, or a train station café, at a certain time, racing towards each other, with reckless abandon.

Personally, I wanted to bang their heads together after the traumatic emotional turmoil they had caused me. I felt dragged through the mill and depleted of everything in through this tragic love story. I had lost count of the nights I had sat up crying with Nailah, comforting her when she was inconsolable. These two individuals had bedraggled me, stained me with their dramatic love story and then, nonchalantly walked off, without so much as a 'Thanks for being there. x.'

I vowed never to become entangled in anyone's love life ever again. Exhausted, depleted and angry, there were days that I imagined setting fire to the advert cupboard in our living room - the place I would sit for hours and write those stupid handwritten notes to The Daily Jang. Would I ever come to laugh in hindsight about this episode of my life? seeing it clearly for all the farcical, archaic and painful practice it had been? I wondered how many other families were out there, having gone through the same protracted process, or was it just us?

Suitorland: The Pakistani equivalent of Blind Date, the

popular TV show of the 1980's and 1990's. If I were to set up a reunion of Daily Jang successful suitor matches, would it fill up a small town I wondered? But more importantly, would anyone be brave enough to even admit it?

"Life is too short," said Brenda, her friend from work, who Nailah had confided in for years. She was like Dotty to Laylah. The older sister, the confidante, the maternal figure we needed, that wasn't mum. "Go... go now and get him! You only live once, do it!" Was her instruction to Nailah. She cajoled and bullied her young friend to take a leap of faith and 'just do it'. Here was free-thinking Brenda on one side and on the other, an unrelenting mum who had opposing opinions. To who would Nailah listen to? Brenda did not mess around. She was a straight-talking, hard-wired Bradfordian woman having grown up in the roughest and toughest estate in the city.

"Marry her or *bugger off*!" were her exact words to Numan on the day she organised a meeting between them, which she chose to mediate. He needed to hear that. She interrogated him with the fierceness of a Rottweiler from the Holme Wood estate. There were no pleasantries with Brenda; she cut straight to the chase. "I'm here for her," she growled in a thick Yorkshire accent, pointing at Nailah. Numan was backed into a corner, literally. Brenda physically poked him in the chest, pushing him all the way up to the corner of the room until he was ambushed.

She continued, "You better get your act together, she's

good stock that one and she deserves the best and God knows why she fell for you!"

It was clear that she had her own opinion of him, but that aside, a decision had to be made; one that her young friend needed tearing out of him. Brenda was the only one who could fight for Nailah this way. She was fuelled by rage, having seen her friend suffering for him, on top of everything else she had witnessed her go through, over the years. Mum would never have been able to fight our corner as Brenda did. We needed someone of her sensibility. A no-nonsense Yorkshire-grit woman, who made it known that Nailah was protected and there was an army behind her. Brenda was her army. We all needed a Brenda in our lives.

During the months of separation, Numan had been preoccupied with sorting the messiness of his situation. He had surrendered everything he had worked for, including the manor house, to the mother of his children. It wasn't as straightforward as we had imagined. This clean break not only left him broke, but it also divided his entire family, who had depended on him financially. They too abandoned him. He was left with very little and alone. That was when he saw the fragility of it all. How lives can be transformed overnight, families divided; a lifetime of things evaporate into thin air. It was all so brittle, but through his losses he realised what mattered to him. And what mattered was genuine, unconditional love. The kind he had found with Nailah. She had made it clear that she didn't care for 'his stuff,' as many others had and she was prepared to start from scratch, with nothing. Just to be with him; that was enough. The wedding plans started.

One particular day in the midst of planning, I curiously asked mum whether she was happy with her daughter's choices. She disdainfully turned to me and announced, "Kothay naal shaadi karlay - she can marry a donkey for all I care." This 'sturm und drang' - storm and stress, had also left mum exasperated.

It was the most exuberant wedding our family had ever seen. Mum planned it with precision, to be hosted at a venue she had always loved and dreamt about for her daughter's send-offs. The Mumbai palace. One of the biggest restaurants in Bradford at the time. It was impressive; nothing was going to hinder this epic moment for mum -the mother of the bride. It was her moment, just as much, if not more she thought, than the bride and groom. She wanted it to be perfect, so of course, it came with more secrets. No one was allowed to mention Numan's previous life to the relatives or guests. There was always going to be something she picked on, like a stain in every situation.

Mum would always find a reason to shroud some element in shame and attempt to hide it. Tuck it away, just like the imperfections in the cloth she was paid to make perfect by the worsted mills in the 1970's. Her distorted image of reality and incredibly ambitious standards were a combination of fear and conceit. How would anything less than perfect reflect on her? "What would people say?" she would gasp to justify her naïve, irrational and somewhat skewed perception of the world. Who were these people, and in hindsight who cared? The same people she was referring to were most likely to be in the same boat as us; trying to navigate the same rocky terrain of messed up east-meets-west values.

Nailah's wedding day was spectacular. It was everything mum had dreamt of for her daughter. The whole family attended; some travelling from overseas for this long-anticipated day. The seven-course banquet she had instructed be prepared by the restaurant lived up to her expectations. Unlike Numan. Mum seated herself as far away as possible from him, for fear of landing him a tight 'chupayr' slap for what he had put us all through. *No man* would ever meet her impossibly elevated ideals, but the fact that her daughter was happy with him, that was all that mattered in the end and in spite of everything; it was one of the happiest days I can remember celebrating joyously, all of us together. Mum, Laylah, H, Zainab and me - the family entourage; held each other tightly as Nailah walked away that day, heading into her new life. We wept tears of joy and sadness, filled with the gravity of emotions that only we, as a family had known collectively. Forever invested in each other, entwined in solidarity through our struggles, and through our happiness.

Finally; *we had found the one.*

Chapter 23

The Imposter she painted brown…

With Nailah now married and settled, the attention swiftly turned to Zainab. Mum was on a roll and was not prepared to waste any time finding the right suitor for her too, whether she was open to it or not. It was obvious that this particular suitor-search was never going to be plain sailing. But nothing prepared us for the bombshell that was delivered in the form of the painted man.

The mid-nineties were beginning to look optimistic for us; the world was opening up in so many new and exciting ways. We were growing up and the tables were beginning to turn in our favour. Mum, now looking to us for support and guidance in a way that empowered us. For Zainab, climbing the career ladder was at the forefront of her mind; not to mum's chagrin, marriage. She was confident, beautiful, intelligent and tenacious as she ran up that ladder, excelling in her corporate job. The new 'It' girl about town, she was different; in a league of her own, compared to the older girls and myself, her younger sister. Zainab had always been much savvier and more streetwise; certainly not one to surrender to any restrictions that mum placed on her, without a full and plausible explanation.

She also saw through mum's futile attempts to control us through her emotional outbursts and blackmail, from feigning illness, exhaustion or her fear of being judged by the community and her family. The kind of statements that mum brandished at us like weapons included: "Never. You cannot ever leave this house without shaadi - marriage; what will your uncle Raad say? You know his wife hates us already, she'll be dancing...and it will kill me!" These words resonated and we believed them; if not duped into submissiveness. Zainab was the only one to challenge this control, marching to the beat of her own drum. She was never going to have the conventional 'send-off' that mum imagined. They would clash regularly, and she knew it was time for her to escape.

"I have searched the length and breadth of London for you, ungrateful little churaayl - devil!" mum uttered under her breath, feigning her usual overly dramatic breakdowns. "Tell me, what am I doing wrong, where the hell is this 'farishta'- angel?" This would usually be followed by a staged and predictable feigned hyperventilation. "Chamree lai-lo! - Take my skin!" she would sigh. Another over-embellished phrase indicating defeat, when there is nothing left to give, but 'skin'. We would try not to laugh too loudly as she carefully choreographed her fall to the ground. She even attempted to threaten us that the pool of eligible men was beginning to get smaller to which Zainab would snigger, "It's a pond mum, there's never been a pool, considering the frogs that come for us." Mum would retort with a curse, "Fittay moo! Shame on you! - may your face be smoke!" Holding up her palm in a cursory manner. The suitor search for her most problematic and argumentative daughter was a thankless task.

"Parray-parray: Away-away" - The bizarre term used to describe how Zainab would be shunned or pushed away; cast out if she married outside of the culture, let alone religion. Forever an out-cast. "You'll always be an outsider and never fully integrate anyone from a different culture into this family. Parray-parray you'll stay." These were mum's exact words to her. Whilst she challenged them, the words haunted her for years. It meant being left for dead, even by your own family, if you married outside of the Pakistani community and Islam. Even when there was genuine love, as there had been with the Mancunian biker, she knew it wasn't enough for her to brave the hurricane of being ostracised and the colossal fallout that it would bring. Ironically, beneath the bravado, she was a frightened young girl, afraid of the consequences of being cut off forever. It terrified her. Until Dale that is.

The ridiculously handsome, blonde haired, blue eyed Scandanavianesque man visiting her workplace, for whom she had held the lift door open. As he slid through the closing doors behind him, it was one simple knee jerk reaction from him - a wink, for her to become completely infatuated at first sight. The lift door and the corny wink changed the course of her life forever. 'Away - Away' was beginning to feel like a place she could call home.

As always, I was her confidante; the only one who knew

about him. The guardian and keeper of all of her secrets. I was also her alibi for the times she needed to sneak out to meet him. I would be dumped at the local library, having pretended to mum that we were going out together, then left to catch a bus home a few hours later, to meet her at the garden gate. We would walk back into the house, as if we had been together all day. It worked for me, I enjoyed the time alone in the library, the place I found my own get-away for a few hours. My only job was to keep schtum.

There was something different about Dale; he was uncomplicated, straightforward and credible. A giant standing at 6ft 2 next to her petite frame; he had the deepest bluest Prussian blue eyes and the finest golden-blonde hair, in stark contrast to our thick dark hair and dark eyes. He was our polar opposite. I could understand why she was attracted to him. It was mutual, they were obsessed with each other, and she was adamant that he was going nowhere. She would never let him go and devised a plan, which was masterminded and executed with military precision.

I first met him at a party that mum allowed us to attend, after we convinced her, it was girls only. Dale was there. He exuded a warmth, a genuine kindness and positivity, with no agenda other than just to be happy, which was refreshing. He was without a doubt a good man, but I wondered where this would end up for Zainab. What did she want from this, knowing the boundaries were non-negotiable with mum. The only thing in her favour was that she had already negotiated her terms and conditions in Suitorland, which gave her the option to assist the search in her own way. Mum had agreed to it years ago, after Zainab left home and was reminded on the day when she announced, "I met someone at work mum, I think you'll like him."

We were told of a man she had met at work called Jed, which I thought strange, given that she was madly in love with Dale. She told us that Jed was mixed race; his father Pakistani Muslim, his mother white British. She knew that a mixed-race Muslim was more acceptable; the religion obviously standing in his favour. The prospect of the third of her four daughters being married-off, filled mum with enough excitement to bypass the minor details. But no one expected what was actually in store for us the day that Jed came to visit.

The meeting was conducted as a regular suitor date. I helped prepare the food as always, hoping and praying for the millionth time, that this would be the last banquet. Given that the highly likely prospects of Jed being the one, we went all-out on the delicious spread, even adding new dishes to the menu. Tandoori lamb leg, roasted slowly in the oven. Our oven now being used for more than just storage; I introduced mum to a world of roasting, baking, slow cooking and a clever recipes that included tandoori naan bread and other dishes, without the need of a classic tandoor oven. It cut down on labour and mess, that used to be generated from the multiple bubbling pots on the stove top. Our repertoire of impressive menus was also growing. Menus which many a suitor had returned to sample again and again, sometimes even forgetting why they had showed up, like Greg, the munching, moaning medic.

For this lamb leg to taste superb, all that was required was a rich, thick, tandoori marinade made from a medley of ground tandoori spices - cumin, coriander, chilli powder, garam masala, fresh ginger, garlic, chillies and lemon juice - all blended with yogurt and rubbed over the lamb which was left to marinade overnight. Slow cooked the following day in the oven, the meat would be so tender; it fell off the bone.

When the doorbell rang, I elected to open it and greet the man who I was hoping would be my new brother-in-law. As I opened the door, I was met by an exceptionally tall man wearing a Pakistani sherwani - a traditional shirt, usually worn over trousers, but today, over blue jeans; the first time I had seen this combination. He was smiling at me nervously, which was when I looked closer and saw that he looked vaguely familiar. His piercing dark eyes were staring at me a certain way. I definitely felt I had met him somewhere before but couldn't quite place him. His ashy brown hair was patchy in areas. A stain at the top of his forehead suggested it had been coloured recently and had left an inky residue close to his hairline. That was not unusual, as many suitors coloured their hair; we knew the tell-tale signs well and often joked about them after they had left.

In a quivering and hesitant voice, he said, "Assa-lammaleekum." His eyes shifted to the side which signalled he wasn't comfortable with mouthing the greeting. He was thinking hard about his pronunciation, which also struck me as a little 'off'. It felt as if his greeting had been practiced several times. It was then that I realised that it was definitely rehearsed if not contrived. In fact, everything about him was out of kilter. Painfully rehearsed and choreographed. His now suspiciously dark piercing eyeballs were staring straight at me. I wondered why his skin tone was also mismatched, in amongst everything else going on around his discombobulated appearance. It had an unusual deep orange hue to it. That was it - he had been painted with cheap fake tan! I couldn't hide my astonishment as I stared at him wide mouthed. It was at that moment, he knew he had been rumbled. Jed was in fact Dale. What had she done? 'I hope it washes off!' was all I could think.

His beautiful Prussian blue eyes, disguised with the dubious brown contact lenses, were struggling to stay in one place, wobbling around his eyeballs, causing him to squint. I felt a strong urge to push him back out of the door, knowing that if I could see through him, so would everyone else. Could he stand the humiliation? Zainab had outdone herself with her outlandish attempt to symphonise poor Dale into mum's criteria. It showed just how far she was willing to go to stretch the truth or bend it in this instance. After he pushed past me, to greet mum in the hallway, I noticed that he had failed to cover the back of his ears with the fake tan; they were glaringly white. Once again, nervously, he pronounced, "Assalamma alaykum walaikumsalaam - Hello and goodbye." Mum, standing in front of him with a knowing smile, suggested she had been waiting to meet 'mixed-race Jed'. Her smug, contrived smile didn't falter as she watched Dale-Jed, become a proverbial lamb to the slaughter.

I ran to the kitchen to check my own lamb in the oven and to confront Zainab. "You could have bloody told me! We made 'aloo paratha' yesterday, we had more than enough time at the chapatti station for you to have filled me in you silly mare!" I whispered, on the verge of dissolving into laughter. Zainab was frozen, her eyes were welling up; she too was on the brink of dissolving, but instead into tears. I knew then that this ridiculously desperate scenario was not to be made light of. She was prepared to do anything, even if it meant stretching to the preposterous in the name of love. I reached out my arms, hoping that our embrace would give her comfort and to know that she still had an ally in me; whatever the outcome. Our hands clasped tightly before we fell to the kitchen floor, howling hysterically, trying to catch our breath as we considered our next move. She stood up and reached into the cupboard to retrieve her car keys. It looked as though she was about to do a runner. "Don't you dare!" I warned her. "If you truly love him, you'll stay."

Mum sat through the whole meeting with Jed, disingenuously making conversation, occasionally nodding politely, whilst thinking up questions that might trip him up about his so-called mixed-race ancestry. She already had her suspicions and had, unbeknown to us, followed Zainab on more than one occasion, where she had seen her with Dale. "So, what city in Pakistan again was your father born? I might know it. Have you ever visited your homeland? Do you have relatives there?" Her quick-fire interrogation of him was relentless. He tried his best to keep up until he was defeated; stumped, shrugging his shoulders, when he had no answers left to give. Agonisingly looking to Zainab for help.

He didn't touch the tandoori lamb that I had made. Dale was vegetarian and only sipped on the 'karak chai' tea I made for him. After seeing him struggle desperately to keep up with mum, I was hoping that he would find comfort and strength in this sweet simmered, milky tea infusion; enough to get him through this nightmarish ordeal. His hands were wrapped tightly around the cup as he sipped and succumbed to mum's intense interrogation. When he eventually left, mum turned to Zainab and proudly announced, "He is not Jed, he is Dale!" Her smug upper handed tone signalling to us that she was in control, and despite how frayed she appeared to us, she would never fall prey to having the wool pulled over her eyes. This, the most inconceivable of all meetings would draw Suitorland to an end. It also saw the end of this relationship. Or so we thought.

After months of relative inertia, Zainab came home one day after work to deliver another unexpected blow. Whilst mum was tending to her multiple plant pots in the greenhouse, Zainab stood over her looking down from the glass door and announced, stoically, "I married him!" As mum looked up and before she could even react, Zainab opened up her loose-fitting trench coat to reveal a small protruding bump. "And we're expecting a baby."

I couldn't believe that she hadn't told me. I genuinely thought her mood swings and consumption of copious amounts of mum's mango lime pickle over the last few weeks were down to heartbreak and comfort eating. Little did I know that her cravings for piquant spicy food were the result of growing a baby. Not even I had detected her bump, "We already performed our Nikkah Islamic vows months ago." She continued whilst showing little if any sign of emotion. "How? What? When?" were the only words mum could muster, in her confusion; confronted with so many shocking revelations, one after another. "But Nikkah can only be done in Islam, and he was pretending to be one of us," mum said, alluding to the fact that Jed was not, to her knowledge a true Muslim. In her eyes this marriage was defunct. Zainab interjected, "He is Muslim now, we did that too, he read his Shahada. It's official, I'm a married Muslim woman mum and have been for some time."

That was the last thing Zainab said before turning away and walking up the path from the greenhouse to her car. She drove away that day and didn't return until she was called back to make it 'official' to our relatives. And this required another ceremony.

Jed had in fact converted to Islam a good few months before. He was now officially known as Amjed; ironically, Jed for short. It all made sense now. What started as an elaborate lie was now bathed in honour, through a genuine and heartfelt conversion to the faith of Islam. He had found religion through Zainab and she too had re-discovered her faith in a way that felt natural and more congruent to her values than it ever had in the past. They were welcomed by a kind-hearted, knowledgeable scholar who had shown her what 'real' Islam represented, redefining it from her past traumatic experiences, that had done nothing but turn her away. I was elated for them both and excited that she too had found 'the one' for her.

The only day mum genuinely did pass out, was when she was issued with a Fatwa from the local mosque, instructing her to acknowledge and accept her new son in law. Mum knew she could not contest this union now. She herself would be in breach of her own religion if she attempted to dispute it.

The weeks that followed were traumatic for our entire family. I couldn't imagine how my pregnant sister felt, as we rushed around her, haphazardly making calls to our bemused relatives and friends to organise a shotgun wedding - possibly the first of its kind in Bradford. Another elaborate tale was constructed to explain why the wedding was so rushed, giving those invited only a week's notice to make their travel plans. The ceremony took place in our home as there was no time to secure any kind of venue in this tight time frame. And Zainab's bump was growing by the day. To add more complexity, (as if we needed it) a Nikkah ceremony could only be performed once, but given that it had already happened, this posed another problem. The relatives wanted to see and witness this important ceremony for it to be plausible.

Somehow, and from somewhere, mum hunted down an old Muslim Imam, who she talked into to 'staging' another Nikkah for the sake of saving face and convincing her suspicious relatives that this marriage ceremony was taking place for the first time. It didn't quite go to plan, when the dithering old Imam inadvertently told uncle Raad that it was all forged. But it didn't matter, as many of them had guessed from Zainab's bump and, a few months later, an unusually early arrival of a baby.

Shop shut

It really was now the end of an era. After this wedding, the doors of Suitorland were firmly closed for business. Mum and I breathed an immense sigh of relief.

Chapter 24

I found *me*

The college years

"Are you an actress? Do you study at the theatre? Can I have your num..." I ran so fast that I didn't even hear the end of his questions. I had just climbed off the tube in Leicester Square station, dashing past the row of stationary commuters on the escalator heading to Charing Cross Road, to run to college. The youngish student-type looking man who had been sitting opposite me, was jogging briskly behind me, trying to catch up. I had felt his stare all the way from Regents Park, doing everything he could to catch my eye, smiling through it all. At one point I reached into my bag and briskly pulled out one of my books. The Phenomenology of Perception, a heavy hitting art theory book which I thought might deter him; a book that sent out a clear message - I'm clever enough to understand this, are you? And with this, I hoped he would back off.

I pretended to read it just to dodge his relentless gaze and annoying smile. He didn't stop. As the tube pulled into Leicester square, I saw him climbing out of one of the other carriages, so I bolted as fast as I could, hoping that he wouldn't see me, corner me or worse still try to speak to me. Still walking briskly behind me, he caught up. "Are you an actress?" he shouted again, through the crowds of tourists who were always congregating outside the Apollo theatre. I raced past the theatre down Soho Street, through a short cut which led to the back door of my studio, my heart pounding. A sigh of relief; thank God. I had lost him. I was terrified of men.

This happened often during the time I studied in London, and I hated it. It would always start on the tube; in that narrow space that forced you to sit or stand next to someone in such close proximity that it was inevitable for them to look, or stare at you relentlessly, to catch your eye if they found you attractive and then not let go. At twenty-three years old, this was the first time I had lived away from home. I came to London to study at one of the most prestigious colleges in the world. London was intoxicating. It had been on my radar for a long while leading up to this point, having been enticed by the galleries, museums and culture that was far superior to that of Yorkshire at that time. I was naturally drawn towards this dynamic city. It oozed avant-garde, cutting edge, and it felt like I was exactly where I needed to be. This was my opportunity to do what I wanted to, more than anything else.

Suitorland; now a world away, was the very last thing on my mind; I had done my job there for my sisters. I was here to make waves in the art world, to see how far I could go; push the boundaries of a discipline that had become an obsession for me. I knew that there was much more for me to learn about life, and I was here to make the most of it. The foundation had been set in Yorkshire where I had studied hard to get here. The only one of mum's five children who made it to university, I was determined not to waste this opportunity; unlike many of the other more privileged students on my course; sons and daughters of aristocrats and Lords. It was obvious that there were no expectations of them having to earn their keep. We were poles apart; my daily two-hour commute would see me in the studio at 9am on the dot, whilst they would roll into lectures at midday. They would enjoy the social life that came with living away from home, whilst I returned home daily, to make roti for the family at 6.30pm sharp. It was as if my day at college and evening at home were two separate entities, polarised. Life and chores at home would never be compromised, it had to fit in with my studies, that was a given.

A sanctuary

Art was my sanctuary, my sanity, my retreat. The place I could be alone, uninterrupted, to think. It was the place I could make sense of the world around me and it re-framed everything, including Suitorland. It was my conduit to understanding life a little better and navigating my way through it. I discovered new ways to express myself, which opened up a world of possibilities. I also realised that my critical intelligence was much more evolved than my emotional quotient. I was so much more adept in this world than the one I had inhabited growing up - that was messy, traumatic, noisy and confusing. That place made little or no sense to me now. But through art, everything was crystal clear.

I would use this time to practice, to create, to paint, to sculpt, reinvent and push boundaries at a cerebral level. To process theories, engage and stretch my brain in ways I never thought possible. It truly was my escape; a refuge and the place I found my sanity. This was my passion, when not preoccupied with making feasts in Suitorland. That world to me, now appeared chaotic, if not ludicrous. My perception was widening, and I had outgrown many things to find my true calling. So, when my name was put forward for a paid scholarship to the prominent London art school, I grabbed it and ran. My lecturers saw my passion and commitment and they also saw the working-class girl from Bradford with a lack of privilege but a ton of ambition. Someone like me would never have made it into this elite world without financial help. And that was the only way I was able to make it to London. Through art I was confident, self-assured and free.

But I inhabited two different mind-sets which would eventually be my nemesis. I was divided. The altruism of my younger self who naively went about her chores, slowly began to evaporate. I learned, just from my daily commutes, that it was not easy being a woman, let alone a Pakistani woman straddling two conflicting cultures. I empathised and identified with my sisters more than ever. Is this what they too went through? I had a newfound respect for all the things that I had judged them for - their rebellious discerning nature and their lack of compliance. They had pushed against the glass ceilings with little or no support; they were the true vanguards of change.

London was a colossal leap from the life I had known in Yorkshire. The impact of it was however buffered by the fact that I was living with extended family. I stayed with my uncle Raad and his new wife, Zareen. This was the same uncle Raad who had previously been married to Diya - the force behind the 1970's power couple we were once in awe of. After the breakdown of his marriage to her, we were all devastated and he was left broken. He had spent years in darkness, before mum encouraged him to marry Zareen - a woman from their hometown in Pakistan. Raad travelled to Karachi, where he married her promptly, surrendering to the belief that he was getting old, as mum advised him, "Jaldi Jaldi!" hurry hurry! make children.

His new wife was a far cry from Diya - the impressive, fiercely independent cosmopolitan and a fashionable woman that we were all obsessed with. Zareen was her polar opposite. Introverted, kind, soft, naïve, accommodating, if not over-accommodating as many 'import brides', as we called them, were at that time. She was not in the same league as Diya. I could see that the old uncle Raad had disintegrated without her and was a changed man. He was constantly angry, argumentative, resentful and bullied Zareen at any opportunity he could. He picked on me too, as

I inhabited the tiniest corner of the basement apartment, they lived in. I tiptoed through that apartment, only being present at mealtimes to help prepare food.

"Try harder to integrate more in London!" I heard him scold her. "Don't wear clothes that make you look too Pakistani" he instructed her; and "try to diversify your palette, it's always curry curry curry… don't deep fry - it stinks the house out." Examples of his daily cutting, judgemental belittling words, chipping away at her confidence. It was obvious, that he was still in love with Diya, but it filled me with rage that he persecuted his new wife *and* got away with it. Through no fault of her own, she had entered into this union, unknowingly becoming a replacement for the love of his life.

It didn't surprise me that Diya had left. Maybe he displayed the same entrenched bigoted behavioural traits to her too? She would not have stood for it. He was not the only one of his generations to subjugate their wives. It was happening everywhere, and it sickened me to my stomach. I felt that there was a reason I was here - to open my eyes to it. I entered this home and unhappy marriage, witnessing their daily arguments and growing contempt towards each other. My perfect image of him and shining example of a successful marriage and functional relationship; the only one we had ever known, had crumbled. If something as brilliant and un-flawed as this could fail so easily and die, what hope was there for us? It taught me that life can mutate in an instant, promising situations disintegrate and turn to dust, leaving only vague reminders of what was and what will never be again. I learnt that nothing is perfect, and nothing lasts forever.

I would make excuses to take my aunt out at weekends, usually on the pretext of going to college and needing her help in my studio. We never did go to my college though. Instead, we would frequent all the markets that London had to offer - Portobello Road, Brick Lane, Church Street and others. It was there that we would satisfy our food fantasies and cravings for everything that uncle Raad forbade us to eat in his house. We would feast on hot deep-fried samosas, watching the oil drip down our faces, giggling just to spite him and his contempt of Pakistani food. We ate Indian street food that looked slightly iffy when cooked in the open air, but we didn't care. We tried cuisines we had never tasted before such as Balinese, Indonesian, and Malaysian. We became regulars among the food stalls and markets, both of us expanding our knowledge of cuisines from around world.

On returning home, at the risk of upsetting Raad, we would recreate some of the delicious meals we had eaten such as Malaysian Laksa and Vietnamese Pho, which we both agreed was the same as the mutton bone broth we knew as 'Yakhni'; the base used to make pilau rice. Now that mum was no longer my food companion, I had my aunt in her place. Those weekends were my only outlet to experience and create food again, away from Yorkshire. It was an adventure and an education for us both. Most of all, it was a culinary release that I still needed. These were some of the most enjoyable days spent with my naïve, accommodating and kind aunt.

I embraced everything London had to offer within my comfort zone, I made it my home and I had planned to stay well beyond graduating. I was determined to keep climbing, pushing myself, being the best I could be. Whether that meant entering a world of academia - an art critic, a writer, a professor, who knows? but I was here to stay. A world of opportunity beckoned, and I planned to take full advantage of it. There were even times my now married sisters would come to see me in my new surroundings. We were all growing and evolving in our own quite different ways. I would take them to galleries, open their eyes to my world, and what made me tick. This world intrigued them, and seeing how passionate I was about it, they admired my fervour, cheering me on through every achievement. It could easily have been different had they been resentful of the opportunity afforded to me; this kind of freedom allowed me to escape the pressure of marriage and what they had to go through.

They truly celebrated me, knowing that I had earned this freedom. The decade or more that I had diligently put in, slaving over the suitor spreads of food; dutifully sacrificing my every weekend for their benefit, had finally paid off for them. They owed me BIG TIME. London was my reward which allowed me to dodge Suitorland for now. But had I?

No one quite expected the sharp turn of events that was just around the corner.

I wanted to stay

It - divided - us

After gaining my degree, I had put plans in place to stay in London. It was everything I had worked towards, and it was all coming my way effortlessly. But mum had other plans. "You cannot stay with your uncle Raad forever you know - it's not the done thing, come home!" she instructed me over the phone on the day I graduated. 'Hang on', I thought to myself, 'that was not the plan! Why would I return to Yorkshire now?' I thought she knew that. I begged and pleaded with her, trying to convince her, every way I could to let me stay in London. I even attempted to bargain with her. "I'll work here during the week and come home at weekends. I'll catch the National express bus, it will be easy," I argued. She threw every obstacle at me she could to stop me, "And where will you live? Certainly not with your uncle now, they need their space," she replied curtly.

I had already found a place to live; a shared apartment with my friend Emma who studied with me; I had it all planned. But mum used an argument that I had heard many times in the past to validate her senselessly flawed rationale.

"Shaadi-to-baad - after marriage do what you like." This had to be most opposing statement she would use to perpetuate ownership as if permission needed to be granted to make our own life decisions. If it wasn't under her watch, it would be under someone else's - a husband to whom we would now be accountable for our freedom. Was that even freedom? Had she even considered the ramifications of our new gatekeeper / husband saying, 'permission not granted?'

It was bad enough that our value was always being measured against marriage, but even the price of freedom was heavily knotted in betrothal. What would happen if you ended up with a rotten husband? I went from being perplexed to repulsed. Could it get worse for women of my generation whose ambitions; dreams were still incumbent on gaining permission from a man, whether that was a father, a brother, a husband. Mum knew she could trust me, I was not here to do the thing she feared the most - be led astray, which in her eyes once again, involved a man. I had seen too much drama played out with my sisters for that to happen. This was not even about religion and observing the parameters of my faith. I quoted her the rights of women, but still, there was no compromising. Mum would not bend on this.

So, I was forced to return to Yorkshire, leaving my dreams of London behind. How could she do this? allow me to fly high, then clip my wings? I returned as she demanded, with a bitterness and a knot in my stomach. A mixture of anger, sadness, surrender and disbelief. My divided self fully prevalent. The same girl who would fight to the death for her art, never backing down; that girl, was nowhere to be seen when it came to standing up to the twisted cultural hypocrisy we faced. It made me resentful of mum and it slowly divided us.

Her words rang angrily in my head day after day, night after night, as I turned them over and over. I fought hard with myself to make sense of them; find ways to appease her and keep my dream alive. Trying desperately to make an unworkable situation work. It made no sense, but my logical brain needed it to. It felt like a standoff. One that I never imagined myself to be in, especially with mum. Why had my right to pursue my dreams turned into a skirmish with her? I continued to battle with the injustice, searching for ways to enable them to happen. But I never imagined my freedom would come at a price that devalued everything I stood for as a woman.

Devastated and depressed at the prospect of having to start again up north, I came back to Bradford and took a job at the local Asian radio station - Daybreak Radio. It was brain fodder for now, but something that kept me occupied, whilst I quietly continued to work on mum. That was where I met DJ Haz. Hassan, his full name, but shortening it was a thing that almost every young Pakistani male did. Appropriate their beautiful symbolic names into three letters to the utter dismay of their parents. It wasn't unusual to be either Taz, Baz, Jaz or Kaz. We all knew at least half a dozen of them. Haz showed me the ropes in the early days of getting started on the decks at the radio station. He also stared at me incessantly which I found extremely irritating.

A delivery man by day and DJ by night. He was not someone I would ever have a deep and meaningful conversation with, but he was pleasant enough apart from ogling me and distracting me as I tried to do my job. One particular day he offered to drive me home, after I missed the last bus, so I agreed. On the way home, he candidly asked me something in his broad Yorkshire accent, "You don't see girls like you up 'ere, you're too good for this dumpy station what you doin' 'ere?" I was taken aback by his acute observations and by the fact that this was the first time anyone had cared to ask what I was doing filling my time at that tired old radio station. I paused, wondering whether he would listen or even have the wherewithal to understand. I felt that it could take the best part of the night to fill him in on patriarchy, bigotry, control and subjugation of women in the Asian community.

Something prompted me to ask him, "Do you have sisters?" To which he replied, "I do yeah… two real sisters, two 'alf sisters." This intrigued me much more than my reply suggested, "Oh, ok, that's interesting." I wanted to learn more about his half-sisters, wondering whether like me, he was from a broken home and maybe his 'alf sisters' were the product of a parent remarrying. But I stopped myself. He interjected before I could say anything else. "One of ma sisters escaped though." Again, I was fascinated, which further prompted me to ask, "What do you mean, escape?" He shrugged before saying, "Ah she ran off din't she… t'other side o' world." I asked him to pull over to the side of the road, where he parked his car under an orange street light, and tell me more.

This was becoming more intriguing by the minute as I asked, "What? Where? Why?" I continued to probe, now with much intrigue. "She did a runner and I 'elped her" he continued, giggling. "Yeah, she's 'appy, lives in Oz now, livin' the dream… ar lass, ar Shay." His face glowed, reflecting the orange haze from the street light above us, which made his last statement sound comical, if not surreal.

It turned out that his youngest sister Shay, short for Shayla had fled to Australia when forced to marry a man that her parents had, without her consent 'chosen' for her. She hadn't stayed long enough to even consummate the union, when Haz helped her to leave abruptly, that same night, in true 'midnight runner' style. He drove her to a safe house, from where she made arrangements to be relocated overseas through her work, to Australia. She couldn't have moved further away. The practice of forced marriage did still happen, at the hands of misogynistic community leaders which Haz's family had trusted to guide them. Shay appeared to be an educated woman like me, working as a business analyst for a company with offices all over the world. She must have been an intelligent, strong, articulate woman, but hopeless when it came to standing up for herself. She sounded more and more like me. How many of us were out there? I wondered.

Whilst irritatingly ogling me at the radio station, in what I arrogantly assumed was wonderment, Haz had actually been comparing me to his sister Shay. He saw Shayla in me. He was perceptive enough to have noticed the frustration on my face, in between playing Bollywood tunes on repeat and delivering road traffic updates. I was impressed with his intuitiveness. He looked at me now, in the stationary car, as if to say, 'I know you' and asked again, "You don't want to be here in Bradford do you?" That was when I pressed my fingernails sharply into the palms of my hands, to cause a piercing pain; something I did to stop myself from crying. "You're right," I whispered, trying to fight back the tears, "I don't want to be here. It's my mum, she won't let me stay in London and just... you know, just live there." It all came flooding out as I continued, "I'm not interested in marriage, and to her, that's the only way she says it's possible." He looked at me pensively, as he rubbed the day-old stubble on his chin.

"So, what will it take for you to escape back then?" he enquired. "No, no; NO! it's not like that," I replied, wiping my eyes with my cuff; assuming he was suggesting I too, do a midnight runner like Shay. "I wouldn't do that," I sniffed. "Oh, ok, I get you. So, if the only way you can get away is through marriage, then just get married?" he said, shrugging his shoulders and raising his hands. "Are you stupid? did you not hear what I just said?" I scowled. "Oh I 'eard everything. Just get married." He repeated leaning in towards me to say it close-up. Now I was annoyed by his glowing orange face; this was not a joke. That was when he dropped the next bombshell. "Let's get married, let's do it. I'll marry you, you marry me, together let's be free?" he said, whilst swaying his head from side to side. "Are you having a laugh, shut up!" I growled half amused, half vexed. "Nah, deadly serious," he whispered menacingly, looking deep into my eyes. "Unlock the door; I need to get out," I snapped, as I unbuckled my seatbelt.

As I was about to leave the car, he grabbed my arm with intent. "Farah, listen, I will help you. Think about it." His face had changed from jovial, to sincere as he continued to look at me, unwavering, directly into my eyes. "No. There is nothing to think about, I'm out." I slammed the car door shut behind me, briskly walking away. Thinking about his ludicrous proposition, I laughed to myself walking the last few miles home.

I saw him the next day at the radio station looking sheepish and embarrassed. He walked over to me. "Please don't bother… It's not happening," I joked. "I know, I know, I came to apologise, to say 'am sorry." "It's ok… but thank you for the offer you idiot!" I quipped as I walked back to the decks.

A few weeks later, I saw an advert in the job section of the Guardian newspaper. A paid bursary to work at the newly built Tate modern gallery in London. I wasn't even sure why I bothered applying; I knew I would not be able to go in any case; mum was still standing her ground on this. A letter arrived a week later, with a paid postage stamp from the Tate. I opened it to read:

Dear Farah

Congratulations, we are delighted to inform you have been awarded th....

I scrunched the letter up; refusing to read the next few lines. I wanted to scream as I tore it into tiny pieces, scattering it over the floor, then spitting at it. Mum would never allow me to leave. Why was I torturing myself? I hated what I had become; I was as defunct and as torn as that letter. I hated myself and my weakness.

Later that day the most furious row erupted between mum and me. I called her a 'pathetic controlling bitch'. I had never sworn at her before. She broke down as I walked away. Her ill-informed, flawed, redundant words ringing in my head, 'after marriage, do what you like', I hated them, I hated her and I despised my life. I once told myself that I would never acquiesce. I knew my truth, but I also felt that my dreams were slipping away day by day and she was the one in control, as always, controlling all of us. And I was enabling her. I had to do something. That night I called Haz.

"Let's do it. Let's get married."

Chapter 25

Passport to Freedom

*I didn't love him, but I liked him. He was safe; he was
my passport to freedom.*

I may as well have been bundled into his car at midnight and driven to a safe house. Just like he had done with Shay. Such was the parity in our desperate situations. Haz had helped her to escape and now he was doing the same for me. But we had to package this getaway differently. Shay had fled, cut and run, left without a trace. She evaporated and would not return for years later, hoping that when she did, the dust would have settled. But it never did. Her dramatic exit left her parents devastated, broken and disgraced within their tight, indoctrinated, community. Being dishonoured or disgraced by a child, was often considered more unbearable for a parent than losing them to the run-away culture which was rife in the Asian community in Bradford. The repercussions included vicious gossip and being ostracised from the judgemental community, which always hit harder than the loss of their child. Their pride never allowed them to try to bring their child back and put things right with love, care and respect.

When Shay finally returned, almost a decade later, it was to attend the funeral of her mother, where she was told that it was her selfish actions that finished her off. No matter how justifiable her getaway, the guilt would always lay heavy on her heart, and she would never forgive herself for that. She regretted not building bridges sooner to her misguided, aging parents, who had been coerced into her being forced to marry a stranger. Their biggest crime was ignorance and indoctrination by the militant community leader who was perpetuating archaic and redundant values. It was easy for them to be manipulated and feel isolated in a restricted social circle. It was all they knew, and they did not have the tools to break the pattern. They would never fully understand the repercussions of their actions on the next generation.

That was the serpentine nature of intergenerational trauma, it played out in so many disparate and knotted ways. It would always leave a scar on you, even if you felt you triumphed by escaping the oppression. Escape may have appeared to be the path of least resistance, but there was actually no such thing as 'escape'. At some point, trauma and guilt would come and bite you on the backside. Our generation would never be free of our sinuous shackles, no matter how far we fled.

Which is why I could never cut and run. Instead, I was here, now arranging my own marriage. A marriage, not for love, or any of the values that my inexperienced emotional quotient had in its vocabulary. Not for anything other than to be free of mum. This union was to be an 'arrangement' that afforded me permission to live my life as I pleased 'after marriage' - in mum's own words. So, I began crafting my plan for everyone who mattered, to see me leave plausibly, under the guise of 'izzat' - respect. And that would be afforded through a wedding, a marriage, rather than the shroud of shame, had I chosen to do a runner.

I could never do that to mum. We had braved enough storms together in Suitorland for me to know that any more drama would actually kill her. That collateral damage was not something I needed on my conscience. This way at least, I would be guilt free; to live out my dreams and aspirations as I chose fit. Her words now began to resonate differently - *after marriage do what you like*. It didn't seem that bad a concept after all. I was following her instruction to the letter and all I needed was an accessory, not a husband in the conventional sense. Haz was my willing accomplice in this marriage of convenience. No one would be any the wiser.

It didn't feel wrong...

Was it wrong? Surely not, we had both clearly and willingly consented to it. It was an unwritten pre-nup; a consensual agreement, the terms and conditions were crystal clear. I was adept at over-analysing things, so I had rationalised it already, unpacked it and re-analysed it as I would a research paper. By the time I was done, I had stripped all symbolic meaning out of the concept of this marriage and murdered it. And it all fell into place effortlessly. I gently eased mum into the idea that I had met someone, who on paper would fit all her criteria. If anyone knew the gravity of mum's pen to paper it was me. The Daily Jang letters were my training academy, those letters and lies still etched in my brain.

I knew exactly how to hit all the right notes to pass the plausibility test with her, in order to get Haz through the front door. I briefed him on how I needed to 're-fashion' him a little to fit the mould. So, we elevated his DJ status to 'composer', which wasn't questioned, after I explained it's congruence with my arty nature - we were a perfect match from this point of view. I had her trust, and I knew I had every tool to engineer the perfect package of a suitor. I executed this operation with the precision that I was already so well-versed in.

No one else in the family passed comment or judgement, as they too trusted me. Bar one; it was Zainab who smelt a rat and interrogated me. "Wait a minute, you don't even like men! You've always got your head stuck in a book - what's your game?" she said, after she had heard through mum, about my sudden plans to get married. She was the only one, sharp enough to corner me into confessing and the only one to whom I came clean, "I'm doing this to live my life. I'm not going to waste it here at home; waiting for someone to give me permission to live my dreams. It is the only way - you should know that!" I scowled. Zainab did know how being imprisoned felt, having lived under mum's jurisdiction. We had all suffered it, but still she voiced her concern and deep fear for my plan.

I pointed out that her own jail-break was engineered and

choreographed and that her big day itself was staged, but she pointed out the obvious difference. Painted-man-gate was done in the name of love. Her endgame was love, pure and simple love. I was engineering a conduit to liberty. She warned me of the fallout if it all went wrong; the repercussions on my future for seeking this kind of immunity. This plan could backfire, badly. "Are you sure that your freedom is more important than love?" she asked. Was it worth the gamble?

I didn't know what this meant. I had never been in love. I had only witnessed how it felt vicariously, through her, in our younger days at the roti station, during our daily chapatti huddles, the place where she confided her secret escapades and adventures. I had lived through her experience of love and whilst it was exciting and exhilarating, it always ended in heartbreak. That didn't interest me; I found my excitement in other things albeit less audacious. I was ashamed to admit that I didn't know what love felt like, so I feigned conviction and responded, "I am as sure as I have ever been. I know exactly what I'm doing." That too was a lie.

I was left to make all the necessary arrangements for my own wedding, which suited me fine. I organised the venue - a small restaurant for a very small gathering, restricted only to immediate family, no friends. This sham needed to be contained. I qualified all my decisions for keeping it low key, by telling mum that I did not want the usual 'tamasha', the fuss and drama that an Asian wedding would usually involve. Mum was unusually compliant, accepting all my decisions without any resistance or interference. It was all happening seamlessly.

And it came around far faster than I had imagined. On the days leading up to the wedding, I began to experience episodes where I would struggle to catch my breath. Whilst I didn't recognise it at the time, my fight or flight instincts were on high alert. I was functioning in panic mode; my adrenaline high was pushing me to the finish line; my goal - freedom. The place where I could finally breathe. I was doing everything in my power to shush the loudest voice in my head, kicking back against the subconscious cries. The cries that were trying to tell me something; the cries that were eventually screaming, 'NO! don't do it'. But I kicked back and swam against a tide that was dragging me further and further away.

I could see freedom on the horizon, I just needed to swim a few more miles to grab it. 'Just keep your eye on the prize' another voice said. The prize: I visualised my life back in London, in the art world, picking up from where I had left off only a few months earlier. Haz knew this; he was quietly laying low in the background, knowing his role in this charade. He expressed no signs of nerves, as he continued to go along with my every instruction, my every detail in this plan. I would constantly remind him that this was a marriage of convenience and nothing more. But I failed to ask him one vital question, 'what was his payoff in all of this?'

The day of the *wedding.*

As I left the hairdressers, my hair heavily pinned into a bridal bun for the day, I remember feeling uneasy. My throat tightening and hands shaking as I climbed into Zainab's car. She looked over at me whilst driving, to see the colour from my face was completely drained. I was sullen, clammy and my head was spinning. I gripped the car door tightly until we reached the road leading up to our house. Before turning into our street, she slowed down, recognising that we were at a critical juncture, both physically, and mentally before taking the biggest leap of faith of my life. "Let me know if you want me to keep driving," she said as she looked me in the eyes.

It was a pivotal moment. My future rested on the answer I would give her. I stayed quiet. She repeated, "I can keep driving Farah... I can keep going." It was clear what she wanted me to say; almost prizing the words out of my mouth. Could I do an about turn now? Did I want to? But I didn't want to let down my guard either; she was my big sister and would have taken control in a heartbeat if she sensed me wavering, even for a second. If I expressed any kind of emotion now, it would be disastrous for my plan. So I kept my head still and my expressionless face forward. "Go to the house as planned. I need to get ready," I instructed her.

As I walked into the house, I saw the living room had been decorated with flowers from mum's garden. It was hydrangea season and mum knew they were *our* favourites.

It was rare, if ever, for her to cut them out from her garden. But today, she filled the room with them, placing them all around with care and attention. Their peaceful, pastel blossom brought a sense of grace and elegance into the tired surroundings. Some were in vases on the window sill, some on the coffee table, and others perched on the wooden fireplace. She placed a few next to the chairs where we would be seated to perform our Nikkah - Islamic marriage ceremony. The room calmed me. It was still, and I was able to catch my breath for the first time that day. Mum knew exactly what she was doing.

Haz's family had sent my wedding gown the evening before, which I hadn't cared to look at until now. I unwrapped the tissue from around it and held it up, feeling the weight of the 'gota patti' - the heavy gold embellished trim of the lehnga skirt as it dropped down. It was a bright red silk, heavy with gold embroidery. Only Zainab was allowed to help me quietly dress. There was a purple velvet covered box under the dress which I opened, to see Haz's late mother's gold jewellery, given to him after she had passed away. It was everything you would expect of 1940's Pakistani gold 'zavar' - wedding jewellery. Delicate, filigree details on the gold elements, carefully held together in an exquisite arrangement, interspersed with rubies and diamonds. It was mesmerising. I closed the box abruptly and put it away; it didn't feel right to be wearing her jewellery today. I imagined her looking down disapprovingly on me and what we were about to do. Instead, I wore an artificial set of jewels and pushed my hands through the snug fitting red and gold glass bangles that were sent with the dress.

Before heading down the stairs to be greeted by the small crowd of relatives, I glanced in the mirror, half expecting the image I would see in the reflection. I had always hated the colour red on me. I never wore it despite being told, 'you just haven't found the right shade of red,' whatever that meant. I knew it clashed violently with my skin tone. I was right; any bit of colour in my face was now completely drained and sucked out by the shrill contrast of this particular shade of red. I felt like a corpse bride.

The Nikkah, our religious binding, took the Imam less than twenty minutes to perform. After that, we headed to the small, low-key restaurant that I had chosen for our reception where, for the first time, our respective families met and passed pleasantries. I tried my best to look happy and express emotions, knowing this sham had to look convincing to our guests. It was almost over, and I was doing well. The last leg of this day involved returning to our house for the 'rukhsati' - the formal send off, where traditionally, a bride would be led away by her in-laws to her new home.

I looked around me as I left the house for the last time as mum's daughter. It was then that it suddenly hit me - I was now somebody's wife. All of the values that mum had filled our heads with growing up, that I was now fighting against; stripping bare of meaning were beginning to emerge and they would hit me a lot harder than I imagined. This farce of a wedding was not as clinical as I hoped it would be. Paradoxically I was also numb; devoid of emotion towards the gravity of what I had just done; having talked myself into getting to the other side of this charade. I was still trying to convince myself that 'feelings can be dealt with later' and just to run to the finish line.

There was only one thing that would break me, and mum knew it, as she stood next to the door, looking at me intently for the first time that day. I had avoided eye contact with her the whole day, and she had tiptoed around me, as if she had read my body language and kept her distance. As I stood in front of her, she looked at me and held out her hands. I knew my emotions would erupt if I moved even an inch closer to her. She continued to hold out her hands; quietly begging me to take them. We stared at each other in silence. I could feel a solid lump forming in my throat and a tightening in my stomach. I told myself that I had to remain composed. If I let my guard down now, having played deadpan all day, even for a second; any slight display of emotion would see me begin to waver and crumble, falling to the ground, feeling the weight of my choices. I saw the gravitas on her face, from her sullen expression to the disappointment in her eyes. She knew what I had done.

I clenched my hands, pressing my fingernails deep into my palms; feeling that sharp pinch to stop the tears and force them back. It felt like there was nobody else in the doorway, just the two of us, even though everyone's eyes were firmly fixed on us. I saw her throat contract as she gulped heavily. At that moment she turned away abruptly, swallowing her tears. It was evident that she did not want me to falter either.

Standing beside her; Zainab's eyes were glazed with tears as she gently handed my Koran to mum. It was wrapped in the same fabric cover she had sewn over two decades ago. It was now worn and frayed where I had kissed it each time I prayed. Mum raised her right hand and held it over my head in a symbolic gesture linked to protection, as a bride walks towards her new life. The Koran was passed to Haz's brother, who began to lead me slowly to the car, ready to drive me away.

As I walked up the path, I knew the consequences if I dared turn back now and look at mum. But I couldn't stop myself turning my head slightly, to notice her through the edge of my veil. Mum had buried her face between her hands and was sobbing uncontrollably, consoled by my sisters. I could hear her cries in a way I had never heard them before. Instinctively, I turned and began to run towards her; my veil pulled down as Haz grabbed my arm and whispered, "You can't do that!" I lifted the heavy lengha from under my feet; the entire veil fell to the ground and was pulled completely away from my body as I ducked down and just ran for it. It felt as if I was being pulled by an invisible force heading straight into mum's open arms.

The next thing I knew, we were locked together tightly,

gripping each other and sobbing, in a way that our entire bodies felt as if they were engulfed in tears. I had never seen or felt her cry this way in my life. Her aging hands, that once had fed me soft roti as a baby, began wiping the heavy tears off my face, away from my eyes, as she looked into them and said the words that I had never heard her say to anyone. "I'm so sorry meri jaan... my darling, 'mahfee' please forgive me."

Mum had known my plan all along and she had played along with it. She was giving me her permission to leave the only way she knew how. She was too old and too weary to fight anymore, but her love was still fierce, and her instincts were acute enough to know that I would be ok. She was confident that I was strong enough to brave this next chapter of my life, always having told me that I was her bravest daughter. I didn't believe her until now. She would never have played along with my plan if she thought otherwise.

Her youngest daughter, her baby, now married; her duties fully discharged. Her job was done, however flawed her rationale had been along the way. For the first time we were equal in our messy irrationality. She too had reached her own finish line that day.

Touché mum.

Chapter 26

Blurry lines

My bags were packed, ready to catch the 11.15am train from Leeds to London Kings Cross.

It had been two months since we married. Enough time for the prying questions of relatives to dissipate and we were now left alone to live our lives as planned. "What's ya rush?" Haz asked me whilst rolling his second joint of the morning. "To live my life," I shrugged. "Don't you think it will look odd?" he said with a sinister stare; a look that I had seen once before in his car, the night of his first proposition. "But we agreed a couple of months here and I can leave?" I said, beginning to feel uneasy. He glanced sideways at me, spitting out the tobacco that had leaked out of his joint as he licked the paper to seal it. He twisted the end of it and lit it, taking a deep drag, then blowing the smoke into the air above him. His head rolled back as he closed his eyes. The room held the woody, earthy, smell of ganja. I opened the window so the smell of it wouldn't stick to my clothes.

His stare was relentless and teasing, as if he was trying to intimidate me. I walked towards him, attempting to hide my uneasiness, "Wait a minute, that was not the plan," I argued. His eyes rolled upwards, slower this time, as he took another long drag. He was getting more stoned by the second. He hoisted himself up off the chair and pulled his face close to mine; his blood shot eyes looking straight at me now. "Ya not goin' anywhere t'day," he growled as he slowly staggered out of the room.

My legs suddenly weakened as I dropped down, slumping onto the bed behind me.

What the hell had I done?

THE END

Acknowledgments

I set out to write a cookbook with anecdotes and it turned into a novel with recipes...

Thank you to everyone who helped to make this book happen.

In memory of my late dear friend Julie McSorley, who cheered me over the start line but sadly passed away before it came into being; your wit and humour was with me as I wrote every chapter.

To Natalie Anderson, who visualised my story as more than a book and opened it up to a whole new world of possibilities.

To Shobna Gulati for your wonderful friendship and wisdom, and to Christine Talbot for your support and enthusiasm.

To Gill Laidler, my guiding light who always puts the right people in my path, including my publisher, Rick Armstrong, who read only the synopsis before investing in me. Forever thankful.

To my darling son and daughter, you are my world.

For you all, I'll be eternally grateful.

Printed in Great Britain
by Amazon

33884030R10162